Unwanted Heroes

a novel
Alon Shalev

Three Clover Press
P. O. Box 4221
Walnut Creek, CA 94596-0221

For information about special discounts for bulk paperback
purchases, please contact Three Clover Press.
three_clover_press@sbcglobal.net

ISBN: 978-0-9819553-9-1

Published in the United States of America

DEDICATION

To Irwin Bear (1933-2010)
A mentor and a mensch
A war veteran and a philanthropist
A friend to the City and the underdog

To my Dad
Served his country in World War Two
Has never stopped fighting

To all those who fought and are still fighting.
To those who gave up and to those who struggle
on.
All heroes.
Some unwanted but always heroes nonetheless.

1: The Disappearance of Mr. Tzu

Monday mornings are tough at the best of times. The Financial District of San Francisco swarms with people craving their caffeine turbo charged as they transition from weekend wildness to the cubical and office. The line for coffee snakes out of The Daily Grind onto Spear Street and I, the barista, marshal my staff to satisfy the needs of my newly adopted city.

Nothing can stop me as steam rises from the Beast, our espresso machine, which hisses and whistles as I concoct cappuccino, mochaccino, latte, espresso, nonfat, low fat, decaf, skinny. I am focused. Nothing can take me out of the groove as I serve the suits, the ripped jeans, the police uniforms.

Police Uniforms? One is a huge ruddy-faced officer while the other is smaller, mustached and maybe Hispanic. I'm still too new in the US to accurately place the myriad of people who make up the melting pot of San Francisco. But I do notice that the smaller officer wears wraparounds even inside our coffee shop.

"Are you the barista?"

"Yes sir. My name's Will … Will Taylor. What can I get for you?" What are the customers thinking? *What did he do? He made such a nice latte. Who would have thought?*

"Good morning, Will. I'm Captain O'Connor and this is Sergeant Mendez. We're SFPD." Two badges flash against the fluorescent lights held in front of the midnight-blue uniforms. "We'd like to talk to you about your employer, Mr. Tzu."

"Now?" I glance at the line then my watch. It is a few minutes to nine o'clock and the rush is almost over.

"Can we move this away from the counter, gentlemen, and maybe give me just five minutes here?" My tone is a mix of impatience and a fear of authority—especially in a land I am not used to. "Why don't you sit over at that vacant table, and I'll bring you coffee?"

As I continue to work our espresso machine, I recall a conversation on Saturday with Tabitha. Tabs was due to replace me for the afternoon shift but, as she often did, she came in early to hang out, as the weekends are pretty quiet.

Tabitha was my first true friend after I arrived in the US, and we have remained close since. She is young, thin and has a tendency to wear body-clinging clothes that appear to have shrunk several times over. Her mousey blond hair is straight and looks fashionably neglected. She has piercings everywhere. Tabitha can be dead cool or apple pie fresh; apparently, it is somehow related to the moon's cycle.

"Hey Hemingway," she said with a chirp.

When we first met, I made the mistake of trying to impress upon her my desire to become a famous writer with a Hemingway quote. I'm pretty sure she uses the nickname as a token of affection.

Tabitha is supposed to be an art student. She is enrolled at the nearby Academy of Art, although she seems to attend with varying degrees of intensity. She never likes to discuss her art or her studies and I have learned to avoid the topic.

Our relationship is purely platonic. She's been to my apartment a few times for dinner and a movie. Twice she slept over as it was late; yet there was no suggestion of anything sexual. She could be my little sister—I always wanted a younger sibling to bully.

On Saturday, I had been cleaning the Beast, which our boss demands must sparkle and purr. Mr. Tzu was apparently one of the first to import such a fine espresso machine from Europe and was extremely proud of it.

"The Beast looks good," Tabitha said, patting the metallic giant. "You take good care of …" Her voice had faded.

I stopped cleaning the machine and turned to her. "What's up, Tabs?"

"Tzu chewed me out the other day." Her voice quivered, and she played with a hanging lock of hair. "He was brutal."

Though Mr. Tzu is my boss, I know little about him. When he saw that I could not only function as barista but also as shift manager, he had me running the opposite shifts to him.

An elderly Asian American, Mr. Tzu is nearing retirement. He's prompt, quiet and formal. Although there is a high staff turnover, I've never heard of someone being yelled at or fired acrimoniously. Tzu provides health benefits, not a given in this line of work, and we enjoy the informal work environment and compensation.

"What did you do wrong?" I asked.

"Nothing really." Her tone was sulky, bottom lip pouting. "I hadn't cleaned the Beast properly in his eyes."

"He is very protective of it," I replied, trying a sympathetic approach.

"The coffee machine wasn't the reason!" Tabitha snapped. "He was really pissed, Will. There's something going on."

I pause, puzzled by her response. "I'm sorry he got mad, but what do you mean?"

"Well, you know. He's married and has kids somewhere. I've never had a meaningful conversation with him, but I sense something is eating at him—something serious."

"Hmm." I had nothing else to say.

I hadn't given it any more thought. My shift finished and I spent the rest of the weekend writing vigorously on my laptop. In fact, this whole scene had slipped my mind until now when the police entered the coffee shop.

"Again, I'm Captain O'Connor." A thick hand is extended and soon crushes mine. "We're here about Mr. Tzu."

"Why? What's happened?" I sip a glass of water I have with me.

"He's disappeared, Will. No one has seen him since Thursday. What can you tell us about your boss?"

"Not a lot. I'm curious. A grown man disappears for a few days and the police are already involved?"

"Listen, kid," replies Captain O'Connor, a big muscular fellow with an imposing mustache and balding head. "San Francisco might seem like a big city to an outsider like yourself—an Englishman no? But we still have neighborhoods, communities, and we still look out for each other. Mr. Tzu is known around these parts and there's a history. Let's just say that this isn't the first time, okay? Now please, tell us what you know about your boss."

I shrug. "Probably less than you. When he hired me, he was looking to reduce his hours. He's getting old; probably thinking about slowing down. I've considerable experience as both a barista and sommelier, and I studied business for a while in college. I really don't know him. Once he saw that I'm competent, he pretty much has had me working the opposite shift to him."

I sip more water and try to think of something else. "There's a Mrs. Tzu and kids, grown up I think, but I'm not sure how close the family is or where the kids live." Both O'Connor and Mendez display bored expressions, and I say, "I'm not telling you anything new, am I?"

"No, you're not," replies O'Connor. "Think of something that might be relevant to his disappearance. How's business? Any problems come to mind?"

"I think business is pretty steady," I say. "But I don't see the books, so I can't be certain."

"What else is sold here, kid?" The second cop, Mendez, leans in and speaks quietly, his voice a fair James Cagney. "Anything, you know, on the side?"

I stare at him for a few moments wondering if he's joking, but he just stares back blankly awaiting my answer. Mendez, in contrast to his partner, is a small, dark man with jet-black, greased-back hair and sunglasses. We're a month into a gray San Francisco winter and he's still sporting sunglasses—indoors. His badge, on the other hand, is extremely shiny and glints when it catches the café's ceiling lights.

"What do you mean?" It's about all my brain can muster.

"Drugs, gambling, numbers, you know?" Mendez no doubt reels off such a list a few times a day.

"None of that stuff." Is he joking?

The Hispanic cop wiggles his nose as if trying to pick up a scent. "You said that he has you working the opposite shifts to himself, correct? Ever thought he did this on purpose?" He stares at me over his steaming coffee cup. There is some froth on his dark mustache. "Perhaps he's keeping you away from something?"

"Of course not," I answer. "I told you he's just slowing down and feels he can trust me."

"Yes, you did." He takes another calculated sip of coffee. More foam beds down in his moustache. "Any of the staff mentioned someone coming into the coffee shop and arguing with him? Or have any of them argued with him?"

I glance at Tabitha thinking about her argument with Mr. Tzu over the Beast but shake my head. "No, not that I know of."

"Anyone fired recently?" Mendez is certainly persistent. "Perhaps someone left feeling like he screwed 'em?"

I'm really no help. "Maybe you should talk with the other employees," I say. "I need to get back to work. Do you have any more questions?"

"Not for now." O'Connor says handing over a business card. "If anything comes to mind, call us."

As the captain walks out the door, his partner leans back in still holding his coffee cup. His James Cagney tone is little more than a whisper.

"Keep an eye on the girl." His eyes flash toward Tabitha. "We know about their argument, and we know you didn't tell us. It's all about the espresso machine. If it ain't treated right, we can tell." He taps his nose with a thick, gold-ringed finger. "The customer always knows."

2: The Letter

I stare at him in bewilderment as he strides out of the café. I cannot decide whether I admire or fear him and conclude that probably a bit of both is most prudent. Turning back to the counter, I see Tabitha watching me as she hands change to a customer. I feel a sharp wave of panic.

"So they're onto me?" Her tone is flippant when it is just the two of us. "It's the addiction, Will. Caffeine and a full moon. Such a fatal combination." She raises her cup and flutters her eyelashes as she sips.

"Until Mr. Tzu shows up, we'll have to rearrange the work roster," I reply somberly. "I assume Ginny has been filling in for Mr. Tzu over the weekend, but you have more experience. You're going to have to pull the shift opposite mine."

"But then we won't get to work together! Who's going to train me, nurture my career, and bring out my full potential?" She does a credible job pouting like a spoiled child. Then stretching out her hands, she bows her head. "I'm still your humble apprentice, Will, my lord, my barista."

I relax. "Be mindful of the Force, my young Padma," I say in my best Yoda-ese, "and keep the fucking Beast clean. Remember, the coffee flows through the Beast." If only my school counselor had let me pursue a career as a

Jedi Knight. "Right now, you're the only other person supremely qualified to run shifts," I say, getting back to business.

"But what about the wines?" Tabitha asks.

"George and I will alternate," I reply.

"Carrot Face?"

"You're going to call him that to his face one day soon and I might not be around to protect you."

We both laugh. The prospect of Carrot Face or George and I going a few rounds over Tabitha's honor is amusing. George is a recent addition to our staff. He knows little about coffee but worked on a vineyard in Napa for a few years. He is skinny, spotty, awkward and … well you can probably guess his hair color.

"But you're gonna work a lot of hours," Tabitha says, concerned.

"It'll only be for a few days. He'll be back soon." I hear the doubt in my voice.

I serve two businessmen, who take their drinks swiftly to a table—their discussion never stopping.

Tabitha shrugs. "I bet the bastard rented a sports car and is in Vegas denying his age. Men are jerks, you know."

"How would I know that?" I roll my eyes.

"You're a writer, Will. You must've noticed them. Jerks." Tabitha manages a disdainful expression.

"I'm also a man—never mind. The other day when Mr. Tzu chewed you out, has that happened before?"

"No, I'm actually a wonderful asset to the business!" Tabitha replies, her voice feigning hurt, then she frowns. "Hey, Will, you're worried, aren't you? You're not convinced he'll be back in a day or so?"

"I don't know," I say. "I wonder what made him crack."

Tabitha shuffles and stares down at her scuffed Doc Martin boots.

"Tzu's always been kinda tight, y' know. Not big on the conversation, but he's not a screamer either. That day, though, he was really pissed and not just because I failed to clean the Beast to his standards. He later chewed out Carrot Face after George quipped that, though it was his brother's birthday, he was ignoring it as they weren't close.

"Tzu heaped him a nasty lecture about family and loyalty. It wasn't a fatherly rebuke either. Tzu was really pissed. I figured maybe it's an Asian thing. They're very family oriented."

Tabitha puts down a wineglass that she's been polishing and sighs. "Look, I don't know Tzu. I've always been a bit scared of him 'cause he never talks or anything, so I've kinda kept my distance. You never know what's going on in his mind. It's intimidating. I'm not a barista or a wine freak like you. I'm expendable. As a woman, too, I feel vulnerable around him. Asians are pretty patriarchal, y'know, and I'm at the bottom of the food chain."

"Yeah." I'm feeling increasingly uncomfortable. "Let's get back to work."

A few minutes later I see Tabitha hovering by Tzu's desk in the back of the store. She's holding a badly crumpled piece of paper and calls me over.

"Will, look. This letter appeared the morning Tzu wigged out on me and Carrot Face. It had been slipped under the door before we arrived to open the café. I picked it off the floor, but Tzu grabbed it from me and read it immediately. He had it in his hand or his back pocket all morning. Later, I saw him put it in his desk drawer."

Hoping for a clue, I take the letter. It is dirty and creased, and I just stare at thick, black Chinese characters.

I return the letter to the drawer of Tzu's desk. It will be here when he returns—probably tomorrow. But Tzu doesn't return and as the week passes, the whole staff begins to worry for Mr. Tzu and our jobs.

Early Wednesday, an elderly Asian woman enters the café. She wears a thick heavy coat and a green-silk scarf covers her head probably to ward off the chill. I turn to serve her as she approaches.

"Will?" Her voice is unsteady and her English heavily accented.

"Mrs. Tzu?" I hazard a guess.

She nods. "Please, bring green tea and sit with me." She shuffles over to an empty table. There is a heavy flow of customers. I don't like the other staff members seeing me sit while they work, but this wasn't presented as a request.

Mrs. Tzu sips the tea and stares at me. Her face looks tired and worn.

"I'm sorry about Mr. Tzu. I really am," I say. "Is there anything I can do to help?"

"Husband will come back." She nods as she says this but without conviction. "He says you are good boy. He says you can be trusted."

"Thank you, Mrs. Tzu. That is high praise." I am pleased to hear this. "I love my job and the coffee shop."

"Good, good." She nods. "You stay and run place. Mr. Tzu will soon return and give you reward. Okay?"

"Sure, Mrs. Tzu. Do you have any idea where he might be? Could he ... could he have gone home to China?" Last night, I dreamed that he had returned there to die, but I don't feel it prudent to share this.

"Mr. Tzu is American." She shakes her head. "Left China as very small boy and feels no love for China. Love 49ers and Giants. For him, America is home."

"What do your children think? Have you talked with other relatives?"

She again shakes her head. "I speak with children. Speak all the time. No brother or sister. This disappearance is very strange. He has gone before when very stressed. Has something in past, something from war."

"So you don't think he's been kidnapped or anything? He doesn't have any enemies, does he?"

She looks at me for a moment perhaps to see if I am joking. Then she leans forward, her expression serious. "Mr. Tzu is good man. Very fair. Many in city know him. All have high respect for him."

"I'm sorry. Didn't mean to imply—" I didn't know what I didn't mean to imply, and we both fall silent.

Then Mrs. Tzu leaned forward. "I am from China. Parents die during time of Long March, I think. Maybe later. China was chaos. Hard life then. I brought to US to stay with aunt. Meet Mr. Tzu in city. America is good but for me not home. Mr. Tzu is my home and so America is my home."

She leans back and sighs. "49ers and Giants, they suck. Coffee not good either. Bad for Shen, for spirit.

Green tea is good—keep you young." She winks. Then she laughs, and I try to laugh with her.

I feel a wave of sympathy toward this brave woman who, like me, is far from her home. I swallow hard. "Mrs. Tzu. I don't know where he is. I don't really know him." I'm getting repetitive perhaps feeling guilty that I haven't tried to befriend him. "But maybe you could come into the café more and sit here to help look after the staff and customers?"

She flashes the briefest of smiles. "Thank you. Mr. Tzu is right. You are good boy. I go down to visit children in Ventura for few days. Help them not to worry." She smiles and looks proud, so I think that they have invited her. Then she asks, "You good son to parents, yes?"

I'm a little bewildered by the change of direction but manage to say, "Despite the distance, I try. My father passed away about ten years ago, but I think they were always good to me. My mum's still in England and I miss her—both of them, I guess."

"Maybe you send mother flowers to show you think of her? Write letter. I come back and check, yes? After I return from Ventura."

Write a letter—shit! The letter! I reach into my pocket but something stops me. Mrs. Tzu rises pushing down on the table as she straightens and shuffles out. I remain seated staring at her cup of still-steaming tea, which she hardly touched. Mrs. Tzu could probably have translated the letter her husband received on the day he flew at the staff, yet some strong impulse holds me back. I shrug. I can show her the letter another time.

I pick up her warm cup and hug it between my two palms. As I stare at the door she has just exited, I have a strong feeling that I am getting sucked into something that shouldn't be part of my life yet unequivocally is. Shit! Maybe I should give up coffee for green tea. It's bad for my Shen whatever that is.

3: The Daily Grind

AHHHH!

The scream is loud and piercing.

I am in the storeroom in the back and immediately run to the front of the coffee shop, where San Francisco Financial District's finest are packed around tables steamy cups in hand. Passing the big freezer, I rip open the door and grab a blue ice block fearing burning coffee is hideously scarring someone's unblemished skin. With great concern for my customers and an inevitable impending lawsuit, I think, *Not on my bloody shift!*

"Fuck man! You've spilled your coffee on my papers. You clumsy asshole! I've gotta submit this today. My professor will kill me!"

Oh no. A law student!

"I'm so sorry. I tripped on the strap of her Timbuk2 bag," the middle-aged businessman replies, pointing to the adjacent table. "At least it missed your laptop."

Oh no, an optimist!

"If you'd spilled it on my laptop, I'd have sued your ass."

Assault with a deadly drink ... graduating this fall; no doubt plotting to make partner next year!

"Well, I'm glad it missed ... oh, wow, is that the new MacBook?"

This man clearly has attention issues.

"Yes, a spanking new one! Look, I've gotta finish these corrections." She picks up the soggy pages. "Just move on."

But the guy just can't. Then his tone shifts. "Why did you print it out if you're still editing? A waste of trees, don't you think?"

"It's easier to spot..." She glares, ready to pronounce the death penalty. "What the fuck do you care? I'm trying to..."

This is my cue. I am the barista: a master of the mocha, a connoisseur of the cappuccino. Well, that's my pick-up line. With careful delivery, I believe it sounds sexy, like a hairstylist, a DJ or an open-heart surgeon. I know from experience—I brew coffee at the corner coffee shop on Mission Street isn't likely to elicit the coveted phone number.

But for now, I play mediator. The law student accepts wet napkins to clean up the mess and the sympathy of Tabitha. I escort the man to a vacant table on the other side of the coffee shop as far as possible from the threat of litigation. Both receive complimentary drinks, and soon the buzz of many conversations restores normalcy.

The law student stops me when I pass her table. "You're alright for a Brit, Scarecrow."

Scarecrow is a nickname that seems to follow me. I am reasonably tall, five-nine I think, thin, and with hair that refuses to be subdued by even a highly disciplining gel. About five minutes after grooming, I am left with, on a good day, the controlled scarecrow effect. I automatically move my hand to flatten the offending spikes and she laughs.

"You look fine." She giggles.

"And you're alright too." I mumble, flattered to get her attention. "At least for a law student."

Our café borders the financial district and the Embarcadero as well as some law and business schools. This prime location attracts refugees from the intensely caffeinated work culture by day and draws an eclectic crowd in the early evening when The Daily Grind transforms into an intimate wine bar. We also serve tourists who have lost their way to the nearby Ferry Building and the attractions of the Embarcadero.

Like all coffee shops, our weekday has its ebbs and flows. The morning is a madhouse as no self-respecting San Franciscan can possibly begin the day without their caffeine fix. By seven in the morning the line snakes outside our shop. With regulars, I try to remember their usual orders; a good memory ensures that loose change finds its way into the tip jar. If I can't recall what they drink, I make an educated guess and am rarely far off. Even then, I apologize and explain how I evidently confused them with an actor, singer, sportsman or politician. Compliments generate tips just as effectively as a good memory.

As the day wears on and eventually draws to a close, we place aromatic candles on the tables; vigorously air out the place to lessen the robust coffee aroma and turn on carefully placed spotlights to highlight the heavy, oak wine racks lining the walls. Polished wineglasses take prominence over coffee mugs while jazz plays softly in the background.

The crowd changes, at least in its intent. Tired businessmen and women seek a ritual to cleanse themselves of the workday stress. Couples huddle in the corners wondering over a deep-red Merlot if the person facing them might just be the one. Life is a Cabernet, my friend, and a soul mate is waiting to be found.

It's a job, a good one, and it pays for my other life. You see, I'm not only a barista. I'm a writer. A well-worn book about famous writers who spent time in San Francisco sits by my bed. I've walked in their footsteps, frequented their coffeehouses and wine bars, and opened my Mac in search of the same inspiration.

One day soon, I'll be a famous author. Someone once defined an author as a writer who never gave up. I'm far from famous, but I'm also far from giving up. Like others of my tribe, I've saved the rejection letters—evidence of the emotional scars that all wannabe authors bear.

Let me show you my world: the parallel realities of the barista and the writer, the highs and lows of an aspiring artist, the pitfalls that await a lonely young man with much to give. But first, let me introduce you to San Francisco, the greatest city in the world.

Yeah, I grew up in London with fog rolling off the Thames, but I do not recall locals stopping to admire it. Other cities share similar traits to San Francisco: Rome has hills; London has immigrants and culture, and Paris the artistic mystique. But San Francisco has all of this and it is not thrown in your face. It just is.

I lean over the rails on the Embarcadero and stare out at the looming Bay Bridge, gray and partially veiled by early-morning mist. Next to me stands a metal woman eighteen feet high—a creation welded from hundreds of recycled pieces of junk. She holds hands with a child about eight feet tall and together they stare out to sea.

The metal woman lacks the elegance of the Statue of Liberty. That is what makes San Francisco special. It works without pretentiousness. I am told that the metal mother and child stand at the annual Burning Man festival in the Black Rock desert. Fire courses through her body and out of her hand into the child.

We could do with a fire right now. I shiver as I watch wisps of cloud hover above the water. It is very early and I must open the coffee shop. Despite the cold, I love this hour of the day when the city slumbers but is not asleep. It is simply preparing for the onslaught. In two hours, tens of thousands of people will spew out of the BART and MUNI public transport tunnels. Others will stubbornly drive in searching for elusive and pricey parking spaces. The more enlightened drivers have recruited passengers from the casual carpool pickup points scattered around the bay thereby paying less for the bridge tolls and utilizing the carpool lanes. The passengers, for their part, get a free ride into town.

Walking down Mission Street, I see Clarence, a huge African American dressed in a shiny black suit. I cannot tell if he is awake behind those big black sunglasses until he raises his saxophone to salute me. The shiny instrument gleams, even in our fog-filled streets, and Clarence lets rip a short riff to announce the barista has arrived!

Clarence customarily stakes his position in the early morning. There are more street musicians than ever these days and, with only a few prime spots, Clarence must claim his territory. But at this time of day, he plays only for me and I feel like a king. Clarence knows I do not have spare change to throw in his open sax case— perhaps he would feel insulted if I did.

19

Later, around 9.30, when the herd is safely corralled into their office cubicles and Clarence's muscles are aching; he will come and rest in The Daily Grind. When I think Mr. Tzu, the owner, is not looking, I leave a cup of coffee on Clarence's table. I used to mutter under my breath that some jerk had changed his order after I had already poured his cup and there is no point wasting it. After about the fortieth time, I figured Clarence had picked up on my ruse so I just place the steaming cup on his table without a word.

No thanks, but I know the gesture is appreciated just as I appreciate Clarence playing for me as I pass him in the early morning. He will sit for an hour or so then slowly move off. I know little of Clarence, but he is part of my life—another strand that weaves this urban tapestry called San Francisco.

Two weeks ago, a bunch of students entered The Daily Grind and their clothes were covered with 'New Orleans' insignia. They were excited and boisterous as they passed Clarence at his regular table. From the way Clarence eyed them, I thought that their intrusion annoyed him, but I was wrong.

"Hey! What's with th' shirts? What y'all doing with New Orleans?"

A young woman, blond, thin and tanned, excitedly explained how they'd just come back from a week helping rebuild houses damaged by Hurricane Katrina. "You should've seen the damage that hurricane did," she said.

"Ain't no hurricane did that, gal," Clarence replied with a growl. "Weren't no nat'ral disaster. Don't let 'em bull ya'. The hurricane would'a done some damage, but if those levees had held, if those bastards had built 'em like they should, well, ain't no one have died there. My grandma's house waz swept away. Broke her, it did. Such a proud w'man."

Clarence rose and moved heavily to the door but then turned. We all watched. He spoke now in a softer tone. "But I thank y'all for going down there t'help. It's import'nt y'all show ya' care, that some'n shows they care."

We saw his tears as he walked out the door and left behind a heavy wake of silence. I could not stop myself. I nodded to Tabitha to cover for me and followed him out of the café.

He stood on the corner of Mission and Spear caressing his saxophone and let rip the most beautiful, soulful jazz I have ever heard. He was not playing for me that time; he was not even playing for San Francisco. I could almost see his tune rolling out of the bay along with the fog making its way to the Gulf Coast.

When he finished, I approached unsure what to say. We stared at each other.

"I'm so sorry," I said. "I'm so sorry."

I had spoken with Mr. Tzu, that day. I had an idea and from that week, every Friday at lunchtime, Clarence played in The Daily Grind to a packed audience. Big jars were scattered around the tables with labels: All Proceeds to New Orleans Relief Projects and as the music touched our customer's souls, the jars filled, because San Francisco has a heart, and that heart was bleeding for a sister on the Gulf Coast.

4: The Law Student

The Financial District and its surrounding neighborhoods boast some universities and campus branches—two art academies, a culinary school, a music conservatory and various business schools all offer flexible schedules for those employed in the financial district.

Then there are the law schools. It's easy to spot a law student. Even though they dress like other students, carry the required Timbuk2 bags and are wired to iPods and MP3s, there is something unmistakable about them. Maybe it's the ever-present, harried facial expression. They scan the drink menu while recalling a court case or legal precedent. They probably know what we offer by heart but still scrutinize the small print.

During the semester, they cluster around tables deeply engrossed in focused discussions. Thick books are consulted and their legal jokes, such as I hear them, are incomprehensible. But it takes only a cursory glance to know when finals are approaching. They inhabit the same tables, but each student becomes an island meticulously following a devised study schedule.

It's never a pretty sight to see the tears when they crack. I started work before the end of the last semester and it apparently happens with finals lurking. The honeymoon is over. They no longer get a kick out of telling people "I'm a law student." They're probably still on top of their course work, but the finals are approaching fast.

Gray, puffy rings appear beneath their eyes. Either they lose weight because they are too nervous to eat or they balloon up because their diet has disintegrated into junk food, and they can't remember when they last hit the gym.

The guys sport the unshaven look—it is an art and, if correctly cultivated, can be ruggedly attractive. The women wear their hair carefully mussed. The lone curly strand that elegantly falls down the side of the face while the rest is regimentally confined shows the tight discipline needed to maneuver the precarious straits of finals.

However, the mask occasionally drops in public, and over a cup of soy latte it can get particularly ugly. Today I should not have put folk singer, Janis Ian, on the music system. That was blatantly irresponsible.

I cannot see her face as her forehead is buried in folded arms on the table. Adjacent are her laptop, an open legal pad and a large uncovered latte that I note with some concern is seriously in danger of getting cold. Her shoulders are gently shaking, and I know what I must do since I am, after all, the barista.

There are few customers. It is late afternoon and several hours before we will entertain the spirit seekers. I sweep the floor and, as I approach her, watch her rhythmic shudder.

I fill two glasses of water and ease into the chair opposite her, while smoothly snapping a plastic cover onto her coffee cup.

"Here, have some water." I gently squeeze her shoulder and she raises her head.

"Is it deep enough to drown myself?" she asks, mumbling.

Her face, though potentially attractive, resembles a pathetic, abandoned puppy. I've never liked dogs. I hand her tissues from the supply I keep nearby for my allergies.

Her long, delicate fingers pluck at the tissues, but there is nothing delicate about the way she blows her nose. Then she looks up at me mournfully and mutters. "Change the fucking music. Janis Ian. At this time of year. Really?"

I dutifully obey and when I return, Calypso music is coming from the speakers. She has sprinkled some water on her face and is back in finals mode. My presence is no longer required, and the tissues lie abandoned on the table beside the laptop.

"How many units?" I ask.

She looks up, perhaps impressed that I know the lingo and the source of her sorrow. "Nine." She makes a face acknowledging that this is more than she should be taking.

"Do you have to take the bar before you can legally drink?" I ask.

She shrugs. Any sense of humor is generally beaten out of the law student sometime before the first-semester break.

"I appreciate your kindness but unless you can provide me with a precedent for corporate libel being struck down in the higher circuits, I need to concentrate. Actually, I need to eat." She begins to pack her things.

I take a deep breath. "McDonald's versus Steel and someone, Royal Court of Justice, London, 1998, or thereabouts. Later struck down by the European High Court of Justice around the year 2000." I gulp for air and she stares at me as I brave on. "Try Googling McSpotlight dot com or dot org. Something like that."

Her mouth is still hanging open, and I would gladly give an extra large, nonfat moccachino with whipped cream to know her thoughts.

"That's British law," she says once recovered, "which is different enough in itself, but their libel laws are particularly archaic and quirky." Then she smiles. "But I'm impressed and I'd like to take you out for coffee to reward your valiant efforts."

She sees my barista frown and smirks. "Fine. Wine. I'll take you to a wine bar in the Mission. It leans toward sophisticated jazz rather than suicidal folk singers, but you'll cope. And you'll have to wait until after my finals."

With that she gathers her things, comes round the table and pecks me on the cheek. As she leaves, I think I detect a slight, provocative swing of the hips.

The tips aren't necessarily only what finds its way to the jar.

5: The Afterglow

The sun is setting when I leave a wine bar near the Embarcadero. The fog and threatening clouds burned off a while ago. Now the sun's rays cast a soft hue over the intimidating towers of commerce.

Walking about San Francisco feeds my imagination. Though my stories are largely fictitious, they reflect real people, real encounters and real places. Yes, I could be writing about you! Ha! That's probably the last time you'll smile at an earnest young man sitting alone in the corner with a Mac and a Merlot.

Content comes from the chance encounter on the bus, the surfer girls down at Pacifica with their muscled, blue-eyed knights, and the Chinese herbalist who never says a word. They come from Clarence the musician, the law students, the businessmen and women, the nonprofit advocate, the writer, mother and homeless person. They are the silks that make up the tapestry of San Francisco and I have the honor to weave them, as my fingers dart around my white keyboard.

I alight from the Muni K line and walk toward home. I share a house located in the Sunset neighborhood, named—as far as I can make out—because a few times a year the fog and clouds dissipate and afford us a beautiful Pacific sunset.

I live three blocks from the sea and was excited by the location when I moved in. Any self-respecting, struggling writer needs a wind-swept beach for morose walks and inspiration.

Chad is crossing the road coming from the beach. His long, blond curly hair flutters in the breeze and he looks as though he's just auditioned for a part in Jesus Christ Superstar. Women ordinarily melt in his path when they stare into his blue eyes.

"Hey, Will, you've met Louise," he says, extracting his arm from around a slim, bleached haired woman, who looks good in a light summer dress. "We've just been walking on the beach."

Louise nods, her face still squinting from the sun on the ocean, and glances down the street. "Hey, there's my bus. Gotta run." She pecks Chad on the cheek. The kiss is not reciprocated, but she seems content with his warm smile.

"Sweet," I say, as we stand at the corner admiring her swinging, retreating hips. Then I remember. "I thought you two split up?"

"Uh-huh." His voice emanates warmth. "But we're still friends."

This is an impressive trait. Chad is never lacking a woman by his side or in his bed. Yet, despite the active turnover, there seem to be no arguments or bitter recriminations. We often bump into past flames on the street, and they always greet him amicably if not wistfully.

Chad and I head for home in comfortable silence. I appreciate his easygoing nature and his desire to see the uniqueness in people. He takes a genuine interest in my writing as he does, I know, in anyone's passion.

"How was work?"

"Fine. The usual crowd."

"And how's Tabs?" Chad has only met her a few times, yet they connected quickly.

"Pretty upset, I'm afraid. Mr. Tzu apparently laid into her last week. Quite harshly, it seems. Now he's disappeared."

"Poor girl." Chad creases his brow. Then after a moment's contemplation says, "It's strange for an old Asian guy to lose it. The ones I've known always seem so reserved and in control of themselves. He must be dealing with something pretty heavy."

I glance over at my friend. The sun shines through his long-blonde curls and it suddenly occurs to me that he just might be the Messiah. Chad is pretty perfect even if he can't cook and clogs the shower drain whenever he washes his hair.

I unlock the front door and a meow greets us. Five of us live in this house including a cat that doesn't pay rent but is wise enough not to precipitate an allergic attack every time our paths cross. His name is Harrison and he is a hefty tom who has lived here the longest. He eats our leftovers and has a surprisingly shiny coat considering our atrocious culinary talents. He also enjoys Seinfeld on TV and has a permanent half-hour spot every night on the couch.

"Coming through," says a voice from the street and another housemate, with bicycle balanced on one shoulder and a pile of textbooks and DVDs precariously jammed on his hip, dodges through.

Julian is Jewish and hails from Los Angeles. His hair is long and dark. He sports a permanent tan, evening shadow and infectious grin. He surfs, plays guitar and also is thronged by female admirers. He is rarely seen wearing anything but shorts, sandals and a Hawaiian shirt. I wonder how his limited wardrobe will handle the winter months. Julian is an undergraduate studying cinema and is continually explaining how this is one of the best majors that San Francisco State University has to offer. I suspect that he needs to justify coming from LA to San Francisco to study the movie business.

"Party alert two houses down," Julian says. "Guys from lit class tipped me off." There are always parties on the weekend and daily at the beginning of semester. This is student land. "Shower time. I call first!"

I can hear the water already running in the shower. I assume that Bear, our fourth housemate, is already in there and, if he doesn't know of the party, might take awhile.

The Sunset neighborhood borders San Francisco State University, a huge academic monolith whose ethos epitomizes the 'celebrate diversity' theme that fuels this city. Of the thirty thousand students, many are immigrants or first generation seeking to pull themselves up the social ladder with academic advancement.

"What's with the DVDs?" I ask, grabbing them from Julian to prevent them falling to the floor.

"War movies and protests," he replies. "They're all about war vets, you know. I need to write a paper on '70's political movies."

"There was a rally downtown last week," says Chad. "War vets demanding that more be done about Agent Orange. I walked with them for a while and heard about some of the suffering from this shit. These guys should be treated as heroes. It was a bummer that they need to demonstrate after all they've done for our country."

I look from one to the other. Part of my brain is telling me that something important is being said, but if it's party night for four young single men, then preparations must be made.

"I'll get Bear out of the shower," I say, hearing the water still flowing from the direction of the bathroom.

I'm not sure what Bear's real name is, but he has an iron-man body. He is always happy to explain his weights regime and flex you a demonstration. Bear is big, has muscles on his muscles and eats like a—well, like a bear.

This makes him handy to have around when one of us gets the urge to hit a club in the Tenderloin. He doesn't drink from fear of affecting his performance (I think he's referring to his workout routine) and, because his size is threatening but his temperament nonviolent, he can be counted on to get us out of a tight spot without anyone getting hurt.

Although Bear is physically the opposite of me, we do have one thing in common—Bear doesn't have a girlfriend—he hasn't for some time and appreciates my balancing out the social scales. Sharing digs with Chad and Julian and their legions of girlfriends would otherwise be unbearable for our young, delicate male egos.

6: First Contact

"Wanna buy me a drink?" The question is posed through full-red lipstick surrounded by a thin yet definite black line.

My eyes widen. I have never been picked up in a bar. Usually, I am in my own little world shared only with my laptop or surrounded by better-looking and more extroverted guys. I never even noticed her approach.

"Been waiting to all evening," I reply, stunned at how smoothly it came out. There is something to be said for spontaneity.

"Smooth." She smiles. "That would have to be spontaneous."

Because I've been living in America for a few months now, I allow myself to plead the fifth.

"What's your name?" she asks.

"Will. And you?"

My question is ignored. "Whatcha drinking?" She peers into my wineglass. I now notice heavy black eyeliner and short, dark hair.

"A Merlot." I cringe keenly conscious of its lack of machismo.

"Oh, I thought it was Bud Light." She deftly picks up my glass and takes a sip. "Not bad. Get one for yourself, Will."

"I thought you were—" I give up and turn to order a second drink.

The barman grins back and already is filling a second glass. No doubt, he has seen it all before.

"Now, let's see," she says, probably wondering how to follow up such an entrance. She smoothly compensates by crossing her legs exposing slim, firm lower extremities from under a short, black skirt. "A laptop in a wine bar in North Beach. I assume you are a struggling writer with a message to save the world. So what are you writing about?"

"Maybe you."

"Really?" she arches a finely penciled eyebrow.

"Not yet," I say with a smile. "I'm still trying to work out if I can make you remotely believable."

She laughs. "Probably not. But I'm most intense at the beginning. After that, my victims either run away or suffer a nervous breakdown. If I focus, they'll have a nervous breakdown while running away. Now, I wonder, how will you react?"

I smile, drawing my sharpened English accent from its sheath. "None of the above, I suspect. I am but a humble writer, m'lady. I merely record what the story wishes to reveal. Nervous breakdowns and narrow escapes only follow success. So what do you get when you fail?"

She exaggerates a panic-stricken expression. "A relationship!"

I raise my newly arrived glass of wine. "L'chaim!"

She taps my glass with hers. "You Jewish?"

"No, but this is San Francisco," I reply. "Let's celebrate diversity."

Her smile is warm: "You catch on fast, Englishman. So what are you really writing about?"

"San Francisco. I think it's a magical place."

"No shit?"

"It's a book about love," I explain. "I love San Francisco, so it's my protagonist. I love wine and coffee so they play supporting roles. I love myself, so there's ample room for tragedy."

She laughs. "And do I have to get you to fall in love with me to land a lead role in your book?"

"Not necessarily." I sip my wine to hide my excitement. "But it might help."

Her grin is perfectly evil. "Sweet." Someone calls her from a noisy group at a nearby table, but I miss her name. She turns back to me: "I'll go make my excuses. You for real?"

"Unless there's a guy sitting there who's over six foot and very upset with you making a pass at me," I say.

She jumps off her stool and looks at me closely. Without warning, she leans over and pecks me on the cheek. "Alright. I do need a few minutes. Don't move."

The thought doesn't cross my mind as her hand gently squeezes my arm and she walks to her friends.

I watch trying to discover how she looks despite the darkness. She is shorter than I am, maybe five foot four, which is good because my ego was severely bruised when I failed to make the London Pygmy basketball team. Past girlfriends have had to sign a contract promising not to wear heels within a twelve-foot radius of me.

I note the black boots to match the dress. I fancy her hair is colored black as well but cannot ascertain whether it comes from a bottle. I chuckle to myself, happy with the scene, and turn back to my white MacBook. I feel secure that the boundaries are clear—a writer's prerogative.

As she returns, I have a better view. Her nose is small and pierced. I deduce this from the occasional flash off her nose. There is something undeniably electric about her and, as the locals say, I'm stoked.

"You didn't try to escape, fool." She punches me in the arm. It is playful but slightly forceful and undeniably intentional. She has a leather jacket with her now—black of course. "Dare to move this relationship to a table and turn your laptop off?"

"Let's take it slow," I reply, "and begin with the table." But I turn the computer off and follow her into the darkness.

She chooses a small round table in the corner lit only by a tea candle. There is mournful jazz music in the background, and I smile. Only a couple of months off the boat, and I am in a trendy North Beach wine bar with a cute Goth listening to jazz. Lord, I have made it! I have discovered America!

"So," she says with a purr. "I guess you come to wine bars instead of coffee shops for a change of scenery after spending all day grinding beans?"

I am suitably stunned. "Um, how do you know where I work?"

"Ah hah! Not so confident outside your natural territory." She misinterprets my blank stare. "Your coffee shop? I've seen you working there. The maestro. The barista. Here you're more easily intimidated, bean-boy. Cute!"

"You've been stalking me?" I try to mask that I find this prospect quite flattering. "So what made you decide to make your move?"

She swirls her wine proficiently around the glass; then smells it eyeing me all the time. Then she leans forward.

"You snooze, you lose. The women line up for you. Cute law students, sultry businesswomen; it's only because you're so busy auditioning characters for your stories that you don't notice. Still, it's only a matter of time before one assertive girl makes a move herself."

"So, I'm lacking confidence and I am socially inept, huh?" I say. "And, of course, you hold a psychology degree I assume, Doctor...?"

"Final year of a PsyD at the CIIS. It's near the Haight."

"Oh, that school," I reply.

"The Californian Institute of Integral Studies."

I shrug. "I'm pretty up on my law schools, you know."

"I bet you are," she says, and I gulp, waves of guilt engulfing me as I picture the law student I've been flirting with for the past few weeks. Goth woman leans forward again—her lovely cleavage exposed forcing me to fight a hopeless battle not to peek. "That's why I decided to make my move, bean-boy. The field's getting kind of crowded. Go ahead and look. It's why I wore a dress that promises."

I now appreciate the darkness the wine bar offers, as I am no doubt blushing. But I have permission and I peek. Well, I gawk. She laughs and pulls her dress front up.

"The good thing about making first contact on a Thursday is that you can now ask me if I'm free on the weekend. I suggest you start with Friday night or Saturday. That way if it goes really well, you have the option to push for an additional Sunday date."

I stare at her for a minute trying to catch up. "So," I say eventually, "got any plans for the weekend, say, Saturday?"

"Actually," she replies, "Saturday is pretty empty. What do you have in mind?"

"Let's see. I finish at the coffee shop at two-thirty. Since you clearly know where that is, we can meet down by the Ferry Building next to the iron statue and hang out. If it's nice, we can catch a ferry to Sausalito and watch the Italian fishermen."

"Not bad," she says. "How long have you been in the city?"

"Two months."

"That explains it. Are you suggesting an itinerary that you've already done or plagiarized from a tourist book?"

"The Newcomer's Handbook for Moving to and Living in the San Francisco Bay Area: Including San Jose, Oakland, Berkeley and Palo Alto." I pathetically flash the book at her from my bag. "It didn't help me find a place to live or a job, but I know where to find the best panini in North Beach."

"A fine sense of priorities," she acknowledges. Glancing round, she sees that her friends are making to leave. It is getting late for a weeknight. "Saturday then at two-thirty by the Ferry Building."

She stands and slowly puts on her leather jacket. Then she smiles. "You've passed the first hurdle, bean-boy. Congratulations." She pecks me on the cheek and whispers in my ear: "From here on it's all uncontrollably downhill."

Damn! I never even asked her name.

7: Tzu's Brother

We meet as arranged near the Ferry Building under the gaze of the Bay Bridge. My date is leaning against the railing staring out at the water. I approach slowly enjoying the first good look—having only seen her in the dark, wine bar. The angled sun warmly lights one side of her face.

She looks very attractive, yet not in a Barbie-doll way. Her hair, partially covered by a black beret, is colored black, shoulder-length and curly at the ends. Bangs are meticulously scattered across her forehead. Her dark eyes are overshadowed by black eyeliner and eye shadow, while her lips are amplified by red lipstick with a black outline carefully applied. Her cheeks are red, though I attribute this to the fresh breeze.

Her entire outfit is black: leather jacket, lacy blouse and short skirt. Thin legs are encased in black tights and knee-high, laced-up boots. Delicate lace gloves complete the outfit.

For a fleeting moment, I fantasize walking up and just planting a kiss passionately on her lips. It will, however, remain a fantasy. I realize she's now watching as I assess her.

"What're you thinking? Rule number one, you must be honest." She holds up a finger to reinforce the rule and puts her other hand on an arched hip provocatively.

Lying isn't my particular talent. "Honestly?" I ask, and receive a serious nod. "Well, I was thinking this would be a great spot for a first kiss. Nice story to tell the grandchildren when they come to visit."

She laughs. "I already kissed you."

"A peck if I recall. Merely a peck." My English accent comes out when I am unsure of myself. "I mean the first real kiss."

She laughs, but it is a throaty, turned-on laugh. "So what's stopping you?"

"I don't even know your name."

A finely penciled black eyebrow arches. "Kiss me first. Depending on how good the kiss is, I'll decide what to let you call me."

I take a calming breath and move in. I open with a shallow, nonintrusive caressing of her lips with mine. Encouraged by her response, I intensify my approach and am rewarded as her hand moves behind my head and fingernails grip my neck. I am on fire and inspired. Tongues meet.

A lifetime later, she holds my head close to hers— our foreheads lightly touching—and looks me in the eyes.

"Cleopatra," she says. Her voice has become husky.

"That good?"

She nods and releases me. "My real name is Jane, but I'd hate to belittle your technique. Do you always kiss a girl like that so early on?"

I shake my head. "No, but you did ask for honesty."

Jane laughs. "And you passed the test." With that, she angles her face upward and puckers her lips.

Ten minutes later, we find seats in a wine bar at the Ferry building.

"Then Mrs. Tzu left the café," I say, still confused from the turn of events, "and I never showed her the letter. I was so certain that I shouldn't."

We are sitting on bar stools leaning close to hear one another as I grapple with why I felt so compelled not to show Mrs. Tzu the letter that her husband had received. Yet here I am confessing to a complete stranger—a stranger I have just seriously kissed.

"I still don't understand why you held it back, Will. It's kind of weird given that she probably could have translated it."

I shake my head. We are drinking wine overlooking the picturesque bay, but I am still haunted from the visit by Mrs. Tzu and my inexplicable decision. I pull the letter from my pocket and show it to Jane.

"Mrs. Tzu has gone to visit her children in Southern California. I can't show it to her until she returns," I rub my forehead, "and now I can't stop thinking about it. I need to find out what's written here."

"Is this how we're going to spend our first weekend—investigating a mysterious letter?" Jane seems intrigued at the prospect.

I nod. "Want to?"

"Do you have any clues?"

I shake my head.

Jane nods. The tip of her tongue moves across her top lip. Though seductive, this is apparently part of her thinking process; then she pulls out her Blackberry. I stare, impressed as small, delicate fingers barely exposed through her black-laced gloves dart across the tiny, black keyboard.

"What if I help you get the letter translated and give you moral, emotional and physical support during the weekend? Will you drop the subject for now and notice me and this perfect San Francisco ambience?" Her hand sweeps theatrically around.

"Sure." I feel a pang of guilt as Jane dials a number and dwell on the offer of physical support.

"Hi Susan." She winces. "How's life? How's your mother?"

There is silence at our end for at least a minute.

"Well, being best friends doesn't necessarily mean seeing each other every day," Jane says. "Okay, so three months isn't exactly every day. I concede the point.

"It's not completely true that I only phone when I need help or have split with some jerk and yes, I'm with someone."

Jane pauses to listen; then says, "Very happy. No, we haven't been together long enough to know how much of a jerk he is."

She stops again. "Yeah, I do need your help," she replies. "Actually, New Jerk needs your help. Your mother's a professor right? What did she study?"

My Goth companion listens to the answer. "That's great," she says. "When can we meet her?"

She brushes hair out of her eyes, and says, "Anytime tomorrow after 2:30 would be perfect; then New Jerk and I will take you out for dinner if you're comfortable with that. Thanks, Susan, I owe you.

"I mean I owe you even more than I did ten minutes ago. You rock, sweetie."

She puts the cell phone down and points to the bottle of wine. "And you owe me big, New Jerk. Pour me some wine." After she drinks a few gulps, I receive an explanation. "Susan is an ex of mine. She thinks I used her to try out lesbianism."

"Did you?"

"Probably." Jane hesitates for a moment. "But she's fucking hot, New Jerk. She'll have your eyes popping out, and she's sharp and witty. If she wasn't so committed to being only with women, I wouldn't risk introducing you so early in our relationship."

"I'm very happy with what I have now," I say, and blush at such spontaneous intensity; then try to mask it with suave machismo. "Still, you must be feeling pretty confident introducing me to your hot ex. And while I am truly stoked at the prospect, why exactly are we going to see her?"

"Susan's parents are from China," Jane says. "Her mother is a language professor. We are assuming this letter is written in Chinese and not Japanese, or Korean. Whichever it is, I'm guessing Susan's mother will know."

"I'm impressed. May I call you Sherlock?"

"It's elementary, my dear. What do they call you in the café? Don Corleone."

"I believe they call me Hemingway."

"Sure, to your face," Jane says with a purr, "but behind your back."

We take the bus to the Mission District near her apartment; then sit in a tiny restaurant ordering Vietnamese food.

"I need to make a phone call," Jane says. "I am presenting a case study next week with a friend and need to tell her something. I'll be a few minutes. You can whip out that laptop of yours, stud."

When Jane returns, she finds me pounding the keyboard.

"Has the Mission inspired you?"

"Everything that happens around me is material," I reply.

She sits. "What are you writing about?"

"Just a writing exercise." I blush and am sure she can hear the guilt in my voice.

"About what?"

"About you and Susan," I reply, trying to work out if I can close the computer before Jane reads it.

"What's that?" Jane points out the window, and I follow her finger. She leans over my shoulder and reads a few sentences.

"Men! You simply have no idea about women with women."

"We simply lack avenues of empirical research and observation." I open my hands in supplication.

She laughs. "Well, I can't help you with observation, but if you survive tomorrow with Susan and still want me by the time we've finished, I might give you some graphic material to work with."

"Why wait until tomorrow? I might forget some plot lines."

Jane laughs. "Good try, but I need to do some prep for this case study and I need a good night's sleep so I can study well in the morning. Do you know what bus to take?"

After we work it out, Jane walks me to the bus stop.

"She'll wear something very hot tomorrow," Jane says. "It'll be a test."

"For you or me?"

When I visit someone, I take a bottle of wine or coffee. For Susan's mother, though, I take a risk and invest in a potted orchid from Trader Joe's. She seems happy enough with my offering as she makes a space for it near the window. She offers us coffee but smiles when we both indicate a preference for tea. A delicate taste of jasmine soon enhances the experience.

Susan's mother is small with shiny gray hair collected up in a disciplined bun. Her eyes are sharp and her skin healthy. Although clearly old—Jane places her in her late sixties—Mrs. Lu wears her age well and seems genuinely excited to see Jane.

"It is so nice that you visit me, Jane. Most of Susan's girlfriends drift away when they break up. You are the only one to keep in touch."

"I'm very fond of Susan, but I guess I'm just not cut out to be a lesbian," Jane replies without embarrassment.

Mrs. Lu isn't perturbed by her daughter's sexual preference or at least doesn't show it. Her house is small and impeccable—located just off Clement Street, a heavily Asian neighborhood. It is decorated in tasteful Eastern décor.

"You like Chinese artifacts?" she says, watching me examine ceramic figures in martial art stances.

"He's a writer," Jane says with a hint of pride. "Actually, he's like a bath sponge naturally absorbing anything he sees."

"A writer! Am I going to be a character in your book?" Susan's mother grins. "Who will play me in the movie?" She makes a display of vainly patting her hair: "Hmmm, Meryl Streep, I think?"

We laugh as she sits back in her chair.

"So what can I do for you? I was waiting for Suling, but she seems late for a change."

I sit down at the table. I am wearing my writer's jacket, a blue tweed masterpiece picked up from a San Francisco secondhand institution called Out of the Closet. I wear plain dark t-shirts underneath, as I have observed that John Grisham dresses like this in most of his book-cover photos.

"I have a letter here. I need to know what it says." I pull the letter out from my breast pocket and hand it to her.

She holds the yellow, crumpled letter delicately and begins to scan it. Just then the door opens behind me and a voice calls. "Mother, I'm here."

"Hello, Suling." Her mother lifts her head showing gentle annoyance.

"I'm going to the bathroom," says the voice trailing from the entrance hall. "Be there in a minute."

Jane turns to me. "It has to be an impeccable entrance."

Susan's mother laughs. "But it is always worth it, no?"

It is. Susan isn't just hot. She's steaming. She is taller than Jane and the shiny knee-length boots help accentuate this. Her attire combines black with purple stockings and a minute purple skirt. Above this is what looks like a black, low-cut tight leotard encased by a purple jacket. The jacket is a perfect foil for the purple makeup that highlights an already exquisite face. She is high-boned and her hair is long, black and shiny with a few subtle streaks of purple.

She goes straight to her mother and they embrace. Jane and I stand and she gives Jane a strong hug. When they draw apart, Jane turns to me and asks, "Was I right?"

I open my mouth but nothing emerges, so I just nod.

Susan saves me by extending a hand, and her grip is vice-like. She stares at me unflinchingly in the eyes with a look that makes it quite clear how I'm not only unworthy of her but also unworthy of her ex.

"Go easy on him, Susan," Jane says, with a tone that sounds as if she might be pleading. "I'm pretty fond of him right now."

Susan glares at me and, pretending that only I can hear, murmurs. "Make sure you keep it that way."

I hastily sit down and turn to her mother—safer territory. Mrs. Lu glances at the letter again; then looks at me gravely.

"This is not addressed to you," she says, her disapproval clear.

"I know," I hear myself say. "I assume it is addressed to my boss, Mr. Tzu. He's gone missing, the police are looking for him, and I'm getting worried. I feel … I know something is wrong and I need to help him. I can help him."

She stares at me surprised, as am I, by my intensity.

"Nonetheless," she says, "should we be reading it? Where did you get it?"

I scratch my head. I know she's right and I haven't even mentioned not sharing it with his wife. "Mr. Tzu received this letter the day he disappeared. He became very hostile to the staff and then was gone. I know this might look fishy but my motives are honorable. This letter might be the key to finding him."

The silence is heavy. I feel that I should add how he's been good to me, helped me off the boat, etcetera, but I feel ridiculous as we've never spoken at length and I know so little about him.

Mrs. Lu stares at me clearly struggling to determine the correct course of action.

"Why don't you first read it to yourself," I say. "Then decide whether to tell me. Just in case it does provide a lead."

Mrs. Lu dons a pair of half-moon reading glasses and begins to read. I take out a small notebook and a pen from my jacket pocket preparing to transcribe her words.

"Is he a cop?" Susan's tone is disdainful.

"No, he's a writer," Jane replies. "He needs to get ideas down when they come to him." I feel a wave of appreciation while realizing I don't want to be abandoned alone with Susan without Jane to protect me. What a stud!

Susan's mother frowns as she reads, makes fretting tuts and shakes her head.

"He is in a bad way," she says, her brow creased with concern.

"Mr. Tzu?"

"No, the writer of the letter. He is homeless and, I would venture to say, mentally unstable."

She takes a deep breath and reads.

My dear Chang,
We both know this letter would eventually come. I am leaving it for you under the door of your coffee shop

in the middle of the night so I know you will not be there. It is better this way.

You are asleep in your bed with your lovely wife, comfortable, and, I hope, content. Sleep eludes me, as usual. We homeless do not sleep well at night: afraid of being attacked or abused, afraid of what we might remember if left alone. But another fear keeps me endlessly pacing the streets. You know of what I speak.

I hear them more and more these days—the voices, the screams, the gunfire. I can't go on anymore. I seek silence, rest, tranquility. I seek the quiet that will forever elude me while I am alive.

I am sorry that you must bear witness, Chang Tzu, sorry that I could not have been stronger like you, my brother, that I could not have rebuilt my life out of the ruins. I wish I had died in Vietnam, then I could have been revered as a hero; then the family would have been proud of me. I have only stayed alive this long so as not to dishonor the family name, but I cannot continue.

The voices, the screams, the bombs—forgive me, Chang Tzu, my brother. I cannot go on.

Forgive me.

There is silence. It feels as though Mr. Tzu's brother is here in the room with us. I pick up my cup of tea. It is cold. Then I look up. There are tears in my eyes and in Mrs. Lu's as well.

"Honor for the family is everything to us," she says in a low voice. "Your boss probably never even told you that he has a brother."

I shake my head and stare in disbelief. "Me? He never even told his wife."

8: Gnocchi on a Knife's Edge

The deal was that we take Susan out for dinner. There is nothing I can do now about the letter or Mr. Tzu. I invite Susan's mother to join us, but she politely declines.

We eat at Delfina, an Italian restaurant in the Mission. It's a lively place, but we can easily talk. We quickly decide on our order and I am granted the honor of selecting the wine. Susan is impressed with my obvious knowledge and, I'd like to think, my credible Italian accent. When the waiter shows his approval, she leans over.

"Do I detect some Italian blood?" Susan asks.

"I wish. I spent a summer there as a teen," I reply. "I learned to love coffee and wine. Actually, I learned to love." I blush—a mistake.

"Well you must be doing something right." Susan sighs and glances at Jane.

I believe Jane squirms in her seat.

"So what do you do, Susan?" I ask, valiantly trying to change the subject.

"Corporate law," she replies, hackles back up.

"That must be exciting." I'm sure I don't sound convincing.

"It's power, Will. I enjoy the power." It's scary the way she relishes that word. "I enjoy seeing rich, smug men entering a board or conference room—calm, arrogant, composed, undressing me with their eyes. When I finish with them, they leave crawling on their knees." She picks up a slice of garlic bread and, taking it between her teeth, rips it apart.

I gulp some wine.

"So," I say as coolly as I can muster, "what do you do for fun?"

"Kickboxing," she replies. "I studied Kendo, Japanese sword, but there was not enough physical contact between opponents. At least not enough to satisfy me. Kickboxing is similar to the courtroom. When men enter the ring with me, they are excited. I enjoy taking them down. How about you, Will? Can you defend yourself?"

I reflect on the years I learned Tai Chi, the soft, meditative martial art. I recall how Tai Chi Chuan means Supreme Ultimate Energy; how some master had been laughed at when he had demonstrated Tai Chi at a martial arts exhibition then beat everyone who challenged him. I also thought of how Susan would make mincemeat out of me without breaking a sweat.

"My pen is my sword," I say; then with growing fortitude, "Bones heal in a few months but a character in a book lasts forever."

She stares at me looking bewildered, and I sip my wine. Out of the corner of my eye, Jane watches our sparring. But Susan, although she'd allowed a slight smile to escape, has not finished with me.

"If I was to arrange to meet you later this evening," her voice becomes deep and sensual, "just the two of us, and I try to seduce you, what would happen?"

I almost drop the wineglass.

"Um, err." I stall. Falling back on honesty, I say, "I would probably helplessly melt under your spell, pathetically underperform and feel like shit afterward." Then I add with more conviction: "But I would feel a shit toward Jane, not you or me."

Nodding and smiling, Susan looks at Jane then at me. "Good answer," she says her tone almost conciliatory. "You'll live another day."

I'm relieved that the food arrives before we can trade a few more rounds, and I dig into my gnocchi. My mind returns to the letter.

Jane looks at me. "You back on your boss?"

"Yeah," I reply. "Sorry. I just think Tzu's brother might be the key to finding Tzu. How could he not have told his wife about his own brother?" I shake my head.

"My mum doesn't think Tzu kept it from her," Susan replies. "She thinks maybe Tzu's wife simply doesn't acknowledge the brother because he's apparently shamed the family's good name. Honor means so much to our people and the way you behave has significance for the entire family."

I stare at her. "Can you imagine that?"

"Yes," she replies. "Stop thinking like a white European colonial pig, Will. We Asians uphold a strict code of honor. The older the people the stricter the code."

I struggle to see the Asian, rather than the purple, Rambo-Goth side of her, but Susan continues. "I can also see your boss being so tight-assed that he'd not tell his wife, because he doesn't want her to think that his family had a dishonorable black sheep."

I nod trying to see it through her eyes.

"Maybe he isn't family," Jane says. "Maybe he's a soldier from the same unit, and they were close enough to call each other brother."

The conversation turns. Susan and Jane catch up as I mull over the different scenarios. Jane speaks of our relationship almost apologetically at first but becomes more assertive as she talks.

Susan is between relationships. She never seems to have problems finding a girlfriend, but it appears that she is not usually the one to initiate the breakup. There are chinks in her shiny armor. I think of her domination and try to imagine her and Jane together.

I realize that they have stopped talking and are looking at me. Apparently, they asked me a question. "I'm sorry?"

"What are you thinking about?" Jane asks.

"The two of you being a couple." I blush realizing how that line could be interpreted. "Not that way." My tone is defensive, though no accusation had been forthcoming. "You are both very strong; very assertive. I'm trying to imagine the dynamics."

"It was very rocky from the start." Susan's tone softens. "Like pieces of flint and steel connecting, we initially fed off the sparks and fire we generated. But it burned too hot too fast."

"The yin and yang," I say. "Two great yangs clashing as they try to come together."

"We both have our soft sides," says Jane, a little defensive.

I'm not sure I should be encouraging an alliance between them, but I plow on remembering Mrs. Tzu. "Inside each yang, there's a seed of yin and vice versa. It's what enables change then transformation."

"So there's still hope for us?" Susan taunts me by taking Jane's hand.

"I didn't say that," I reply, feigning worry.

For my efforts, I get my leg squeezed under the table. It goes unnoticed by our guest. Jane isn't going to put on a show that might hurt Susan's feelings.

"So how are you gonna proceed with the letter and your boss?" Susan asks.

"I'm not sure. I need some help." I have been mulling this over. "Tomorrow, I'll try to find a homeless guy I know."

"Oh, so your friends are homeless?" Susan sounds both mocking and impressed. "Do you play a round of golf together at the club on Sundays?" She has apparently made a fair impression of Jane's mother and both women laugh.

But at the same time, I'm beginning to feel despondent. Relying on a homeless guy suddenly didn't sound too good. Playing with the last gnocchi on my plate, I shrug. "I'm a writer. I listen. When I listen, people talk."

I'm glad when dinner finishes and we leave the restaurant. Without thinking, I suggest we walk Susan to her car. They stare at me incredulously.

"You want to protect me?" Susan, hands on hips, one leg slowly rising with foot pointed, clearly a weapon ready to wreak havoc in the nearest groin.

I bid a swift retreat. "Actually, I was worried for the other guy."

They laugh and Susan embraces Jane, who promises not to wait three months to call again. Susan turns to me and, surprisingly, gives me a friendly hug. Then she playfully punches me on the chin martial arts style.

"Maybe you are okay for a guy. Take care of my friend." She points a finger at me. "Or else!"

We watch her walk-off then, arm-in-arm, move toward Jane's place. A man stands on the street corner slumped against a newspaper case. He wears an old black coat and a red cap that is losing a battle to contain wild, white hair. He has a scruffy, graybeard and holds a sign in his hand. I notice a Safeway shopping cart where two American flags are attached to opposite ends of the handle and waving patriotically in the wind.

I can't read much of the sign but make out the word vet. I stop and turn to the old man and offer him the leftovers from our meal.

"They're still hot," I say.

He takes the bag and stares at me. His eyes are dark and he nods slowly.

"Good night," I say, and force a smile.

Jane has invited me to her apartment. Though I've been told I'm not staying over, Jane tries to create a romantic setting lighting candles and playing Carole King in the background. Contrary to the general state of my libido, I'm not in the mood. I'm thinking of Mrs. Tzu, her brother-in-law, and the homeless man's eyes are haunting me as well.

"Why did you sigh like that?" Jane, realizing soft candlelight won't work, has just brought in a tray with two cups of hot chocolate laced with brandy.

"Like what?" I haven't even realized.

She gives a credible impression as she sits close to me.

"I don't know. I'm worried about Tzu, the coffee shop and the letter. It's cold outside. Almost winter." I put my arm around her resting my hand on her shoulder. "I'm glad I found you."

"Hey!" She elbows me in the ribs. "I found you, dude."

"Yeah, I'm glad you did," I reply, and kiss her cheek.

"You did well tonight, seriously. I learned a lot about you." She passes me a steaming ceramic cup. "Not many men can go an evening with Susan and still be standing at the end ego intact."

"I had a good bodyguard."

"No, you did it yourself. She hugged you at the end. That was genuine. Susan doesn't do false, and she didn't disembowel you like she threatened on the phone." I hear admiration in Jane's voice. "You did well, Hemingway."

9: Trial By Fire

For my birthday, I buy a Timbuk2 bag. It's not something I can usually afford, but with the strength of the sterling and a family across the pond who feel beholden, despite the distance and my inconsistent letter writing, to mark the occasion, I splurge.

I love my Timbuk2 bag and the story behind it. The company, a local to San Francisco, originally made letter bags for usage by mail carriers. As mail carriers moved from mailbags to vans in an admission of defeat to the onslaught of junk mail, the company lost its main client, the Post Office.

The bag company did everything not to fire its workers, and everyone across the board had their salaries and benefits cut. When the company changed direction and these über-trendy bags brought great success, management shared the profits with the workers that stood by them paying three years worth of back salary.

I love San Francisco.

There are certain accoutrements successful alien immigrants living in San Francisco require: an iPod, gym membership (lugging a yoga mat around the Financial District is regarded as optional), a Blackberry (or equivalent, equally obnoxious and slim) and an Apple laptop.

This is America, the West Coast, and San Francisco—where life is lived at the cutting edge. Though Californians are remarkably tolerant when it comes to race, sexuality and gender, people make statements using their accessories with remarkable informality.

Coming from the land of the stiff-upper lip, I have a sincere admiration for this informality. It enables a group of razor-thin, but wickedly curved young women to sit at a table during their lunch breaks with hair regimentally tied back, yoga mats unabashedly laid on the table while sporting an afterglow—evidence of a brisk workout.

Why are they not sitting in a juice bar knocking down a shot of barley grass with a chaser of orange juice or perhaps a fat-burning, high protein smoothie? There is a natural juice bar just two blocks from here with plastic grass as window decoration and many choices for the self-loving, health freak, New Age yuppie.

However, they choose to sit in our coffee shop accessories at arm's length. I recall the first time I served a nonfat, decaffeinated, sugarless, Free Trade latte with no whipped cream. God Bless America. I knew then I had arrived!

Tabitha receives these women at the coffee bar. One rubs her lower back and admits that she overstretched herself at class. Without hesitation, Tabitha says with authority, "Mocha latte for muscles."

"Where did you read that?" the woman asks.

Tabitha doesn't miss a beat. "In my Woman's Health magazine. A study discovered drinking two cups of coffee after exercise reduces muscle soreness more than pain relievers do. Apparently, the caffeine dulls the nerve receptors."

I stare at my assistant, but the customer nods her approval and the deal is sealed.

"I want to see that article," I demand, my tone half admiration and half skepticism.

"Here," she replies, and without missing a beat takes out the magazine and flicks through a few pages. She then reads, "A further study from the University of Nebraska demonstrated that exercisers who drank only decaf experienced the same fitness gains as daily caffeine users." She taps the magazine with authority. "I just read this during my break."

Still unsure if she is kidding, I take the magazine from her. 'Eighteen students took a 200mg supplement of caffeine and eighteen took a placebo.'

"That's a great magazine," the customer says. "I read it for health, finances, and relationships—essential for twenty-first century survival."

Tabitha has another surprise for me. She produces a notebook with articles cut out and stuck on the pages. I read aloud. "Swedish scientists found that two cups of coffee a day reduces the risk of liver cancer by 43%. They researched eleven studies analyzing 241,000 people …"

There's a general nodding from staff and customers. Feeling somewhat bewildered, I choose another. "A study at Brooklyn College found that four or more 6oz cups of full caffeine a day might reduce the risk of dying of heart disease by 53%. The study tracked 6,500 people for two years …"

Again, there's a general hum of consent from my audience. I realize I'm preaching to the converted. I turn to Tabitha. "Why do you collect these?"

Tabitha shrugs. "It's important information for the customer. We provide a service not just a product. This is, after all, the Age of Information."

I look at her trying to see if there's a genuine entrepreneurial streak in her or whether she's taking the ...

"Okay," she admits. "It helps to justify our sins."

My smile is smug, but one of our slim, yoga-mat wielding customers says, and she is serious, "Makes perfect sense to me. I have a notebook full of studies about the healthy attributes of chocolate. I'll bring it with me tomorrow."

I share a lot with Tabitha but haven't mentioned Jane. I don't want her to make fun of me if the relationship abruptly nosedives. However, I realize that this won't work as the next time Jane is available is Saturday, and she wants to pick me up from the coffee shop when my shift finishes at two-thirty.

Jane arrives a half-hour early without greeting me and chooses a corner table with a direct view of the counter. She keeps staring at me with an occasional seductive flutter of her eyelids. Every time a handsome man walks in, she makes a display of eyeing him then returns to stare at me—a picture of innocence. I am suitably flustered and she's enjoying herself.

Tabitha waits on her table and they chat. They make no secret about the subject—Jane glances from Tabitha to me, while Tabitha occasionally turns her head to stare. From her expression, I'm sure she's seeing me through new eyes.

I manfully ignore them getting just about every order wrong and undercharging a customer for a mocha drink.

A few moments later and Tabitha is behind the counter with me. As I bend to pick up some coffee cup sleeves I've dropped twice, she crouches to help me.

"Have you noticed that Goth chick in the corner? She's hooked on you."

"Uh huh," I reply as nonchalant as possible.

"She's been asking about you, Will. She thinks you're hot, poor girl. Hate to see a good woman set herself up for disappointment. She started telling me what she wants to do to you in bed. Man, I hope your body is flexible. Might I suggest you incorporate some stretching exercises into the foreplay? She asked me whether you're with anyone."

"And you told her?"

"Yeah, I said that you're single and pathetically desperate. True enough." She raises a thinly plucked eyebrow to add some authority to her words.

"What else did she say?"

"She asked about other women and whether you flirt. You know. I think she's trying to work out if you're gay."

"What did you reply?"

"I told her you hit on law students and stray dogs. So what're you gonna do?"

"Finish my shift."

Tabitha glances at the clock. "You just did. Listen, if she gets you into bed, let me know if she removes those black lace gloves. They're very cool."

I take Tabitha's smirk as a dare and decide she deserves a show. I glide to where my jacket is hanging. Staring back at our customer, I smoothly undo the knot behind my apron. Then hanging it up, I slowly take my jacket and, threading my finger through the loop, toss it over my shoulder. Then I walk to Jane's table. Leaning over, I say as smoothly as I can muster, "Wanna move?"

I straighten and slowly walk to the door. Without checking behind, I open the door for her and she slowly saunters out taking care to clearly brush her body against me. I allow myself only a fleeting glance at Tabitha. Her mouth has dropped open. Victory is sweet!

Laughing, we walk down to the Embarcadero. My hands are in my pockets, and she lightly wraps her hand around one of my arms.

"You owe me big for that one, chump." Jane squeezes my arm.

"Yep," I say smugly. "She won't give me problems next time I tell her to clean the Beast."

"The Beast?"

"The espresso machine," I reply. "It's Italian and Mr. Tzu's pride and joy."

As we stop on a street corner waiting for a stoplight, Jane asks, "Any news of him?"

"No, but I think I might have a lead."

"Great!" Jane says, and nearly steps into the road on the red pedestrian light. A convertible blasts its horn, and a raised, erect middle finger accompanies the driver's yell.

Jane shouts back something questioning the man's ancestry and his voting record based on him driving a gas-guzzler. Then she turns back to me and seamlessly asks, "Who?"

Her abrupt change of tone throws me. "The homeless guy I mentioned. Remember? I'll tell you about him later. Let's cross the Embarcadero first."

We enter the Ferry Building, head for the wine bar and find two seats where we can comfortably people-watch. I suggest a bottle of Chardonnay in acknowledgment of the city's attempt at a sunny mid-afternoon and she agrees.

"So," she says as our wine arrives, "what's the story with Mr. Tzu?"

"Let's not talk about him," I say. "Let's have a normal date and get to know each other." She nods and I continue. "I love people watching."

"You're a writer," Jane says. "They're your subjects."

I feel a wave of warmth.

"Are you really a psychology student?" I ask.

She nods.

"Really studying for a PhD?"

"PsyD actually."

"Excuse me. Aren't they the same thing?"

"To the ignorant and nonacademic," she replies, sounding like a stuffed professor, "it's a doctorate with practical orientation. I plan to practice, not research or lecture."

"And how do your fellow students and professors read you at the school?" I ask, having never encountered a Goth psychologist in London.

"It's San Francisco and the school is as San Francisco as it gets."

We both laugh, and I continue. "I love San Francisco."

"Good," she says with a broad smile. "Otherwise, we wouldn't have a chance." She raises her glass and we clink.

"To San Francisco," I say.

Jane replies with enthusiasm, "And to its writers, its therapists, and all who dwell within its walls."

We enjoy a few minutes of comfortable silence, before I ask. "What shall we do today on our first official date?"

"Pay homage to San Francisco," she replies smiling, and I imagine walking arm-in-arm across the Golden Gate Bridge at sunset. Jane's timing is perfect. "We're having dinner with my parents."

The wine heads north up my nose, and I choke. When I have restored control, I quip. "Next weekend I'm working a double shift, but I'm sure I can fit the wedding into my lunch break."

She laughs enjoying my squirming.

"Is this a normal American mating ritual?" I ask, justifiably flustered. "My *Newcomer's Guide to America* failed to mention it."

"No," she replies, relishing in my discomfort. "But there are advantages. We arrive at my parent's house at four o'clock forcing my mother into a flurry of culinary activity. We'll be free by seven, as they probably have tickets for the opera or theatre or something." She sips her wine and with a huskier voice adds, "After that, we have all night. We can hit the city and have some fun. I will be deeply in your debt."

"What if your parents don't like me?"

She purrs. "Then I will be deeply in your debt, and you just might be awarded breakfast as well. Besides, you don't seem to know how to lie. Listen, at some point, my father will corner you and ask with as much ferocity as he can muster if you're sleeping with his daughter. You will look him firmly in the eye and tell him that it's none of his business, but you'll excuse him this one time. You can then honestly tell him that we haven't slept together. Make it clear that he should never ask you again. He won't."

"And then what?"

"Tonight," she replies matter-of-factly, "I just might fuck your brains out."

I'm going to have a lot of trouble concentrating at dinner.

10: A Brush with Aristocracy

Nerves make me drink fast. At Jane's insistence, I drank another glass of wine and finished hers. Drinking fast makes me light-headed, but the fog effect is pleasantly calming, though the wobble somewhat alarming.

As we leave the wine bar, I realize I'm turning up at her parents' house empty-handed. "Jane, will your parents appreciate a good wine?"

"I wouldn't bother." Jane pats my arm. "You can't afford their taste and anyway, they're never gonna like you."

I feel numb and, accepting my destiny, I hold her hand as she leads me to Market Street and in a few minutes has us seated on the No. 1 bus. When we pass through Chinatown, Jane starts a series of short, high-pitched sneezes that come one after the other thick and fast. After my three glasses of wine, it seems cute.

"Nervous?" I ask with some optimism.

She shakes her head as she produces a small black-laced handkerchief and dabs, sniffs hard and wiggles her nose, which I now notice is slightly upturned. I wonder if she needs to clean the clasp of her nose stud whenever she sneezes. I'll wait to ask until our relationship is a little better established before I ask.

"Nervous?" She gives an evil laugh. "And you? Oh, don't consider jumping out the door just before it closes. You'd get badly hurt."

"You sound concerned."

"No, not in the slightest." She gives me a stern look. "I'd probably push you."

I laugh. "Jane, I'm simply dying to meet your parents. I see this as a major breakthrough in our relationship—one I've been waiting for since we began. Has it really been a whole week already?"

Jane chortles and leans against me letting her head fall on my shoulder. Her hair smells delightful. She whispers into my ear seductively. "They'll hate you, eat you alive, but later tonight I'll feast on whatever's left."

The tip of her tongue lightly flickers on my earlobe. I swallow hard as the bus wheezes up the steep hills.

Pacific Heights sits atop one of these hills. It was one of the first neighborhoods settled by those who became rich from the gold rush—topographically stable in earthquake territory. The stately Victorian houses are unique works of art. Some, I note, even boast turrets. I've read that the families who reside here reflect their houses. They're the aristocracy of San Francisco. I've heard about hopeful social climbers entering these neighborhoods never to be seen again. The owners are surely novel fodder.

Jane pulls the string of the bell requesting that the bus stops. I gulp. "Here?" I ask with a whimper.

"Come on, Daniel," she grins. "Into the lions' den."

We walk off California Street to a small side street that is exclusive enough to have no sign revealing its name. Evidently, either you know the street or you shouldn't be here. But Jane's arm is firmly locked around mine. There will be no escape. We approach a white, blue-trimmed Victorian house. I look up.

"Turrets?" I groan.

"A man's house is his castle," Jane says, flaunting her English accent. "You should understand that, me old biscuit." She pats my arm savoring every moment of my discomfort.

Lacking a drawbridge, we climb, or ascend, a dozen steps. Jane rings the front-door bell and a heavy chime resonates.

"Don't you have a door key?"

"Of course I do, but Mother wouldn't consider it proper to bring in a guest unannounced." Mother has a distinct capital M, I note.

A well-groomed woman comes to the door. She is wearing a matching tweed jacket and skirt with a white blouse underneath. Her hair is immaculately straight with an elegant curl at the ends.

"Jane, my dear. What a surprise!" Her voice clearly shows a distinct lack of surprise and a cheek is offered, which Jane dutifully pecks. "And who is this?"

One sweep of the eyes is enough, and I realize that I'm underdressed for the occasion—not for a first meeting with a girlfriend's parents and certainly not for a first meeting in Pacific Heights. I suspect that I don't even own clothes worthy of a first meeting in Pacific Heights. Moreover, I have just left work and feel distinctly inadequate.

"This is Will. We were gonna get married next weekend, but he needs to work a double shift."

Jane's mother takes this all in her stride. I suspect she's developed a highly sensitive filtering system when dealing with her daughter.

"Come in. Where do you work, young man?" Her disapproving tone reveals no mercy.

"The Daily Grind," I reply, adding, "I'm the head barista."

"How lovely. Do you speak Italian?"

Jane thankfully drags me past her mother and into the house. It is open plan with adjacent sitting room and dining room. I notice a staircase leading up and another going down.

"What's for dinner, Mother?"

"Well, dear," her mother is suitably distracted, "you hardly gave me much notice. Your father and I plan to eat early. We have tickets to the Conservatory tonight, but I dare say I can rustle something up. I hope you and your friend, Bill, can join us."

"Err, Will," I say, correcting her, but I don't think she hears.

She leans down the flight of stairs that disappear into darkness. "James, your daughter is here. She has company, and they will be dining with us." Then she turns back to us. "I will see what I can throw together." She disappears toward the kitchen.

"Does she cook in those clothes?" I ask.

Jane blinks at me in disbelief. "My mother? Cook?"

Dinner is eaten in an intimate pink and white alcove overlooking a small, orderly garden. It's the best meal I've eaten since coming to America and probably for some time before that. We begin with an antipasto and a small-green salad. The main course is salmon, tender and masterfully blended with subtle herbs. There are small garden potatoes and crisp peas.

There is an array of silverware options, each for a different course. Jane's father is seated beside me, and I closely follow his utensil selection. James is a tall, broad man with a tanned face. His hair is gray but plentiful. Even in his home, there is an air of formality about him—in his clothes, his movements and his demeanor. He eats slowly and methodically.

I'm largely ignored for the first part of the meal. In fact, it might have been quite painless if James had not decided, just before the main dish was served, to offer wine. It is a test, and I am grateful that the chosen battleground is viniculture.

"I have a Chardonnay chilling," he says, looking at me. "It won't intrude on the subtle flavor of the salmon."

"Excellent choice," his wife says without looking up from her plate.

James stares at me daring me to respond. If he'd had a white, starched glove handy, he might have slapped my face and produced a dueling pistol.

"It's really a matter of personal choice and the selection of herbs is crucial to the final selection." My English enunciation belies the necessary deference to the subject. "But generally, a Pinot Noir is considered a superior match for salmon."

James eyes me critically, while his daughter buries her face in her napkin, shoulders shaking. I'm not sure whether my English accent is adding legitimacy to my case or merely keeping me from being thrown onto the street.

"Will has trained as a sommelier and supervises the wine bar in the evening," Jane says, but neither she nor I are any match for James's experience. The trap is set and he doesn't bat an eyelid.

"Really? Then I would be delighted if you would accompany me downstairs and select a wine you deem suitable."

His smile is smug and we both rise. My napkin falls to the floor. His does not, and I vow to discover this technique at the earliest opportunity. But I have more to worry about right now as I catch a warning smile from Jane. I follow her father downstairs.

"A man is never master of his own castle when he's married," he says. "But anything underground must be his domain." He points into a room and turns on the light. "This is officially my home office. It is my den, my sanctuary. No, before you ask, I didn't shoot the bear." He then says lamely, "It was my wife's interior decorator's idea."

We pass his office and enter a smaller dimly lit room even after he flicks a switch. There is a smell of wood and earth—air does not circulate here. One wall has wine bottles on their sides in a wooden case. On the other wall there is a wine fridge, two chairs and a small cabinet with glasses, bottle openers and wine paraphernalia. I am in paradise and James smiles appreciatively. His voice softens.

"Have fun. Anything is up for grabs."

I find the Pinot Noirs and peruse the labels. While I am distracted in wine heaven, James speaks—his voice changing abruptly to a cold, harsher tone. "Are you sleeping with my daughter?"

I straighten up slowly a bottle on my arm, label face up. I have been prepared, thank God. My English accent is armed with a steely tone. "Where I come from we don't discuss such topics. But I am your guest and will answer this one time." I stare unflinchingly at him. My voice remains steady but firm. "I have not slept with your daughter."

"This is an excellent wine," he says congenially, pointing to the bottle I am cradling. "Beringer is considered aristocracy in Napa. Been around here almost as long as my family. This Special Reserve is a fine choice."

He takes the bottle and leads me back upstairs to the battlefield.

11: Sex in the Heights

"How long have you lived in the city?" For my valiant attempt to make conversation, I receive a kick under the table from Jane. When James and I surfaced from below ground, we had interrupted a heated but whispered exchange that rings in the tense silence as we rejoin the women at the table.

"The City," Jane says, correcting me, with an arched eyebrow. There is something in the way those who have lived all their lives in the Bay Area manage to pronounce the City with a capital C.

"Since the Gold Rush," her mother replies, and my fourth cup of wine in one afternoon finally proves too much.

"No shit," I say, then hope for the ever-promised earthquake.

James laughs, though a sharp look from his wife has him clearing his throat. "My family has been here for centuries, young man. They beat back the colonialists, I believe. Now who were they?"

"The English, my dear," his wife replies, her expression suggesting she can still hear the cannon fire.

"Have you ever lived anywhere else?" I say, wanting make amends.

"Oh yes," Mrs. van Ness replies with pride. "I studied at Cal, that's UC Berkeley to you. It's over the bridge."

Jane's legs squeeze one of mine under the table—she is enjoying herself.

Her father, though, is casting his mind back over his ancestry and explains that some vague family member fought in some battle. I find it hard to follow but come away with the distinct feeling that some Englishmen hadn't behaved themselves at a tea party in Boston or somewhere. These things happen. When James pauses, expecting a response, I comment that I don't know much about tea and he seems flummoxed.

"I love wine, though," I say, offering him a lifeline. "It's great coming to California and discovering such a rich wine culture."

"Do share with us your global perspective on viniculture." Jane's mother has perfected the social sarcasm—the ability to clearly show what you think of a person or comment without verbally taking them down. "Tell us something we don't know out here in the Wild West."

"Well," I say, struggling through the gathering alcoholic fog. "I can toast in thirteen different languages."

There is a stunned silence. Even Jane seems impressed. "For real?" The question is a challenge. In truth, I usually share this during drinking games, but getting her parents drunk might have to wait a few weeks while we get better acquainted, assuming I am not deported over a bridge.

I raise my glass. "Ganbei!"

"Chinese," Jane says, impressed by my gambit.

"Mandarin." I correct, and she bows her head. "Meaning, of course, dry your cup, a sentiment shared by the Japanese who say kanpai!"

"Go on." Even Jane's mother is intrigued.

"The Europeans prefer to toast one's health with santé."

"That's French," her mother says. "I spent a year in Paris in my youth."

"Drinking wine?" Her husband looks startled. I push on.

"Salud is of course Spanish." I am in full-flow. "Vashe zdorovie is Russian and lechyd da is Welsh."

"You're not making this up?" Jane's brow creases with skepticism. "You know I will Google everything you say."

"The Dutch drink to one's health," I say and plow on, "saying proost! The Irish say sláinte! The Israelis drink to life, l'haim, as do the Italians. Per cent'anni means 'For a hundred years'. The Israelis can, however, top that with ad me'a v'esrim, meaning 'Until one hundred and twenty'. The Germans keep it simple, prosit, meaning what we British say, which is cheers!"

"You still owe us one," Jane says, seemingly upset to discover that I was not bluffing. "You gave two for the Israelis."

"Fine people, the Israelis." Interjects her father, thoroughly lost. "I've done business over there."

"I saved the best for last." I smile at Jane, staring her in the eyes. "Latin is not just for lovers so the Romans said in vino veritas."

"In wine there is truth." Jane echoes, flashing a loving smile then remembering her parents are there says, "I was premed; I learned Latin for a few years."

Silence descends. How do you follow that? Jane's mother looks at her watch and remembers, rather too dramatically, that they have to dress for the evening.

I rise and offer James a handshake.

"It was nice meeting you, young man," he says, and I think he might mean it. As he leaves the room, he turns. "You kids take your time and feel free to visit downstairs. Will, help yourself."

"James!" A voice calls sharply from upstairs.

And we are alone.

"You bastard," Jane says, trying hard to sound hurt. "They weren't supposed to like you. You spoiled my fun."

"I don't think your mother was too impressed."

"Of course not, but my Dad was. I assume he asked you the question?"

"Yup, thanks for the tip. So what now?"

"Let's clean up while they get organized and leave."

Forty-five minutes later we have the house all to ourselves, and I am sent to the cellar to select our next bottle of wine. This, I hope, we will consume in a more romantic setting, so I choose the light Chardonnay that James had chilled for the meal. I return to the kitchen and wait.

I have been instructed not to ascend to the top floor until called and I begin to pace the kitchen floor. I'm nervous. To distract myself, I take Jane's parents' coffee maker apart and thoroughly clean it thinking this to be the least I can do for my new friend, James. Finally, the call comes.

At the top of the stairs, Jane orders me to halt and close my eyes. She blindfolds me, and I'm led to my destiny. From the scent and overpowering humidity, I deduce we're in a bathroom. Jane slowly lifts my shirt over my head, careful not to disturb the blindfold. Then my boots are unzipped and removed together with my socks.

Jane stands in front of me and turns so her back brushes my body. She takes my hands in hers and brings them round to her mouth. She kisses each finger individually then sucks my index fingers. As she does, she moves her buttocks closer to my crotch and makes light, grinding movements. She directs my hands down her chin and neck. On reaching her collarbone, she guides each hand out toward their respective shoulder. Before reaching the edge, I feel a strap, presumably a bra strap, and with my imagination racing, deduce the bra to be black and lacy.

Jane hooks my index fingers under the straps, which are released from her shoulders. She then guides my index fingers down skirting the edge of the bra, and I feel first the swell of her breasts then the cleavage between them.

We both breathe heavily and, as my hands are allowed to encompass the material covering her breasts, I can feel her nipples already erect. Jane sighs and allows my hands to linger then guides them over her stomach. Her skin feels smooth and her stomach flat. A stud announces that I have reached her belly button and I am then directed due south.

My fingers skim the boundaries of underwear, and I enjoy the silk texture. With my hands still above the material, I cup her entire pelvic area and am allowed to slowly take the initiative. I begin searching for that special spot, but after a moment, a willing but impatient hand guides my right hand to the desired location.

The movement of her hips increases with her breathing, and I'm relieved to still be wearing my jeans. Assured that my right hand isn't going anywhere, her hand moves up and pushes the blindfold away.

We are in a bathroom and face a steamy mirror through which Jane has watched as she guides me. We both stare into the mirror, Jane in front of me, and her hands go behind her body and undo my belt. My left hand makes its way up to her breasts while my right hand stays where it was sent. I stare at her firm stomach and see in her pierced belly button a stud with a black stone in the middle.

I trace around her nipples through the bra with my fingertips and she sighs. She turns to face me, kisses me passionately, while holding my face firmly in her hands.

Then she puts her hands behind her back and unclasps her black, lacy bra. It falls to the floor and she positions her breasts close to my chest—her nipples feathering my skin. It is electrifying and we kiss again enjoying the taste of each other's lips.

Jane takes my hand and guides me to a Jacuzzi. Bubbles rise in the steamy, frothy water. She signals for me to enter, and I immerse myself in the warm water.

She turns to bring the Chardonnay—her black-silk underwear veiling her firm buttocks, emphasized by both the thin string of her underwear and her swaying hips.

She opens the bottle and fills two glasses, swings her long legs into the tub, and straddles a corner covered in foam from the bubbles being expelled. A finger signals for me to approach, and I stand and hug her. She absorbs the wetness of my body while I enjoy her dry warmth. Then she presses down on my shoulders and I am on my knees. I have work to do.

To my credit, I take great joy pleasing a woman and tease Jane through her silk underwear. This is, I assume, why it's still being worn. Her breathing becomes heavy and her eyes close. Her hands move across her body and squeeze her nipples.

After a while, she stands, turns around, and leans over the side of the Jacuzzi. I slowly peel off her panties, as I lick and nibble her buttocks. Then she turns back and resumes her position allowing me to resume my work unhindered by lingerie.

Jane picks up a glass and takes a long gulp of wine. She sees me watching and nonchalantly spills some down her body. She shivers as I suck and lick it up and she almost climaxes. I have always been impressed with this Chardonnay and from now it will be my favorite. Finally she lowers herself into the tub, legs either side of me and guides me inside her. She has the jets perfectly positioned to intensify any movement and we move slowly, rhythmically, eyes closed, together.

"What is it?" she says, her voice husky but there is an edge in it.

I have stopped moving with her and have slipped out. I feel myself and discover my erection has gone.

"Don't I turn you on?"

I frown. I am stunned. "I'm sorry." I mumble. "It's not you. I …"

I turn away, not sure what has happened. A wave of guilt has extinguished the passion. Mr. Tzu is out there somewhere hurting, and I am drinking wine in a Jacuzzi with a beautiful woman. I look over my shoulder at Jane, who has rejection written all over her face.

"It's not you," I repeat and explain.

Jane moves toward me and hugs me from behind. There is nothing sexual in her embrace, but it feels so good. When finished, she turns me around so I am facing her. There is a puzzled look on her face.

"Will, is there something more to this that you're not telling me?"

I pull her close. That is also puzzling me.

12: Wisdom from the Streets

When I first arrived in San Francisco, I noticed the homeless and felt ill at ease. How can such a beautiful city allow so many of its people to live on the streets? How can 150,000 men, women and children live below the poverty line? At some point we begin to blame them: they're druggies, alcoholics, and psychos. We don't consciously become angry or judgmental but attempt to shield ourselves justifying our inaction and self-disgust at how we've so quickly accepted them as part of the scenery. We've slipped on the first layer of insulation necessary to survive the American city. It is thick, warm and selective.

I first met Salvador about a month earlier one morning in a small park on the edge of Chinatown. The park is just off the tourist's radar and boasts a modest playground that attracts weary parents and children seeking relief from the tedium of shopping or waiting for day care to open. It also attracts some elderly Asian people who find a little serenity in their practice of Tai Chi, Chi Gong and Ba Gua.

I studied Tai Chi in England and have a deep appreciation of the martial arts. I would love to join them but am intimidated by these elegant ancients who seem so genuine. They don't have a clue that I even know any

Tai Chi and probably see me as just another gawking tourist or pseudo-Eastern wannabe.

"Why don't you join them?" A deep, regal voice asked. "It's clear that you want to."

I looked up and saw a smiling, stout man with wild, salt and pepper gray hair. I nodded politely, unsure how to react. His clothing says he was a member of the 15,000 homeless people who live in the shadows of this beautiful city and make their homes in doorways, park benches and, during the winter, in the shelters around the city.

I signaled with my arm across the bench that he should sit down.

The old man carefully lowered himself. His breathing was labored and his many layers of rags restrict his flexibility in such a simple movement.

"Actually, young man, this is my office," he said congenially. "You're new around here. Where are you from?"

I gave my name and a quick synopsis. Being new to America, I had it down pat. "And you, sir, may I ask your name?"

"I am Professor Espinoza," he replied, sitting up a little straighter. "But you may call me Salvador when we are alone." He turned slightly and pointed behind him. "These are my students."

I looked and saw a shopping cart and a group of cats. Not missing a beat, I told him about Harrison, my furry Seinfeld-loving housemate. We bonded quickly as cat-loving males do.

"Be wary of them," he said conspiratorially, nodding at the cats. "They are closer to Buddahood than we are, though they can be quite catty about it." Salvador burst out laughing at his own pun and his body shook. I imagined him in a Santa Claus outfit surrounded by happy children.

"What did you teach, Salvador?"

He sighed heavily. "Philosophy, young man. Just like our friends over there." He nodded to the elders practicing their Tai Chi. "But I am Western, and, armed with my Western arrogance, I approach the question through the path of intellect rather than daily practice. I assumed that university degrees, high academic status and adoring students would help me reach the peak."

"Did they?" I asked, not sure whether to take him seriously though still captivated.

"Indeed they did," Salvador replied. "But I discovered I had scaled the wrong mountaintop and lacked vital equipment."

"So what happened?"

"I went over the top and rolled uncontrollably down the other side." He scratched his beard and shook his big head. "It's a long way down, Will. Remember never to climb what you cannot descend. When I finally finished rolling, I found myself considerably lower than where I started."

Salvador paused engrossed in the laughter of a young family by the swings. He sighed. "It was crushing, but it was also a sign. It took a long time to get up, dust myself off and decide to begin the climb again. This time, though, I knew I would either have to find a different route or a different mountain." He smiled. "And I learned to pack a healthy dose of humility in my backpack."

I was having difficulty following him. It was early morning, and I hadn't had my first cup of coffee. I tried to fill in the gaps.

"So where did you teach?"

"I am a professor, young man. Professors lecture." He clearly savored the words. "Title is important. But it is also ego and that has been my downfall. My students were too eager to sit at my feet, and I was too arrogant to warn them that I did not have all the answers."

Again he scratched his wild beard. "Then I sought out new students. I foolishly wanted to attempt to climb the same mountain again. I made San Francisco my university and gathered students anew. This bench is one of my classrooms." I reflexively stared at the warped wood covered in graffiti. Salvador raised an eyebrow. "Cuts in Higher Education have hurt us all." He sighed again—patting the back of the bench and smiled as I laughed.

Then he stared at his cats for a few minutes. They seemed at peace, not meowing, playing or trying to climb on the old philosopher. But they seemed ever mindful of his presence and clearly want to stay close.

"They're good students," he continued. "If I'm not a good enough lecturer for them, they'll seek another. They do not stay with me for food, shelter or luxury. Nor is there any prestige to glean from this professor. They're simply here to learn. And they've taught me a most important lesson."

"What's that?"

Salvador smiled and for a moment his eyes sparkled. "That a good teacher always learns from his students. So, what might I learn from you, Will? What might you learn from me?"

I was fascinated with Salvador and searched for his name on the Internet that evening. When I returned to the park the following day, I was glad to see him.

"Good morning, Will. Did you find me?" Salvador was watching the old Asians stretching and preparing for their Tai Chi.

"Yeah, you're here," I replied.

"That is not what I mean. Did you look for me?"

I nodded feeling guilty. "Yes, I Googled you then checked Amazon. Salvador's not your name, is it?"

"It is now." His reply was abrupt, and I suspected that he had not had a good night. "Take what I have to offer, young Will. Find the rest elsewhere. This is why cats make such good students. They are critical but studious, and they don't ask the wrong questions."

He hesitated a moment, then turned to me and spoke softly as if he were my father. "You should enroll, son. This can be a tough city in an unforgiving country. You will need an experienced professor if you are going to graduate from this campus. Come to me when you need help."

I nodded, feeling somewhat spooked. "I will, Salvador. When I need help, I will come."

The old man smiled sadly, looked me in the eyes, and his tone became intense. "Yes, you will, young man. And I will guide you as best I can."

I met Salvador regularly over the next few weeks and we discussed philosophy and other subjects. I discovered that he also taught literature. Today is Sunday, and I plan to solicit his help finding Mr. Tzu. I go to The Daily Grind to help open the morning shift.

Tabitha has not started a shift by herself because we had someone with more experience to work with her. Doing so on the weekend makes sense, as it is always slow on a Sunday in winter. I will return later to help Tabs close her shift and take the second one.

Chad volunteered to help and accompanies me to the café. After Jane and I hooked up, Chad and I spend less time together as I sleep over more nights at her place. Jane will meet us at the park, and I look forward to discover how they will bond. I figure if she could trust me meeting sexy psycho-Susan, I could stand exposing her to Chad's animal magnetism.

About eleven o'clock, I feel comfortable leaving Tabs to run the shift. Though conscientious, the staff is inexperienced. There are only three baristas including Mr. Tzu—an ample complement for a café our size. But the other guy is a full-time student and not able to pick up any slack. We survived the last week because the schools were out.

"You will tell Tzu that I ran the place in his absence?" Tabitha asks for the sixth or seventh time.

Chad sits happily at a table near the door drinking coffee skimming a copy of National Geographic—his mind a thousand miles away in whatever country is featured. I pull my jacket off the rack and turn toward him ready to leave. Just then the door opens and the two policemen that questioned me before walk in.

"Just leaving, were you?" The short, James Cagney look-alike Hispanic asks suspiciously. His large sunglasses prevent any chance of reading his expression.

"It's not my shift," I reply, equal parts defense and irritation. "I just popped in to help the staff get started. We're obviously short-handed."

"Very conscientious of you. A rare trait in the younger generation." He twitches his mustache emphasizing his double-edged compliment.

"Do you need anything from me?" I ask wearily. "We haven't heard from Mr. Tzu, and I'll need to return here in a few hours."

"No, actually we want to chat with your colleague." He nods sternly toward Tabitha, and I feel a wave of unease. Images of bad cop movies fill my mind. Would she break under interrogation and reveal the letter? "You got a problem with that, kid?" He has caught me staring a moment too long. Damn, they're good!

"No, of course not. But it's her first time in charge here."

We all look around. Apart from Chad, there is one couple in the cafe and Tabitha's assistant is furiously concentrating on filing her nails.

"Have a nice day, kid." I am suitably dismissed.

As I glance back from the door, Tabitha throws me a worried glance.

For some reason, I anticipate finding Salvador in the same small park in Chinatown and am disappointed when he isn't there. By the time Jane joins Chad and me, we're all hungry and dive into a cheap Chinese restaurant in the bowels of an old building. The clientele are Asian and the menu is a long strip of white paper that hangs informally on the wall. The dishes are handwritten in Chinese using a thick-black pen. Jane and Chad order fast then strike up a conversation as if they have been friends forever. It occurs to me that I should feel threatened by Chad's magnetic charm, but I don't.

Confused, I focus on piling up my plate from the array of mysterious dishes.

Once satiated, we check the park again then walk down a crowded Columbus Avenue that today is distinctly lacking in homeless people. The few we do ask all know the old professor but have not seen him. Soon we find ourselves sitting outside a small café near the wharves. The winter sun is already at an angle and restricts our vision but gives a welcoming illusion of warmth.

I'm frustrated, as I won't have much time to search for Mr. Tzu during the coming week. I will be working long shifts to cover for him. Instinct tells me that the longer he stays absent, the more serious this will get.

A figure stops in front of me blocking the sun with his silhouette.

"Looking for someone?"

I jump to my feet. "Salvador, what a coincidence!"

"Coincidences have never been scientifically or philosophically proven," he says with a smile.

"Can I buy you a coffee? I need your advice on something."

"I'm not sure the proprietor would appreciate the intellectual panache I would add to his storefront. But I'd appreciate some hot tea and I will meet you ..." He turns and surveys the front. "I will wait for you on the wharf there. I'll go claim the bench."

He notices my companions and to my utter amazement, says, "Hello Jane. Long time, huh? And who is this nice young man?"

"I'm cool, Salvador. This is Chad, a housemate of Will's and a fellow conspirator."

"Charmed." The old man puts down his plastic bags and taps his hat.

"Sweet," replies Chad, flashing his trademark smile.

"Chad and I will get the tea," Jane says. "You two go talk."

As we cross the road, my astonishment shows. "How do you know Jane, Salvador?"

"All who make this fair place their home are my students, Will. San Francisco is not a city. It is a university. It is an institution of great and vibrant learning to those who take its classes." As he hesitates, I wonder at his simultaneous clarity and well, imagination. Then he chuckles. "It is an open university. You have those in England, didn't you?"

I nod.

"I used to teach at the Open University to supplement my income before the advent of the Internet." He pauses as he sets his two bags on the bench then we both lean against the metal railings and absorb the picturesque bay.

"This view is particularly endearing on sunny winter days," Salvador says. "No one can capture the clarity of the colors we see. It is like a wild animal, say, a leopard whose spots are so distinct on its skin, whose walk is so graceful, so relaxed; yet so full of potential. You can only stand in wonder as you stare and take the obligatory snapshot." The professor pauses his lecture to reflect. "Yet when you develop the picture and try to share the perfection of the animal with a friend who wasn't there, they see only a one-dimensional photo of a leopard. Something is lost no matter how exceptional the camera or photographer."

There is silence as we both contemplate his treatise.

Then he smiles, perhaps embarrassed. "Is this relevant to the problem you're grappling with?"

I tell him about Mr. Tzu, his wife and the letter. He nods. Jane and Chad have joined us and when I finish, he takes a minute to think.

"Will, you're new to our lands. Do you know about our wars: Korea, Vietnam and now the Gulf War?"

"I have a grasp of the history. Not dates or battlefields but the gist."

"It's not history that I want to talk about. I picked up a newspaper left in the park the other day. It had a review of Neil Young's new album. Do you know his music?" I nod, and he says, "I once idolized him. He was a voice for change, for promise. A line from his lyrics caught my ear about America being beautiful but having an ugly side.

"You can decide for yourself whether the wars were right or not. The issue is—to what lengths should a country go to defend and promote democracy if it truly believes in human freedom? You can write me an essay, four pages single-spaced." He chuckles wistfully but immediately gets serious.

"But I want to talk about those who came back. What do you hear in the media about war vets in England?"

I shrug. "Not a lot. They come out once a year for ceremonies to recount their tales and wear red poppies."

Salvador nods. "What about those who never adjusted back into society, those whose wounds were internal?"

I shake my head. "We don't talk about it, I guess. It's that stiff upper lip and British resilience."

He smiles. "Possibly. Resilience can be a double-edged sword, Will, a close relation to stubbornness."

"The English can certainly be stubborn," I reply.

"Your people's strength when Hitler and other conquerors were at your gate helped you survive. And today, if someone needs medical help, the National Health System takes care of them, right?"

"Probably."

"It's not like that here. This is an example of America's ugly side. We idolize the strong and the successful but show disdain for the weak even when they are our heroes. America has always wanted to forget each war and move on to the next episode, the next fad or soap opera. Those who couldn't move on were cast aside and often found the streets less judgmental than their families. The streets offer many avenues of escape."

He pauses and sips his tea. It is steaming and he exhales sharply.

"Don't judge the homeless, Will. We are each unique with our own personal stories. No one is innocent, no one guilty. But there is a common thread for those who fought to defend our country and its principles and now find themselves on street corners and sleeping in parks."

"What about their families?" I ask. "Don't they help?"

"Certainly, and I believe in most cases they did and still do. Men returned with emotional wounds and families have varying levels of functionality and resources. Those you see on the street are the exceptions."

"What about Asian-Americans, Salvador? They served in the army. I don't see many Asian vets."

"They're more complicated and, like your British, perhaps more resilient. Their family structure is generally stronger; their emotions perhaps more repressed. I'm no psychologist like your lovely friend here. Asian-Americans had to deal with additional aspects such as being viewed as traitors over there and suspicion from bigots here."

"Salvador," I ask. "Do you know any American-Asian vets? Do you know any American-Asian homeless vets?"

There is silence and he turns to stare at the bay.

"Oh, Will," he says, his voice little above a whisper. "I was hoping you wouldn't ask."

13: In with the In-laws

Salvador won't tell me the man's name. There is a code among the homeless, but he promises to talk to him. He's not optimistic and judging from his troubled expression clearly hasn't told me everything. This must be difficult—a professor holding a diligent student back.

Back in the coffee shop, I prepare the changeover to an informal wine bar. I go about my work immersed in Salvador's description of war vets and can't find the opportunity to ask Tabitha about her police interview earlier in the day.

Although her shift is over, Tabitha hovers. I hope waiting to talk. She watches me anxiously fearing she might have revealed something to the two detectives.

When the place has been aired, I distribute apple-scented tea candles around the tables. Then I dim the lights and put on a Joshua Redman CD. Given the rich jazz scene in San Francisco, I feel obliged to promote local musicians. Once the wine bar is ready, I take a bottle of Pinot Noir, open from the previous night and pour two glasses. Tabitha smiles as I nod to a table.

"How did the interrogation go?" I ask, as casually as possible.

Tabitha puts on an expression of pain, horribly overacting. "Oh God, Will, they tied me up in the back room and turned Tzu's desk light on my face. Mendez roughed me up a bit although those truncheons can be quite arousing if you know the technique." She throws her head back and theatrically mops her brow. "Still I didn't break even when they threatened my mother."

"I didn't know you had a mother!" I say, glad for some mindless banter after such a heavy day.

She punches me playfully on the arm nearly spilling my wine then recounts the true story of the routine questioning. "What did you learn?"

"That America is beautiful but has an ugly side."

"Amen to Neil Young, bro'."

"You know Neil Young?" I'm surprised, though I'm only a few years older than Tabitha. "I thought you ..."

"When someone writes something meaningful, Hemingway, we all get it." Her eyes expand as she displays a self-righteous pout. "People like Neil Young write unflinchingly about the truth, whether it's the '60s; the '90s or the twenty-first century. The truth is the truth."

"Amen to writers, then." I toast.

"Yes," she says mischievously. "To writers who seek the truth. Now can you put your inflated ego on ice for a moment and tell me what you discovered?"

I recount what I have learned this afternoon, and she listens diligently.

"This homeless guy—was it Salvador, the professor?"

"You know him?" Again, I'm taken aback.

"He's a bit of a legend around these parts. My bets are that he'll discover the meaning of life and find that no one will listen. Probably what cracked him in the first place was some cosmic knowledge too great for the human brain. Did you ever see the movie, The Fisher King?"

"Yeah."

Tabs doesn't continue; the question hangs in the air. After a moment of silence, she says, "I didn't mention the letter."

"Thank you." I'm relieved.

"Will, why are you hiding it from the cops and from Mrs. Tzu?"

"I'm not sure." I pause to think and a long sigh escapes. "Tzu went to considerable lengths to cover his tracks. Part of me wants to know where he is and find him, but another part of me wants to respect his possible desire for privacy."

Tabitha is examining me with an intense stare, and I squirm in my seat.

"What's driving you, Will? There's something more here, isn't there?"

I inhale sharply, look away and then rise too abruptly. "I must dust the wine bottles on the display rack. Have a good night, Tabitha."

"Fucking Englishmen."

Sitting up in my bed the following day deeply immersed in a new breakthrough chapter, I pick up the ringing phone without thought.

"Will, this is James."

"James?"

"Yes, Jane's father."

"Wow." So eloquent. Spontaneity was never one of my strong points. "How are you doing, sir?" I ask, trying to recover.

"Busy, busy. Listen, I thought we could meet for lunch sometime this week, maybe tomorrow? Perhaps after you finish a morning shift at that … at your establishment." The lines come out wooden, a bad actor sweating through a script. "Keep the rest of the afternoon free," he says, more assertively.

"Err, thank you." I stutter, floored. "If you don't mind me asking, what's the occasion?"

"I'm not sure. Jane thinks I can help you with something and assures me it is not money or influence concerning a job. She also seems to think it will be to my benefit."

"And you trust your daughter's instincts?" I say this frivolously.

His tone is suddenly intense. "Yes, I do, Will, implicitly."

So, Tuesday afternoon I enter the lobby of 44 Montgomery Street, a huge office block in the financial district surrounded by Starbucks, Peet's, juice bars and gym clubs. I am a member of 24-Hour Fitness and frequent this branch once or twice a week, not because it is in walking distance of the coffee shop, but because it gives out free workout towels something that makes me feel pathetically exclusive.

At the reception desk, I ask the two burly security guards to let Mr. van Ness know I'm here. One uniform looks at me dubiously but phones through. The other leans over to interrogate me, his tone sneering.

"You don't frequent these parts, do you?"

"Actually, I come to the gym a few times a week." I nod in the vague direction of the street corner where 24-Hour Fitness is located.

"Come for the free towel, do you?" There's no attempt to hide his smugness.

I can't resist and, leaning in theatrically, I say quietly and passionately. "They're so soft and perfumed and sometimes they're still warm. I swear I can feel the fabric softener."

The guard quickly retreats. His companion returns the phone to its receiver.

"Mr. van Ness will be down in a moment," he says, failing to hide the surprise in his voice.

The door to the elevator opens and shuts a few times spewing glassy-eyed business suits in desperate need of nearby coffee shops. I know these people well though I've never met any of them. About two o'clock, The Daily Grind experiences a similar rush of expressionless customers needing a fix to see them through the rest of the day.

Finally, the elevator door opens and Jane's father exits. "The car is parked around the corner," he says brusquely.

We exit and moments later stand waiting in the underground garage of an adjacent building. The walls are oppressive gray concrete with thick red pipes running through. James makes no attempt to walk to his car, and I feel a wave of anxiety. Mobster and cop movies rewind through my imagination. Will we have our conversation here? No eavesdropping wires, no witnesses. My writer's mind cruises into top gear. To relax, I let my imagination spin off pondering whether the congenial Mr. van Ness is a CIA operative. In fact, maybe the den in his house has a secret door in the panels leading to his Batmobile. His mission is to recruit me to spy against Her Majesty's government, infiltrate the National Health System or buy him shares in Manchester United Football Club. Will I need to start drinking martinis and differentiate between beverages shaken and stirred?

Neither of us attempts to strike up a conversation, and we stand together in mutually uncomfortable silence. Headlights approach and I wonder who's behind the wheel. J. Edgar is dead—I read it somewhere. The driver will probably become my handler.

A shiny, black Mercedes with tinted windows in the back slowly pulls up and a starched uniform exits stiffly from the driver's side. He almost salutes.

"Your car, Mr. van Ness."

"My chariot," James says, glancing sideways at me.

We get in and I notice that the car is as black and shiny inside as out. He presses a button on the stereo and Miles Davis entertains us. As the car pulls away, I can feel James relax. He begins humming and tapping the steering wheel. Then he remembers he has company and clears his throat, embarrassed. I'm happy to have seen the mask slip though I pretend not to have noticed.

"When was the last time you had a decent plate of fish 'n' chips, my lad?" James asks with a credible attempt at a British accent.

"Not since leaving the homeland," I reply.

"There are many of your compatriots in our land, a fifth column perhaps." Here comes the recruitment. "I have a table reserved and your national dish being prepared as we speak. They serve Guinness too. Though, be warned, it will probably come chilled."

I nod gravely. "Malt vinegar?"

He smiles warmly, eyes still on the road. "Malt vinegar, of course." He dials a number on his cell phone. Malt vinegar—of course!

After passing the Sunset district where I live, then the university, we drive through a gated entrance and down a very long path lined with eucalyptus trees. James pulls up outside what would easily pass for a stately home in England. The gardens are immaculate and the lawns meticulously manicured.

Before our seatbelts have retracted, our car doors open for us and we exit, the engine still running. As we walk up the stairs and into the building, I fight the urge to look back at the car. Jane's father leans over.

"Don't look back. It's not classy." There's an undeniable air of mockery in his voice. "It's taken me years to master that."

Everyone we pass knows him by name, and we are escorted to a corner table overlooking a lush golf course. Since it is the middle of the afternoon, there are not many people dining, but I suspect Mr. van Ness would have received a window table regardless.

A white-suited waiter approaches and asks my host if he wants his usual. James nods and the waiter smiles at me. "And a Guinness for you, Mr. Hemingway?"

I see my host is very pleased with himself, laughing at the opportunity to use my nickname. He probably can't wait to share this with Jane, the snitch! James sits there with a big grin on his face.

"Do you play golf, James?" I ask.

He leans forward and whispers. "Hate the game, but that needs to remain between us. The trick to advancement, Will, is either be an excellent golfer or stay off the green. But you need to be a member of a golf club regardless."

James raises an eyebrow conspiratorially. He just knows I'm going to write this all into a novel.

14: Tombs of Honor

The food is worthy of the olde countrye. The Guinness is good, though chilled, and the malt vinegar is waiting on the table. But this place is anything but your British corner chippy. The crystal chandeliers and starched tablecloths amply attest to the exclusivity.

Still, it has easily been the best meal I've eaten in America. The fish is tender and juicy on the inside and crisp on the outside. The chips are delectable—none of those wimpy, anorexic and pale French fries that incarcerate the New World. The garden peas are fresh, bright green, and make just the right pop when you bite into them. I don't recognize the label on the malt vinegar bottle, but I'm sure it is vintage if there is indeed such a thing.

James works hard to keep the conversation flowing. He talks about his company; how he developed it from almost nothing into a Fortune 500 entity. He regrets that they had only one child, light of his life that she is, and that she is not inclined at all to take over the company.

He would have liked to pass the reins over by now, slow down and go fishing at hotspots around the world. Maybe Jane's intended will be from the business world. Sorry, he adds when he remembers with whom he is talking to, but these are early days yet for Jane and me.

However, he continues, it is most important that she marries for love, for happiness.

His wife has her quirks but make no mistake, they love each other very much. He is very proud of Jane— had he mentioned this already? She is so smart, so vibrant.

And so he talks while I eat and absorb the ambience of the meal. When we finish eating, he suggests we move to the lounge. "Your folks would call it the Smoking Room and change their jackets. But this is California. We don't smoke or change jackets. Why do they change jackets?"

Having no insight into the mores of British aristocracy, I shrug. "Perhaps they don't want to carry tobacco odor on them for the rest of the day."

"I think they didn't want their wives to know they'd been off *scallywagging.*"

He savors every syllable and we both laugh at its absurdity.

We move to a big room where there is a large fireplace with crackling wood. Jane's father chooses two vacant armchairs, and two coffees appear on the table with a small plate of wrapped mints.

"So what's on your mind, Will?"

"What do you mean?" I ask, hesitating for a moment.

"Jane told me that it has something to do with your boss, and I might be able to help you. Does this make sense?"

I nod, take a sip of coffee and recount the story of Mr. Tzu's disappearance. I tell James of my discussion with Salvador and, as I talk about the war veterans, James's expression becomes intense. He leans forward listening to every word.

When I finish, James sits back in his chair and thinks. There are lines across his face that I hadn't previously noticed. Then he turns to a waiter and orders a cognac. He asks if I want anything and I decline.

"I understand now why Jane wanted us to meet. Why does this interest you, Will, apart from the implications at work?"

I shrug. "I've been wrestling with that myself. It consumes me. I can't stop thinking about him. I've tried googling his family and such. Maybe because I'm a writer and I sense a story."

James looks unconvinced. I plow on. "There's some kind of injustice here, I'm sure. I want to write about injustice. I want to use my talent, my creative energy to help bring about change. Why did Jane want us to talk?"

James sighs. "I served in the Marines in Vietnam. Jane knows I was an officer, a decorated officer. There are five medals in a case in my den. My unit was honored by President Johnson, and he spent some time visiting us."

He pauses, staring into a distant past. "Jane knows that while her friends' families organize barbecues on Memorial Day, her father disappears. She knows that in the days leading up to Memorial Day, he secludes himself in his den when he's not at the office, and that he doesn't share jokes or listen very well to his little girl's stories.

"Maybe she sees him drinking more during this time, though I hope not. Perhaps she sees that her mother is uncharacteristically understanding and supportive while stealing worried glances at her husband knowing she is powerless to help."

James stops for a moment and takes a long, contemplative drink and a deep breath before continuing with unconcealed venom. "I hate Veterans Day. I hate that it's a national excuse to party. You know, I went on a business trip once to Israel and the middle of the trip coincided with their Memorial Day. Every man serves in the army and many women too. Everyone has lost somebody. I was being driven from Tel Aviv to Haifa on their equivalent of Highway Five. At exactly eleven in the morning, the driver pulled over. My host had warned that this would happen, but I was still astonished at what I saw. We all got out of our cars. I mean everyone. The whole highway stopped. Six lanes of traffic. People stood in silence by their cars, heads bowed, as sirens wailed from car radios."

There is silence for a few minutes. My host is sitting across from me, but he is far away. Then James looks up. "I want to show you something, Will. Come."

We leave the club in his black, shiny Mercedes and drive about twenty minutes to the military cemetery in the Presidio. There are stunning views of the Golden Gate Bridge, and I stare as we pass through the tall stone pillars and iron gates. The cemetery, like most of the city, is built on a hill. Rows of white tombstones stand in perfect, military symmetry, defined by straight grass borders that resemble a white and green chessboard. A huge flag blows in the wind as I follow Jane's father. I note the flag is frayed at the edges, a victim of uncompromising wind and sea air.

"What do you think the average soldier dreads when he goes to war?" James asks without looking at me.

I think for a moment. "Death, captivity, never seeing his loved ones again?"

James nods. "That's about right. What about an officer?"

"The same?"

"Yes, but there's something else. The officers see the young, fresh faces when they join the unit. Sometimes, if we're embarking together, we see their parents, wives, girlfriends, and children. They hug and cry, while the family steals frightened glances at the officer silently pleading that he bring their boy, their lover or father home.

James stops, standing taut, reliving a scene. His voice has gone eerily cold.

"And a shiver courses through you. You are not God, probably not much of a soldier either. You know you cannot protect them but still you swear a silent oath to try and bring them back alive—as many as you can. Fuck the war, the politics, and the drive to serve your country. All you pray for is to bring your boys back alive. You'd rather face a thousand Charlies than one of these parents, wives or children at the funeral or memorial service."

We stop by a tombstone and he crouches to tenderly brush some dirt from the grave. I crouch with him as he takes a deep breath.

"The last time my wife entered my den when I was not there was about fifteen years ago, Will. She shouldn't have, but her motives were no doubt innocent. She found a small-black notebook. Almost full. I had written a list of names. Mainly women. The names reappeared regularly and there was a column with dates and another with dollar amounts. She found a checkbook from an unknown bank account.

"That evening she confronted me. As far as she knew, we didn't keep secrets from each other—financial or otherwise. Who were these women? Ex-lovers? Illegitimate kids? I screamed back totally out of control that it was none of her damn business. How dare she enter my den, and I yelled other absurdities. We'd never raised our voices to each other like that and never have since. Now, thank goodness, she knows, and I was a fool to think I couldn't share such things with her. She is the rock in my life."

He points to the tombstone, and I notice his hand shaking. He takes a moment to compose himself.

"My first sergeant, Pete O'Reilly, died in my arms. The last words he heard were an oath that his CO would take care of his two young kids. Their mother receives monthly checks from the bank. She doesn't know the source. When his oldest daughter was eighteen, she received a letter about a trust fund set up for her and her brother to pay for university tuition. The youngest graduated from Stanford a few years back."

As James rises, he steadies himself on my arm for just a moment before straightening. We move on to another grave where he says, "His family is devout Catholic. In his faith, one's life belongs to God, and you are forbidden from taking it yourself. He was never meant to be a soldier, should never have been there. I swore his parents would never know how he died. He's buried here as a hero, and so it'll remain."

At another grave he seems lost in thought, while buried memories resurface. Then he turns to me. "What I'm about to tell you neither Jane nor her mother knows. They know I served and that I have taken care of my men when I could—those alive and those that have fallen. But what I am about to tell you ..." He pauses and I nod, understanding the unspoken demand. He continues. "I worked in intelligence as well. I oversaw the recruitment and training of a spy network of sorts. Nothing glamorous. We gave the alcoholics and junkies money for booze and drugs, and in return they supplied us with information. Basic stuff like troop movements. Crumbs. They were the dregs of their society and they knew little. But sometimes they knew enough to prevent some of our troops dying. If we thought physical methods and intimidation would get more out of them, we didn't hesitate in order to save one more life, bring one more boy home alive.

"I didn't care. I could justify it. Not for the great United States nor for freedom and democracy—just to get my boys home alive. If a worthless drug addict's confession could save just one life, then let the bastard scream."

I stare at James as his cheeks flushed red and his breathing rushed. He forces his shaking hands into his pocket and stops to compose himself.

"They were handled by Asians—usually Asian-Americans recruited over here. These people had it hard. They may have had nothing to do with Vietnam born thousands of miles away in a different culture and a different language. They were doing their job as loyal Americans no different from the rest of us."

His voice becomes a hiss.

"But the army saw them as different. They had yellow skin and slit eyes. They aroused all the wild fears and prejudices that permeated the white and black soldiers. They largely hung out together and felt betrayed.

"Then we returned home. To some here we were perceived as heroes; to others we were a source of uneasiness because of the horrors we'd inflicted. For Asian-American soldiers, it was twice as bad. In civilian clothes, they were immigrants who looked like the enemy. They received no honor and no respect from their peers. Sometimes they even faced rejection by their own folks."

He pauses again. I watch his warm breath escape as he exhales into the chilly air.

"Two of my men are still alive, physically at least. They're both loners, pariahs. They've never held down jobs, never married. They wander the streets occasionally returning to a particular hostel for shelter and food. They are luckier than the homeless you talk about, Will. Their officer turned out to be a rich bastard who cares. Their tabs at the hostel are taken care of."

There is silence and we stand both looking around. I search for something to say and put my hand on his shoulder. "You're a good man, James, a generous man."

He turns abruptly, my hand flying from him and looks at me incredulously. His eyes stab and his voice becomes sharp and loud. "I don't do it for them! I do it for me! I do it so I can live, so I can continue! I do it to keep away the nightmares, to prevent the faces of widows and orphans staring at me at every turn."

He stomps off toward the car.

"You're still a good man, James." I shout after him, my voice shaking with emotion. He turns around. My arm sweeps in the cemetery and, with considerable effort, I steady my voice. "They all know who you are and what you did. They still think you're a hero. So do I, sir, even if I can't understand it all."

He stares at me for what feels like hours, and I walk slowly toward him. He is breathing heavily—I see this even though he wears a thick winter coat. When he speaks, his voice is quiet, but steely.

"Find your boss, son. Find him and help him if you can; his brother too if the poor bastard is still alive."

15: Psychology 101

Jane is happy that we bonded and frustrated that she can't pry the entire story about what happened when we met from either her father or me. I work daily and often pop into the coffee shop to check the shift changes. I have become obsessed with Tzu's disappearance, and this is hardly the best way to build a new relationship.

I promise to speak with Mrs. Tzu about hiring an additional barista. When she hears my request, Mrs. Tzu bows her head. It suggests an air of permanence, and we are both upset with the idea. Nevertheless, I tell her about Jane and my need to put time into the relationship. This seems to resonate with her and the old lady smiles for the first time since I brought a cup of green tea to her table.

"This woman, Jane, she good for you, yes?"

"The relationship is early, but we're having lots of fun." I'm not sure chasing homeless eccentrics and facing down scary, kickboxing ex-girlfriends can seriously be defined as fun, but I have a plan.

I share with her that I have booked a short trip to a hot spring retreat for the weekend after next. Truthfully, I had done this last night, but the implication sounds as if it had been on the calendar for some time.

Mrs. Tzu reluctantly gives her consent, and I am a click away from posting the open barista position on Craigslist, a community-based website for jobs, housing and other services. Tabitha has also prepared a sign to hang in the window, and I'm confident that we'll quickly fill the position.

Knowing that I'm near the end of my shift, Jane enters the coffee shop, and I introduce her to Mrs. Tzu.

"He not try to pick me up. He good boy," Mrs. Tzu says patting my arm. Then she lets out a hearty laugh, and I feel a weight leave my shoulders. Mrs. Tzu understands survival.

I move behind the counter to begin closing my shift. I give the Beast a wipe over, although I cleaned it thoroughly not long before. As I look across, I see Jane and Mrs. Tzu deep in conversation. I slow down giving them time to talk.

When I can't think of anything else to do, I pull on my jacket and move toward the table. Seeing me, Mrs. Tzu finishes a sentence and they glance at me. I can feel the warmth emanating between them.

Mrs. Tzu says, "Jane and I talk. What you think, I pierce my nose too?" Then she laughs again, her hand on Jane's arm. "Where you take her, somewhere nice, I hope?"

"Next weekend? We have a reservation at the Wilbur Hot Springs," I reply and try to recall what I read on their website so I can tell her more. There is no need.

"Ah, good place, good food. Have nice fireplace and walking paths in hills. Mr. Tzu and I took many walks; see small deer and rabbits. All wild. Best are the pools." She leans in and says conspiratorially, "You can be naked in pools if you want." She giggles and her wrinkles disappear for a moment. "No way Mr. Tzu go naked even at night. Not proper, he says. Crazy hippies, he says."

"You go to places like that? And Mr. Tzu?" I guess I really don't know her husband.

She looks at me exaggerating a surprised expression. "Where I get such beautiful skin, you think? Avocado? Tofu?" She strokes her wrinkled skin softly then laughs. "You go in naked?"

"I ... I don't know." I'm not comfortable sharing such details with a woman the age of my grandma. I look at Jane for help—no luck. Her arms are folded across her chest and her grin suggests she is thoroughly enjoying my discomfort.

Mrs. Tzu hasn't finished and, as she rises to leave, she turns to Jane. "Chinese men uptight. Englishmen uptight. Why you choose him?"

Jane puts an arm around me. "He has his good points, I guess."

"Yes, yes." Mrs. Tzu looks at me and her tone is serious. "I think you are good boy. Jane is lucky. But next weekend, no need to be too good, okay?"

She shuffles off laughing to herself.

"Did I just get slaughtered by an elderly and fragile grandma?" I say bewildered.

"Elderly grandma maybe." Jane grins, watching her leave. "But she ain't fragile."

The week passes. Jane is writing papers, and I'm working shifts and interviewing. But on Thursday we hire a new barista, and she has a working knowledge of wines as well. She seems confident and competent, and on her second shift makes a few suggestions for improvement. I appreciate the modest way that she does this and by the time we are in Jane's car on Friday afternoon, I feel relaxed. I have promised not to mention Tzu and instead concentrate on Jane. I am determined to deliver.

Once we clear the Bay Area traffic, the journey takes only a few hours. The last part of the trip is a rocky, country road that follows along a stream. Though the weather is cloudy and uninviting, we get out of the car by a wooden bridge and listen to the stream babbling. Jane puts an arm around me and sighs. Nothing needs to be said—it is just right.

At the hot springs guesthouse, we are greeted warmly and taken to our room. We quickly change into bathing suits and toweled robes and gather books and drinks to take with us. Jane wears a tight one-piece that promises more than it reveals. It is, of course, black. Ten minutes later, I am lying in a steamy pool watching wisps of fog play on the mountainside.

An elderly Asian couple walks past. I follow them with my eyes, wondering. My girlfriend clears her throat not very subtly, and I force myself to look back at her.

Jane has brought psychology books with her though she claims that not all are curriculum-required but ones she wanted to read and never had the time. I watch her lying in the shallow pool reading. She is right. I have been self-absorbed with my writing and Mr. Tzu. I know so little about Jane. Is she really a conscientious student under the eccentric Goth image she portrays? A hidden genius? Though she needs to study, I will be there when she wants to talk, walk, and be with me. It will be her weekend, I promise silently.

Now as I watch her reading, I reach for the latest Christopher Moore novel. I love his humor and this vampire story takes place, significantly for me, in San

Francisco. I sigh. I need this break for myself as well, a short break from the city I love.

Once our skins are adequately shriveled (is this what Mrs. Tzu meant?), we return upstairs and shower before dinner. Jane puts on a thin, black dress with a low cleavage and straps tied around her neck. She looks so gorgeous that I contemplate throwing her on the bed right there. However, dinner waits.

The chef is a guest for the weekend. The resort routinely swaps chefs with other retreats or hotels. The point is lost on me, but the food is light and excellent. There is fish and a healthy salad, and we order a pleasant Pinot Noir from a small nearby winery.

After eating, we retire to a spacious lounge room. We find two soft chairs facing each other and put our wine and books on a small table between us. The elderly Asian couple sit about twenty feet from us playing a board game I don't recognize. I will not be tempted to butt in.

I focus instead on a group of young people our age that have staked out the area near the fireplace. I'd noticed them earlier at the pool. They're all very attractive and chatty. Though not yet divided into couples, the dynamics suggest they soon will be.

"So," I say, filling both our wineglasses, "let's talk psychology." Jane stares and arches a thin black-penciled eyebrow in a way that would have made Spock proud. But I continue, unperturbed. "What are you reading?"

"Secrets of Sexual Body Language." She has my attention. "It explains how we consciously or subconsciously send nonverbal messages; how you can tell heaps about a person without talking to them—just by careful observation."

"Really," I say. "Does it work?"

She rolls her eyes and glances at the group by the fireplace. A mischievous grin stretches across her face. She leans in and I follow suit. "Let's do some field work."

She opens the book and reads, "'It was Charles Darwin who first said in the 1870s that some facial expressions are not culturally determined.'" She gives me a stern professorial glare to check that I'm taking her seriously. I put on my best classroom face mastered from twelve years of feigning interest at school.

Satisfied, she continues. "'Many of these expressions are universal based upon common needs shared by all humans. In other words, you should be able to tell whether that guy has a chance with the girl he's chatting up regardless of whether we are in California, New Delhi or Berlin."

"So what is the secret to success?" My chin rests on my hands; my elbows on my knees.

"You need to convey that you are available, likeable and nonthreatening," she says. I must admit that I'm intrigued to see this side of Jane. "That's what you portrayed in the wine bar that first night despite everything else."

"Everything else! What does that mean?"

"Let's focus on our lab rats over there. You see the big, blond guy chatting up the two longhaired chicks? We can't see their faces, but they are plainly interested by the way they are head-on to him. Their bodies are saying, 'I'm here for the taking'."

An evil grin creeps across Jane's face. "This next bit might not be easy for you. Are you ready?"

"Sure," I say, coolly exuding uncertainty and inadequacy.

"Why do you think they're so attracted to him?"

"Well, he's tall, handsome and obviously rich but has athlete's foot and is inextricably tied to his mother's apron strings."

She looks at me trying to maintain an expression of stern academic skepticism but can't help laughing. "Sure he's tall, well built and handsome," she looks me over as though making comparisons and pauses enough to enjoy my squirming, "but he's also emanating that he's an alpha, a leader, and a survivor. He is the evolutionary caveman sending out a strong message that his genes are going to survive and thrive, and these women should take a share."

I gulp more wine. "Probably just discussing the latest movie," I say.

"If so," the comeback is swift, "it is Lord of the Rings. Look how he controls the scene; his voice is loud and confident. He's making eye contact all the time and, I'll bet, the women are the ones who look away from his sheer power."

Jane peers at me and I try to stare her down. She shakes her head as condescendingly as she can but at least squeezes my knee. "Don't bother. I'm not a good fit for alpha males or females. Remember my relationship with Susan? Oh, look at him now. Sweet. He's touching them marking out his space. And see how he interrupts the women without seemingly annoying them. He's the one who finishes any topic. I wouldn't let you get away with that."

"I'm not sure I like psychology."

"Ah, but, though you can't compete with him on his territory, you have other avenues. Your type," I don't like the way Jane uses that term, "show that you are listening, engaging with me as an equal. You nod with empathy and say words like *yes*, and *really*. You make eye contact but not in a threatening way. You are quieter, but you are quick to show your intelligence through conversation or gentle humor. Sound familiar? Such tactics tell a girl that you will take care of her needs, provide a stable home and family, but also allow her the space she needs to grow.

"Now, see the woman over there in the tight-green dress? She's talking to a couple but not interested in either of them. It's not just that she glances in the direction of our alpha male, but her body is facing him. She's smiling a lot suggesting that she's a happy camper even if they are boring the pants off her—assuming she's wearing any. When she knows that she has his attention, she'll touch her hair or eyebrows or engage in another kind of preening. If she's not quite confident in her appearance, she'll disappear to freshen up. But there are dangers in doing this as she'll concede the territory she has established in his range.

Jane pauses for a sip of wine.

"He's also subconsciously noticing. Look at how he changes his behavioral patterns when he sees her looking at him. See how she smiles or makes some kind of eye motion when their eyes meet? She needs to get closer to him." Jane leans forward, holding her breath. "Look." She whispers. "Here she goes."

Green dress moves slowly in alpha male's direction. As she nears, she leans over and nonchalantly picks some nuts off the table. Then she turns from his direction toward the fire and begins talking to another woman.

"Watch the angle of her body," Jane says with anticipation.

Green dress laughs at something the other woman says and then, yes, her body is now facing alpha male. And, there, she glances over.

"And you know the amazing part?" Jane's eyes are wide open with wonder. "She probably doesn't even know she's doing it."

Jane turns to me rather proud of herself. I slowly lean forward and stare at her studiously. "Yes," I say as intensely as I can manage, forehead creasing to exude maximum empathy. "Really."

She laughs. "Forget it, beta male, I'm the pro."

I am suitably quashed.

Then she stares intensively into my eyes, bringing her face close to mine. Her body has turned to me and our legs touch lightly. She slowly puckers her lips and rolls her eyes. In a deep husky voice, she says, "What am I trying to tell you now?"

Over the next hour, beta male's hands are tightly tied to the brass bed frame, while Black Slinky Dress becomes crinkled and sweaty. Later, we float in one of the public pools. We are naked and let our bodies lightly graze each other in the warm water.

Alpha male walks in holding hands with green dress. Jane turns to me triumphantly and pulls me close. She whispers proudly in my ear. "See, they're together. From now on, it's Dr. Jane to you."

16: Progress

I'm standing on a wharf staring across the water at Alcatraz Island. Chad called with the message that Salvador wanted to meet me here. It's cloudy and foreboding. I'm told that San Francisco suffers from bad storms during the winter. Though they last for only a few days, I have been warned that their intensity wreaks havoc bringing down trees and telephone poles; flooding drains and sidewalks.

I wonder what attracts people to Alcatraz. It was a prison—a depressing, violent place where swimming in icy waters with ravenous sharks was often the preferable choice. But this gray island remains an undeniable magnet for people.

Is it possible that people subconsciously connect to being imprisoned even when they've never been physically incarcerated? When people say they feel trapped in a job, a family or a relationship, can they somehow relate to the helplessness and despair that the prisoners on Alcatraz must have felt?

There are no boats on the bay. The wharf and surrounding areas are almost empty. Only a few diehard tourists and the homeless brave the piercing cold wind. San Francisco is bracing itself for an onslaught.

Salvador Espinoza shuffles up and greets me. His cats, having a hard time negotiating the gusting wind, follow. The old man is short with his sentences and eager to move on. He agrees to go to a nearby diner styled after an old cable car. The partially enclosed outside area is empty.

I go inside for coffee and return with two breakfasts. Salvador gives me a dirty look—there are limits to how much charity he'll accept.

"I need to eat, Salvador," I say. "I'm going to work soon." I try to avoid sounding as if I'm pleading. "And I'm English. There's no way that I can eat breakfast with you watching. Please, do me a favor. Apart from which, you're spending a lot of time helping me right now."

We eat our breakfast in silence. Though sheltered, it is still cold and the food will not remain hot for long. It's a basic diner breakfast: scrambled eggs, bacon and home fries. Nothing fancy. But it finds its mark on this gray winter day. Sitting outside, Salvador can share some of his food with his cats that show remarkable discipline and patience.

When his plate is empty, Salvador dabs his mouth with a napkin. Despite his disheveled appearance, he fits easily into the scene, eating breakfast at a local diner; perhaps meeting a fellow professor or enthusiastic student at the school canteen surrounded by young, vibrant minds. Is this time travel back into a not-so-distant past?

Salvador is deep in thought. I feel a wave of affection for him, but he has already warned me against trying to change him or anyone else among his peers. He catches my eye and flashes a warning look as he reads my thoughts.

"The storm will hit about noon," he says matter-of-factly. "We must all hunker down deep for the next few days."

"Where will you go?"

"The shelters. I will go straight from here and claim my place early. Most of the faculty leaves it late; some will leave it too late."

"Will there be room for everyone?"

"No, but not everyone will come looking."

"Salvador, if—"

His glare cuts me short. Again, the boundary that must not be crossed.

"I'm sorry," I say, lowering my eyes.

"You're a good boy," he replies, his tone mollified. "Let me tell you why I asked to meet. My colleague might be able to help you. He was not very enthusiastic about the prospect, and I had to use my considerable sway. He walks a delicate path between sanity and its antagonist. I have much to say on the topic but now is not the time. I cannot promise what state he will be in when you meet or how receptive he will be."

"Who is he?"

"He's an Asian war vet—maybe your boss's brother. They share the same last name, though it might be commonly used for all I know. I had to tell him the reason that you need help. We can meet on Saturday at the Transbay Terminal on Mission Street. What time do you finish work?"

"About two-thirty. Let's say three o'clock, so I don't keep you waiting."

"Good." He laughs. "Because I keep a tight schedule."

I laugh too. Then I take a plastic bag out of my backpack and from this a book. "This is by Thomas Friedman, 'The World Is Flat'. I have just finished it and thought you would enjoy it."

The old man eyes me suspiciously.

"I picked it up at a thrift shop, Salvador. I paid three bucks for it. I usually pass books along. I'm not at a stage in my life where I can afford to collect possessions. I'm still moving around."

He relents and smiles. He knows all about being transient. "Thank you," he says, taking the book. "I can't promise to read it immediately, you understand. I have to keep up with my assignments and students." But he carefully wraps the book and stores it.

"Saturday then?"

"Saturday. Keep warm, Salvador."

"You too, young man. Thank you for breakfast."

We rise and go our separate ways. For a few blocks, I walk along the Embarcadero looking out at Alcatraz. It remains dark and impenetrable. I'm meeting many people incarcerated in their pasts. I think of Salvador, of Mr. Tzu, and now possibly his brother who I am soon to meet.

The storm hits San Francisco with ferocity. Tree branches break and fall, drains are quickly blocked creating small ponds that pedestrians must negotiate, while avoiding minor tidal waves when passing cars drive through. People scamper from cover to cover.

Over the next few days, the coffee shop understandably sees little business and the shifts last forever. I am tempted to pull out my laptop and write.

How many times can I clean The Beast or sweep the floor?

My housemates and I decide to eat together Friday night without girlfriends or other guests. This is rare. One of us always tends to have company, female or otherwise. But the decision is made and we each chip in ten bucks to ensure a feast. Even more peculiar is an unspoken decision to clean up the place and, by the time we go shopping, the house looks almost presentable.

The storm has largely passed though there is still a strong wind. Entering the supermarket, we realize that we haven't decided on a menu. Chad seems serenely nonplussed by this and content to just walk the aisles, but Bear is worried by such an approach.

"Let's begin by deciding on the protein," Muscle Man says.

We stand by the meat counter and watch a man in a white coat dispassionately dismember a dead bird. We compromise on fish and tofu before moving on to vegetables.

I pick out two bottles of wine for ten dollars. These labels wouldn't find their way into James' wine cellar, but they are solid California wines. The heavy weather stipulates that I reject anything white, so a Cab and Merlot are carefully placed into the shopping cart. Chad picks up one of the bottles and reads the label. He smiles approvingly.

"You know your wines, Chad?" I ask, surprised.

"I don't." He smiles back, returning the bottle to the cart and picking up the other. "But how can you go wrong with a wine called Smoking Loon? Have you ever heard the call of the loon, Will?"

"I don't think so," I reply.

"Oh, you'd remember," he says warmly. He frowns as he reads the label of the second bottle from a company called Three Blind Moose.

"The moose are not actually blind." I point out. "They're just wearing sunglasses."

This satisfies Chad, who shows it to Julian, our Southern Californian surfer. Julian is rarely separated from his shades and, despite the storm, still defiantly wearing a Hawaii shirt, a pair of shorts that reach his knees, and flip flops ('I'll never walk around with wet socks'). He looks at me incredulously.

"Tell me there's more to selecting a bottle of wine. My parents spend thousands of dollars on trips to wine regions around the world, belong to a wine purchasing club, and discuss little else whenever we break open a special reserve."

He raises both hands and indicates with his fingers that the term *special reserve* deserves quotation marks.

"Truth is," I reply, putting on my sommelier tone, "a good wine comes in all prices and ages. You can open up an expensive fifty-year-old bottle and it might taste of vinegar, while a Trader Joe 'Two-Buck Chuck' wine recently won an award at a respectable blind-tasting competition. Herein," I conclude, "lies the contradiction."

"A profound dichotomy," offers Chad, philosophically.

Bear hasn't been following. Now he turns to Chad. "A medical procedure?"

We all laugh as we make our way to the checkout. I look at my housemates and feel profoundly lucky. There is rarely tension between us though we're so different. Inevitably, someone gets annoyed at someone, but we deal with it swiftly. We seem to effortlessly reach a level of harmony. Bear says my thoughts out aloud.

"A man's home should be his rock," replies Chad and, unbidden images of Tzu, his wife and children come to mind.

Back at the apartment, we set to work. Bear reverently prepares the fish. Chad the tofu. I make a salad while Julian sets the table and takes care of the music. The discussion turns to women. Strangely, I am the only one in a relationship and find myself talking enthusiastically about Jane.

"She is cool," says Chad.

"And she sounds pretty smart," says Bear. "She balances her studies and social life, while still finding time to work out and stay in shape.'

"Tight," says Julian, popping open the Smoking Loon Merlot.

17: Under the Bridge

I meet Salvador after work on Saturday, and we make our way under one of the on-ramps that streams traffic to the Bay Bridge and over to the East Bay. Thick, gray columns of heavy concrete rise to a foreboding roof through which seeps a steady rumble. It is wet and cloudy, and the devastation from the storm lies all around. We approach a fire contained inside a metal barrel. A tight band of men surround it—their outstretched hands trying to draw warmth from the flames. I can see others huddled in corners or burrowed in sleeping bags.

"The faculty sleeps a lot during the day," Salvador says. "There is little respite to be found during the night. Some are wary of being attacked or harassed. Others fear the prospect of dreaming, of remembering why they are here and what they had before."

I stare at Salvador amazed by his clarity and perceptiveness. With hands deep in my pockets, I have nothing to say and walk with him. We reach the fire and the men make room for us greeting Salvador with respect and warmth. I will later learn that he helps many of them fill out forms as well as read or write letters. They accept his philosophical lectures as part of the terrain. He is appreciated, eccentricities notwithstanding.

They eye me, however, with open suspicion though I am silently invited to share the heat of the fire. I had wanted to bring something, coffee or food, but Salvador had advised against it.

"You are already in a precarious position in their eyes—a privileged student, who has a special relationship with his professor. You will be regarded with suspicion and your request has been widely discussed among the faculty."

I glance around at the faculty. What secrets or memories are lodged deep inside the vaulted walls of their sanity? As I look at their faces, each man drops his gaze and takes an exaggerated interest in the fire.

No one is Asian, and I glance back at Salvador who is expounding to his audience about the rigorous life of the writer. From the way he talks about me, I am clearly a monolith in the world of literature. There is no mockery in his voice, and I wonder, rather too optimistically, if perhaps he is seeing into the future.

After a few moments, he pauses and looks at me expectantly. Am I supposed to say something wise or avant-garde? They all look at me with great interest, but the gruff southern voice of a great bearded man breaks the spell.

"He ain't here for a read'n. He wants to see the Chinaman."

"Indeed he does," replies Salvador, his tone pleasant and in control. "Li Tzu has granted him an interview. We are meeting him here."

They all look around and shuffle.

"He ain't here," says the Southerner, stating the obvious.

"He will come," Salvador replies. "Li Tzu has something he needs to say."

"He can say it to us," another homeless man blurts out.

"Yes he can, and I hope he knows that option is available. But he wants to speak to the writer. Will here knows his family."

Another man, face hidden in a ski mask, asks in a high-pitched voice, "Whatcha want from him?"

"I'm trying to find his brother."

"You be a bounty hunter?" The questioner looks at me seriously.

"No, I am a writer and I work for Li Tzu's brother."

"He owe ya' money?"

I shake my head. "It's not like that. I'm trying to help."

Apparently, this specific phrase doesn't figure among their favorites and I feel them stiffen.

"Well, he ain't here," says the big man. "Maybe he done changed his mind."

I am also wondering this, and I'm not sure how long I should hang around. Salvador must sense this as well and turns to me.

"Will, let us wait in my office. I have some paperwork to attend to."

We walk away and when we are out of earshot, he says: "Don't judge them too harshly, son. It is a bitter life and we become protective of one another."

We sit down on an old truck tire guarded by his cats, his faithful students. Salvador busies himself with his belongings, and I see the book I gave him is carefully wrapped in a clear plastic bag with a bookmark about two-thirds of the way through. I pull out my current book and settle down.

A few minutes pass and Salvador clears his throat. As I look up, he signals with his eyes and we both stand, Salvador with some effort, to greet the approaching man. A faded Giant's baseball cap hides the man's eyes until he is closer. He is Asian and, though he looks much older and his face more worn, there are resemblances to Mr. Tzu. But his eyes lack the gritty determination and confidence I have seen in my boss.

"You are late," says Salvador. His voice is gentle but rebuking. "It is not courteous to leave a fellow student alone with the professor."

Li Tzu glances up at me and bows slightly. This is his apology.

"It's okay," I say, flashing my most congenial smile. "I enjoy the Professor's tutorials."

Tzu cracks a brief smile and Salvador seems flattered by my response.

The three of us sit on the truck tire with our feet inside. We are close, knees touching, and I can sense the fear—the struggle inside Li Tzu.

"Mr. Tzu," I begin. "You know why I'm here?"

He nods.

"Do you know where your brother is?" There is no response and I plead my case. "I'm a friend of his and deeply worried by his disappearance." The old man looks at me. He knows that I haven't spoken the truth. "He is my boss," I say. "He took care of me, gave me a job when I had barely set foot in America and knew no one. He trusted me and now I run the opposite shift to him. I feel ... that I owe him something."

Li Tzu looks away, but I sense he is listening. "I have met his wife and next weekend I will travel to Ventura and meet his children. His wife is very worried about him. She loves him very much."

"H–how did you find out a–about me?" His voice is quiet and though he stutters his words are clipped.

"Oh, I can be tenacious," I say trying to lighten the atmosphere. Salvador smiles and nods at me.

No smile, however, is forthcoming from Mr. Tzu's brother. "H–how?"

"You put a letter under the door of the coffee shop on the day I believe he disappeared. One of our staff found it."

"Sh–she can read Mandarin?"

"No, my girlfriend's ex-girlfriend's mother is a retired professor of Oriental languages. She translated it for me." I see the look of confusion on his face and regret complicating an already sensitive issue. But the old man soon dismisses it. Susan's mother is not the pressing issue.

"Did she not see it was p–private?"

"Yes, and it troubled her to read it to me. But I persuaded her that my motives were genuine—to help your brother. They are genuine now, Mr. Tzu. I want to find him. I want to help him."

Tzu looks up frowning. "His wife," he asks hesitantly. "Sh–she knows about me?"

"No, I swear. I haven't told her. It was initially instinct that held me back. I know your brother is a very private man, and I didn't want to encroach."

"You encroached."

"Yes, yes I did. I still am, but I can't seem to stop."

There is a tense silence. He is struggling with something. When he speaks, his voice remains quiet, but his English is fluent and each word is spoken deliberately. "Thank you for not t–telling her. P–please, do not. It would p–put my brother in a very difficult p–position."

"You have my word. Please tell me where he is."

The old man looks up, fatigue written across his face. "I do not know." He shrugs. "Ch–chang Tzu walks his own path now."

I feel a wave of panic. "What does that mean?"

"He came back from the war and," Li Tzu sighs and rubs his forehead, "it seemed that he could s–seal all the memories, the blood, the fear, all the demons; he could s–seal them in a box in his head. The box remained s–sealed and he continued with his life. He married, opened his little c–coffee shop and had ch–children. He has done well for himself. I am proud of him. It was the right thing to do. It is the way of the warrior, of honor. A true warrior will fulfill his d–destiny on the battlefield, but when it is over, he returns to become a valuable member of s–society. He deserves what he has achieved."

"Mr. Tzu works very hard to build the business," I say softly, "and, from the little I know of him, he is very dedicated to his family."

"No, that is not what I mean. I am talking about the M–medal of Honor."

"Is that some kind of war medal?"

Li Tzu looks at me darkly. Then he smiles. "You are not American? Ah." The old man sits up straight and his eyes light up. "It is the highest m–military honor."

"Will," adds Salvador, "it's the equal to your Victoria Cross."

"Wow! I had no idea," I say in wonder.

"That is my b–brother. He is a true warrior, a true hero."

18: The Promise

A heavy silence descends and drags for minutes. I glance over at Salvador, who is closely observing the veteran and is clearly concerned. I wait for his lead. From somewhere deep inside, Li Tzu finds the strength to continue.

"When we came back, Chang threw himself into civilian life. He moved on. We had talked about going into business together. I would have liked that—The Tz-Tz-Tzu Brothers."

His hollow laugh echoes off the stoic gray concrete pillars. Then he sighs. "I c–could not move on. I c–could not c–close the box in here." He signals with a finger to his head. "I c–could not silence them. Chang tried to help at first, but it was too dangerous."

"Dangerous?"

"That by trying to help me, he would not be able to k–keep the box in his head c–closed. It takes so much discipline even for him when I am not around. But he felt it as he tried to help me; he felt his lid loosening.

"He tried a few times. Once, he just took off—to Tahoe I think. He hadn't slept for days and was yelling at his family. He rented a chalet for two or three days and wandered around the mountains and the lake. When he returned, he couldn't find me. I was still watching him, but he never saw me."

Another pause.

"He needed some space. He said he would go to Italy and learn about c–coffee. He was sure that this was the next wave. He would learn about c–coffee and wine. Then he would decide which would be the most profitable.

"He chose them both." The old man laughs softly. I feel his pride in his brother. "He c–could not decide. He loves c–coffee and he loves wine. You c–can understand that, right? My brother told me about you, speaks warmly of you; he says that you are very similar about the c-coffee and wine. He likes you very much."

"I have a lot of respect for him too, Li Tzu," I say. "That is why I'm here."

"Yes," he nods. "Yes, I know. That is why I agreed to meet you."

"What happened to your brother when he returned from Italy?"

"He c–could not find me. I was losing the fight and knew even then that I c–could never win. He is my brother. I had to protect him at all c–costs. I had to stay away." His voice becomes harsh. "I would not take him down with me and I will not now."

"I don't understand," I say.

"I was already doomed. I knew I would never be able to c–close the box. In trying to help me, Chang would have opened his own and let his demons loose. Remember Tahoe. What if he had c–crashed his car, drowned, or fallen from a mountain? He had a family to take c–care of. The voices." He shakes his head. "They are so strong, so unrelenting. They can disappear for days, but you always feel their presence, always fear their return. You live in their shadow even when they are silent."

He pauses for a moment and drinks from a plastic water bottle. A few drops spill and he furtively wipes them away.

"I would not let the voices do this to him, so I vanished. It is easy to disappear on the streets. Then I hitched down the c–coast for a while. I worked for farmers and got by. But San Francisco is my city. It became a part of me as I grew up, and I soon came home.

"I watched Chang from a distance. I saw his success. His wife worked there until they had children. Then she would bring the children into the c–café to see him. I watched." His voice becomes intense. "My brother was alive—very much alive—and c–complete. The past was not eating him up. He had become a husband and father. He had won. He was moving forward. I was so proud. I am so proud. I was happy to just drop by and watch from a distance. He had no idea."

He again goes silent and we wait patiently.

"Take your time," Salvador says, anxiously watching his friend.

Clearly, Li Tzu is suffering through the narration. Salvador won't press him or allow me to. After a few moments, he is ready.

"Then one day, maybe two years ago, my brother stopped next to a friend, a homeless brother, and gave him some change. My friend thought Chang was me and said my name. Chang Tzu is a good man, honorable, a family man, and he tracked me down.

"We both understood what was at stake. He knew he had to keep his distance. Occasionally, I would try some drugs or some therapy, and he would provide money for this. I never accepted his money for anything else and he respected that. We made a bargain that I would c–come and see him once a month. Otherwise, we would stay apart. I am sure he dreaded seeing me. I am sure he did not sleep in the nights before or after. At these times, I forced him back into the battle in his head, grasping the box, holding the lid down with all his strength for his family and his honor."

Tzu pulls a soiled bandana from a pocket and wipes his moist brow. He is sweating despite the cold weather.

"I saw the price my brother was paying, because I watched him at other times from afar. I swore that I would go away; leave him forever, though I love my brother more than anyone." He bowed his head. "But I am weak and have not been able to leave. I live for those meetings once a month."

He stops abruptly and stands. I make to get up too, but Salvador signals me to stay. Li Tzu walks away for a few minutes then returns. He picks up his bottle, but it is empty. I have a water bottle in my bag and put it in front of him. He stares at it then takes it and drinks. He gulps as though seeking strength and more drops escape down the lined crevices on his face. He wipes his mouth on his sleeve and takes a deep breath.

I sigh. "I'm sorry to …"

"No, I need to say this. I am losing my battle. I feel so tired. The demons c–come more often now—almost every night. I c–cannot c–continue to resist them. They will take me soon and, honestly, I wait for them. Perhaps there is peace on the other side for people like me.

"When Chang Tzu saw that I was losing, he tried to get more involved. He wanted me to get help, go to the

VA. He began to make inquiries. I tried to stop him, but he is strong-willed. He has to be. He has survived."

His head jerks up and he stares at me. "My battle is lost, but you can save him. You must help. It will be easier when I am gone. He will be free to c–concentrate on himself and his family."

What have I unleashed? "What are you going to do, Li Tzu?"

"I will fight and then I will stop fighting." His voice sounds hollow. "It is not you. You must help the living. I am already dead with one foot on the other s–side."

He leans toward me in a jerking movement, and I fight the urge not to lean away. For the first time, he stares me unflinchingly in the eyes and his stutter disappears.

"Help my brother," he says with a hiss. "He must not blame himself. Find him and tell him I am proud of him. Tell him that it could have been different, should have been different. But he must honor me by living on." His voice rises in high-pitched desperation. "He will honor my memory and our family by surviving and by winning. Tell him I love him."

A lump forms in my throat. I take a moment to compose myself and rest my hand firmly on his arm.

"I will, Li Tzu, I swear."

He smiles and nods. "Thank you," he says quietly, and it seems as though a wave of serenity passes over him. "Thank you."

He gets up and moves slowly toward the fire. The men surrounding it open their tight circle then close it around him.

"Allow me to escort you back to Market Street," Salvador says.

We stand heavily—our limbs stiff from sitting on the tire. Salvador, in particular, is having trouble. I resist the impulse to take his arm. It will not be well received.

We walk in silence up First Street. It is late afternoon and most bagel shops and juice bars are already closed.

"What will happen to him?" I ask.

"Li Tzu? He will hopefully find peace."

"Is he going to ..." I hear my fear.

Salvador stops walking and wheels round to face me. "Whatever he decides, Will," his tone is hard and authoritative, "it is his decision alone and we mustn't interfere or judge him."

"But maybe I precipitated something. Maybe talking to me has pushed him over the edge." I feel a wave of panic.

Salvador shakes his head. "Listen, son. He has been fighting this battle for forty years. After each attack, a little less of him remains—only his consciousness has stayed intact. He has been fighting an enemy far more powerful than you. You will be a great writer, Will, but don't flatter yourself. Li Tzu, whatever he might think, is a warrior; only a great warrior can fight and survive for so long."

The old man starts walking again, but slower, measuring his thoughts with every stride.

"Do not hold yourself responsible for what may eventuate. He had to unburden himself to someone, and he chose you, a Westerner, a writer, a friend of his brother. You play a vital role, Will, but you cannot play

God. Fulfill the vow you made to Li Tzu and ease your conscience."

That night, the events of the day haunt me. My dreams are full of boxes, of lids opening and flames. In the glow of the red-hot fire are a burning flag, charred stars and stripes. A medal lies in the heart of the fire, untarnished, shining.

19: The Ghost of Alfred Peet

I work the evening shift at The Daily Grind as I intend to head down to Ventura on an early morning bus to meet Tzu's children. The Greyhound station is only a block away, so I plan a few hours of rest in the coffee shop hoping I sleep well on the bus.

As I enter The Daily Grind, I notice the two dark SFPD uniforms are back sitting at a corner table. The tall, mustached Captain O'Connor and the short, James Cagney-like Mendez are both clearly agitated. As I approach their table, I can see that they're both scowling—Mendez failing to hide it even behind his ever-present sunglasses.

"Barista, wine connoisseur, writer, and now private detective," says Mendez with what sounds like a growl. "Any other careers we don't know about?"

"I've always fancied being a ballerina but not with these hips, y'know."

There are no laughs.

"Look kid," O'Connor's face is flushed, "you need to back off. What we do is also a profession. I'm sure you make coffee better than my partner or I. There's a reason—"

"He's my boss," I snap, "and I'm working my ass off here for him. I feel a certain loyalty, and his wife comes in each day looking more like a ghost." I take a deep breath. I can still feel the emotional residue from meeting Tzu's brother—it has only been twenty-four hours since we met. "What do you expect me to do, sit around and wait?"

O'Connor says, "How would you feel if I started making coffee for your long line of customers? You wouldn't appreciate it."

"He'd do more damage than good," says Mendez, peering over his sunglasses for added effect.

A disturbing image of O'Connor and Mendez abusing the Beast and spilling coffee on customers flashes across my overworked imagination. Then it hits me.

"Has something happened?" A shiver courses through me.

"Our warmest lead to your boss has gone stone cold." Mendez is deadpan.

"What are you saying?" I gasp then realize. "Li Tzu?"

They both nod gravely, oddly in sync. I think to ask how they found him, but it is not really important right now. I take a deep breath.

"He's not talking to you anymore?" I'd ooze sarcasm if my voice wasn't so shaky.

"He ain't talking to anyone anymore, kid," Mendez replies. "We know you talked with him before he died."

I moan and my head falls into my hands. I have been expecting this but imagined Salvador delivering the news.

"His friends ain't too happy with you either," Mendez says gruffly. "I wouldn't hang out under the bridges for a while if I were you."

I stare at him, not sure if that was an attempt at humor. "What do you want?" I ask, defeated. "I need to get the shift going."

"Just back off," says O'Connor. "Let the pros do their work. Feel free to share any ideas with us, and we'll seriously consider them. But let us work, huh?"

"Can you order me to do that?"

"We can request it," replies O'Connor, adopting a more diplomatic tone. I look up at his massive face. There is warmth in his tone, like a father chiding his wayward son. "We can also slap a restraining order if we think you're trying to hide a crime, bury evidence, or confuse our leads."

I nod and look at O'Connor. I want to tell him that I'm not trying to stop them, that I'm trying to help, and that I genuinely want—no—need to find Tzu. I look away.

"I didn't imagine that—" No, that would be lying. Salvador had given me plenty of hints that this might be Li Tzu's epitaph, but would these cops understand? What would they think of my reliance on insights into a homeless former professor who thinks San Francisco is his campus and we all, cats included, are his students?

They stand to leave, and I look at O'Connor. "I'm not responsible for Li Tzu's actions. He's been fighting this for four decades."

"Yes he has," the big police officer replies.

"It wasn't me who abandoned him after he returned from Vietnam."

He lays a massive hand on my shoulder. "I know your intentions are good, Will, and I know Salvador was with you."

He turns and walks out. Mendez readjusts his sunglasses and follows.

On the verge of tears, I move mechanically through my shift. I consider phoning Jane or her father and wish Chad would spontaneously pop in. But, thankfully, brisk business keeps me distracted as we transition into wine bar mode. The couples are low maintenance, but a few regulars come by expecting conversation.

Six hours later, I am sitting with the last remaining customer, an elderly man, surely returning to an empty house. He has bought a bottle of very good Merlot, a Ferrari-Carano from Sonoma County west of Napa. He invites me to join him joking that this is the closest he'll ever get to feeling wealthy. I rarely get an opportunity to taste such a vintage, and I bring over a glass.

The wine is rich and smooth. I can taste black cherries and, as it glides down my throat, I feel it healing the raw emotion inside me. No, it is not healing—it is numbing, but right now that feels equally attractive. When he finally leaves, he gives me the bottle. I have hardly spoken, only listening as he shares his unfulfilled, corporate life.

"This will be more of a comfort for you than me," he says.

By the time I have cleared the wineglasses and candles away, the bottle is empty.

I lay down to sleep on one of the benches that hug the walls. Above me hangs a portrait of Alfred Peet. Mr. Tzu had once called him the Michael Jordan of coffee. Having just arrived in the US, I was not acquainted with the NBA.

"Michael who?"

Tzu had glared at me, not sure if I was making fun of him.

"Do you not know who Alfred Peet was?" He didn't wait for an answer. "The founder of Peet's Coffee?"

I had, to my credit, joined the dots. You couldn't work in coffee without noticing a Peet's Coffee on every street corner of Northern California.

Tzu had shrugged. "At least that," he said, but his tone gave away his satisfaction. He had put on a haughty English accent. "His Majesty doesn't recognize Michael Jordan's contribution to civilization but at least appreciates good coffee."

I laugh as I recall the memory. Then following a big yawn, I look up to the portrait. "Good night, Alfred," I say before falling asleep. "Check if Li Tzu's settling in okay."

I wake immediately. Someone is shuffling around the café, and I see a shadow behind the counter. I lie motionless anxious not to be noticed. I'm very committed to Mr. Tzu and The Daily Grind but not enough to risk my life challenging a burglar.

"Ah good, you are awake. I was hoping to talk to you."

The rasping voice suggests an old man, but I'm not certain and fear keeps me lying frozen on the bench.

"It's okay. I'm no burglar; money has no use for me. Come here, Will." He chuckles to himself. "I prefer Hemingway, actually. An appropriate nickname, yes."

His English is fluent, but there's an accent that I can't quite place, perhaps German?

"No, I am Dutch, though I left Holland many years ago. You were looking at my picture above your head there before you went to sleep. Remember?"

"Peet? Peet's Coffee?" I rub my head feeling the fuzziness of the wine.

"Yes, yes, the very same. And you did drink a lot of wine." He laughs again.

I slowly realize that he's reading my mind. He says, "My father ran a small coffee roasting house before the war, and I helped him. That's how I learned about coffee." He chuckles to himself.

I sit up facing the counter. An old man with wispy white hair is gliding around though he gives the impression he is shuffling. His body seems slow and stiff, but his movements are smooth. I think I see a gray shimmering light, very thin, encompassing his body. Shit! How much wine did I drink?

He peers into the bins of coffee and meticulously examines the Beast.

"I learned from my father the importance of keeping the machine clean and working smoothly. I've been watching you; you take great care of this fine machine." He pats the Beast tenderly. "The secret of a good roast and a good cup of coffee is clean tools. I worked in a forced-labor camp in charge of a lathe during the occupation. The guards saw how I took care of the machine and that probably saved my life."

"When did you come to America?"

He didn't seem to hear me. "I could not believe the taste of coffee here in the United States of America—a superpower, the so-called land of the free, yet incarcerated by instant coffee."

Instant coffee is said with the same disgust a pious person might reserve for a sexually transmitted disease. I ask my question again and this time he answers.

"I arrived in the mid-fifties and got a job in San Francisco importing coffee. But I knew that to make a difference, I would have to begin from scratch. People were unquestioningly drinking gallons of Folgers and Hills Brothers without giving it a second thought. How could they?"

He shakes his head still disgusted after forty plus years.

"I served a long apprenticeship and opened my first store in Berkeley in 1966. Have you been there? It's on the corner of Walnut and Vine?"

I nod. I'd made a pilgrimage not long after coming to the Bay Area. "Why did you choose that venue?" I ask, still trying to decide whether I'm dreaming or drunk—or both.

"Berkeley was alive with new ideas and tastes. The Gourmet Ghetto was in its infancy—Chez Panisse soon to open. An array of memorable establishments that catered to the eclectic crowd of radical students and professors as well as a plethora of connoisseurs."

"Mr. Peet, why are you here? What do you want with me?"

"I've been watching you and am impressed by your commitment to quality. I was committed, maybe too much. Brewing coffee is craftsmanship. Since I was successful, especially after my death, people began to idolize me."

He sighs and pushes back an imaginary lock of snow-white hair.

"But listen, Will. Though I always hired good staff, young enthusiastic people like you, I couldn't delegate and I relentlessly checked every little task they did. My passion for perfection made me insufferable to many of my younger staff despite paying them well. There was a huge turnover. In the end, I burnt out. Do you understand what I'm saying?"

"Yeah, but how does this apply to me?"

His eyes blazing, he sits opposite me. "Listen, Will. You and I share many similarities. You care passionately for quality and justice. You want to save the world, but you can't. No one person can. The more you try, the more you open yourself to failure; to disappointment.

He bounces up again, wagging his finger at me and shaking his head.

"You are brave to try and save your boss. You were brave to confront his brother, but you couldn't win. He'd already lost to his own adversaries, and you couldn't save him. Leave him behind, Will. He wanted only to rest in peace. You must make your peace with him and his actions—for him and, more importantly, for you."

He walks to the beans, stares at them for a moment while scratching his head, and then returns to the table. His voice becomes intense.

"Listen to me, Will. Be the writer. Distance yourself from the tale that is unraveling. Don't allow yourself to be drawn in or it will consume you, and you won't be able to write the story that must be written."

Alfred Peet shuffles around the bar and sits on my table peering down at me. I resist the urge to see if his feet are touching the floor.

"You have much to live for, Will, but you must not burnout as I did. The literary world is full of one-book wonders."

He reaches out a hand to touch my arm then stops and shrugs—embarrassed.

"Delve into the coffee. Learn the ancient ritual of cupping as master roasters have before you. Absorb the aroma, the muddy grounds and, most of all, the taste." He leans in. "Don't forget to slurp. It sure pisses them off."

Again, he is laughing but he begins to fade. Then his tone turns serious. "Also delve deeper into wines but use a spittoon, or it will also consume you, son."

I rub my head feeling the approaching headache from the impending hangover.

20: Wounded Children

The alarm on my cell phone wakes me from a deep sleep. One of my cheeks is plastered to the coffee table and my head pounds. I blame the ringing alarm for the pounding, but my head still vibrates after the phone is quiet.

I gulp a glass of water and rinse my face. Then I swing my bag over my shoulder and lock the café.

Twenty minutes later, I'm sitting on a comfortable Greyhound bus in the Transbay Terminal staring at a gray, graffiti-riddled concrete wall. The bus is crowded. Most of the passengers are Hispanic, and Spanish seems the main language on the bus. Old people stoically brace for the long haul, as small children are already asking, "Are we there yet?"

I sink deeper into my seat, and my head rests on the window, a brown sweater rolled up for a pillow. I'm already dozing when a hand jerks my leg. I open my eyes and stare into the face of a stern, gray-haired, African American woman. I have slipped down and my sprawling legs are preventing her from sitting.

"Excuse me," I say, and quickly sit straight and move to my own seat. For some unknown reason, I say, "Up all night."

She rolls her eyes and eases into the adjoining seat. "Looks like yah met a ghost and come off second best."

Seeing the joke that she does not get, I laugh. Was he real? I know the answer. My hand rubs the stubble on my face, and I realize that I probably look a wreck. Remembering images of Kerouac et al as they crisscrossed America, I smile. The Beatniks. Cool analogy.

The lady, however, tucks her skirt under her clearly defining the border between our seats, and I soon begin to drift. I will use one of the breaks to shave and brush my teeth and hair. I fall asleep and only wake when the driver announces a stop in Santa Cruz. I leave the bus and head for the station's bathroom.

I feel much better when I return to the bus. Having shaved and brushed my teeth, I am narrowly more presentable. I have eaten a banana and emptied a bottle of apple juice. When the bus pulls out, I switch on my laptop and review the questions I plan to ask Tzu's children, Michael and Madeleine. Neither seemed happy with the prospect of meeting me, but I think my earnestness to find their father offered them little chance to refuse.

"Yah researching war vets?" the woman asks.

"Yeah," I answer, deciding not to confront her for looking at my screen.

"Hmm," she says disapprovingly.

"Why 'hmm'?" I guess I'm still feeling a little hung over.

"Ain't it enough that they go and lay down their lives for our country—for you and me?"

"Sure," I reply, having no idea what she's getting at.

"Son, why do yah need to stalk them? Let them be. Give them their pitiful pensions and let them get on with their haunted lives."

"And what about those who can't get on with their lives?" I reply. "What about those who can't exorcise their ghosts? Are you okay with leaving them alone?"

A confused silence ensues. We clearly have our wires crossed.

"Yah ain't checking up on their widow pensions and veteran ID cards?"

I shake my head. Still suspicious, she stares at me. "Yah don't work for no government agency then?" She almost spits out the words.

"No ma'am," I say, probably never having used that term to address anyone. Then it occurs to me. "Do government workers use the Greyhound to travel on business?"

She harrumphs. "Good point," she says, and now peers over at my screen again. "Vietnam vets?"

"Yes ma'am. One—"

"You students all study them 'Nam vets," she says.

"Yes, no, actually—"

"I don't doubt it. What about Gulf War vets? Yah been checking with any of them?"

"No ma'am, but—"

"You see, 'Nam was all draft boys: blacks, whites, Jews. They all went. You get plenty of white boys to research. Yah know any Gulf War vets?"

"Not really. I've met a few passing through but not really—" I tail off knowing she clearly hasn't finished.

"The Gulf War soldiers ain't chosen from the draft. Most are black boys or working-class Southern boys. Them recruiters hang around the schools—the public schools and state campuses. They go for kids that don't have much going. Kids that'll probably not find jobs. They tell them they can leave home, get good money, see the world, and get a better education and a profession. Yah all know where I'm going with this?"

"Er, no ma'am."

"We're going to make the same mistakes again. We're going to let them fall through our fingers and end up living on the streets. The booze. The drugs. We ain't going to learn from 'Nam, because these kids are black."

I open my mouth, but nothing comes out. She sits back then and reaching into her bag, takes out a bottle of mineral water to chase down a small pill.

"I'm a simple working woman, and I worship the Living Christ every Sunday. I don't want them taking our boys away. So I want to reinstate the draft. Yah follow why?"

I shake my head.

"When they draft, they take all colors. All of us. That way they're going to think twice before sending privileged white boys off to fight.

"I lost my brother in 'Nam and now my son is in Iraq. My brother was a good boy. Had steel round eyeglasses and always had his nose in a book. My Pa used to kick him out of the house wanted him to be drinking with the men and chasing them girls and such though Pa sure didn't approve of such behavior come Sunday in church."

She smiles, remembering her father and brother and sighs shaking her head.

"My brother should have become a minister, a servant of Christ. He had no business being a soldier. Pa was real proud of him when he went. Said he'd make us all real proud. We weren't feeling so proud when they shipped his body back all wrapped in white."

She dabs tears from her eyes. Her voice wavers. "I love my country, but I don't care. I want my boy back. I want him back in one piece—all his hands and legs, and I want him in one piece inside." She digs her fingers into her ample chest.

"I lost my little brother then I lost my Pa. He blamed himself for pushing my brother to be a man. He never meant for that to happen. Pa was never the same after that. The bottle took him. The devil and the spirits."

"Maybe they're up there together now," I say. "Maybe they made their peace."

"Amen." With tears filling her eyes, she sighs. "And I hope they are looking out for my boy. I pray they are doing that." She looks out the window, and the small handkerchief reappears to wipe both her eyes.

I wait a moment, and then say, "I'm trying to help a man, a war vet whose life has unraveled. He's just lost his brother, also a vet, and it's affected his family. I'm just trying to ..." I can't finish the sentence.

"They your family?"

"No ma'm. He's my boss." Then I explain.

"It's a holy deed you are all doing, son. A holy deed. Jesus will help yah."

I sigh. "I could certainly do with some help."

We don't speak anymore and by lunchtime the Greyhound arrives in Santa Barbara. When we disembark, she goes off to collect her bag. Then I see her returning—looking for me. We hug warmly.

"Jesus will help yah, son. I'll take it up with him on Sunday. I promise."

My parting recollection of her is the deep, booming laugh. She can still laugh after everything. Despite my atheism, I shoot up a silent prayer. *Take care of her ... and her son.*

An hour later, I'm at the small Greyhound stop in Ventura waiting for Michael, Mr. Tzu's son. It's warm, and I drain a bottle of water. A shiny red car pulls up and the passenger window opens.

"You Will?"

"Yeah. Michael?"

"Sure. Hop in, man. I'm on my lunch break. Clock's ticking."

I get in and the air-conditioning hits as Michael drives to a nearby diner. By way of introduction, he talks about his job. He works in insurance, and his company has just been bought out. Talk is of promotion rather than laying people off. Michael is one of the stars of the company; he's dreaming of a big future.

We enter the diner, a small, unassuming place full from the lunchtime rush. The waitress tells us that there is a brief wait for tables. I ask Michael if this is a problem. "I don't want to get you into trouble with your new bosses."

He laughs and pushes back black, shiny hair. "They're not around yet, and I doubt I'll have to worry much. Everyone is very result-oriented here. Always chasing the next bonus or promotion. No one needs to be watched. You don't last long if you don't get results."

The waitress signals that she has a place for us, and I watch Michael as I follow him to our table. He is very handsome, and his skin is tanned and healthy. He wears a black polo neck that shows off his jet-black hair and a pair of pressed jeans and shiny shoes. His teeth flash white as he laughs that I soon discover is often. There is something in the confident way he holds himself that clearly suggests he is more American than Asian.

"We have until two o'clock. Then I'll drive you to a coffee shop about ten minutes from here to meet my sister. She'll drive you back to the Greyhound station. It was smart to meet me first."

"Why?"

We order lunch. I go for a typical diner meal—the novelty still hasn't worn off. Michael orders a grilled fish that arrives swimming in a healthy salad. I am suitably shamed and tell him. He laughs.

"This is California, dude, and the farther south you go, the more California it becomes. We all surf, spend the weekends on the beach and belong to health clubs. We all get regular massages and aspire to having a Jacuzzi and swimming pool in our yards." He extends his arms. "It's the great American dream."

"God bless America," I say, enjoying his company.

The clock on the wall says it is already twenty after one. I don't have much time.

"Michael, tell me about your father. Anything that may point me in the right direction."

Michael sighs. "Since you called, I have been worried about this. There is a reason why my sister and I live down here when surf and gyms exist in the Bay Area. Our childhood wasn't great. Don't get me wrong. We had two parents who loved each other and us. Everything they did was to try and give their children a great future. We always had food on the table and clothes on our backs.

"But there was always an underlying tension. My sister and I are American. Our eyes might be Asian, but we are integrated in every way. Even though she knows they are out of place, our mother clings to the old ways. With her, it is accepted, and we joke with her about that. Last year I sent her a jade bracelet and a voucher for a massage. She chided me on the phone for giving a woman of her status and reputation something like that. But she was really very pleased. I've forgotten more of her birthdays than I've remembered."

"And your father."

"He bridges East and West. He strives to be as American as he can. He took me to Giants games, whether I wanted to or not, but he never really understood the game. It didn't matter. He wanted to be an American father, and to him this is what they did.

"But he is also a product of China. Honor and family means a lot to him. We know he served in the war. We know something happened, but he never talks about it. He said he was just doing his duty as an American, but we thought he was lying.

"Maybe he was just a simple soldier, but I'm sure he saw action. He never watches war movies and would flinch when he saw a scene by mistake."

"And when you tried to press him?"

"He would get really angry and order us to stop. Then he was the Chinese father. He ruled the roost. But after he calmed down, he took us out for pizza and tried to be jovial. In the end, we stopped asking. We didn't want to rock the boat.

"Now he seems to have snapped. I feel bad, man. Really bad. If going to San Francisco would help, I would be there. I was with my ma a few times. But when we saw it going on, she told me not to come. She knows I work hard. She knows I need to go on."

When we returned to his car, it was nearing two o'clock, and Michael warned me that his sister was more worried and uptight.

"Tread carefully. She'll go on about the government not taking care of its heroes." He laughs. "My old man is kind and stern but couldn't hurt a fly. I doubt that he ever fired a bullet."

Breathing deeply, I get out of the car and turn to Michael. "Thanks for taking the time to talk to me and for lunch. Listen, Michael, I think your father was a hero and still is. I think he saw serious action in the war, and I think he is still fighting it. Do not ever tell anyone what I'm telling you now, but you have to be a fucking hero to be awarded the Medal of Honor."

A woman's voice behind me announces that Michael's sister has arrived.

"Your father was a brave but wounded soldier, and he was good at hiding it from you until he could hide it no more."

"Medal of Honor!" Michael says. "Fuck!" Then his sister is leaning through his open window pecking him on the cheek.

21: Wounded Children 2

Like her brother, Madeleine is fresh-faced and attractive. Having just left the gym looming behind us, she is particularly flushed. She wears workout tights and a hooded Cal sweatshirt. Her wet hair is also black and shiny. It is pulled into a tight ponytail and she carries a gym bag with a small towel hanging out.

We enter a *Coffee Bean & Tea Leaf* coffee house. She orders a decaffeinated iced green tea and, when we sit, lays the framework.

"We have until three sharp. I'll drop you off at the Greyhound station. It's on my way."

"I appreciate your taking time from work," I say, glancing at the clock.

"I'd hardly be working full-time if I could hit the gym and have a coffee with you in the middle of the afternoon." It comes out harsh, perhaps unintentional, as she strikes a more conciliatory tone. "I need to pick my kids up from day care. We decided I'd work part-time until our children are both in school."

"Where do you work?"

"I'm a psychologist at the hospital. I specialize in trauma."

I listen patiently, but have one eye on the clock. We have forty-five minutes, and, as her nervous chatter comes fast and smooth, I sense that she'd happily run the clock down. I stop her.

" Madeleine, I need you to focus on your father."

Her body stiffens. "Didn't get much from Michael, I assume?"

"What can you tell me about your father's disappearance?"

She flicks back a lock of hair that has escaped. "Why do you need to know? What's between you and my father?"

I give her the same explanation I offer everyone, myself included. When she tries to ask more about my motivation, I put up a hand and interrupt.

"Please, I just traveled a few hundred miles. I need to understand more about him, and I need to hear it before three o'clock."

She eyes her wristwatch and takes a deep breath.

"Our father put up walls, Will. Either you accepted these walls or you tried to break them down. Michael is younger than me and, I think, got the message early. Chinese men are stricter with their sons than daughters. Michael likes the easy life and avoids conflict whenever he can. He's very American and if he can sweep something under the rug, then he surely will."

"And you?"

"I'm not like that. I became a psychologist because I want to explore relationships, create dialogue. I believe this is the path to all healing. Does that make sense to you?"

I smile. "My girlfriend is studying psychology."

Madeleine frowns. "Excuse my bluntness, but I'm not sure your girlfriend is a factor. You're British right?" I nod, and she continues. "I think the British are very similar to the Chinese with your stiff-upper lip." She smiles, perhaps regretting her tone. "I'm sorry. I shouldn't be judging you, but after you phoned, I've been tense about talking to you. And please don't judge my brother too harshly. If one of my parents asked him for help, he'd do the right thing, but he'd wait to be asked."

She picks up the spoon and intently stirs her iced tea. The ice cubes clink, and she watches them circling.

"Being the younger sibling, Michael missed a lot. The battles were fought before he knew what was going on. The first time I saw the other side of my father was when I was in fourth grade. A classmate's grandfather died and he was a war vet. My classmate made a presentation about him in class.

"It was very interesting, and she showed us his medals and some photos. The teacher gave us homework to talk to someone who had been to war. Most others had grandparents from the Second World War or the Korean War, but I had no one except my father."

Madeleine's cell phone vibrates and she looks at the screen but lets it go.

"Where was I? Yes, so I brought a pencil and notebook to the dinner table, but he went rigid. I was only ten and was very upset with him. When I asked him why he was being nasty, he erupted and began shouting at me—half in English and half Chinese—until my mother said something sharply in Chinese. Then he stormed out of the house.

"I was in tears. I didn't know what I'd done. I had no clue what he'd gone through. I thought he was being so spiteful." Her voice cracked, and she sounded like the hurt ten-year-old. "I was also scared, as I'd never seen him totally lose control. I cried and cried while my mother held me and tried to explain."

Madeleine wipes a tear away, and then glares at the droplet on her finger.

"Mama told me he was sick—something that no medicine could cure. She told me how he was a wounded soldier but wounded inside. All the time she kept telling me how much he loved me, but I was heartbroken."

Madeleine pauses again to sip her tea. Her watery eyes blink rapidly as her mind seems to be dragging her back in time.

"I'm sorry this is hard for you," I say.

"It's okay. I knew it would be. However hard, things need to be said. This is what I tried to tell him over the years. Anyway, that night he returned home at dinnertime. His face was puffy and I could smell something strange on his breath, in retrospect probably alcohol. He'd bought me a doll I wanted all wrapped up in ribbons. He'd also spoken with a friend and arranged for my mother to take me to see someone who had served in the Korean War.

She pauses again. "But I couldn't let it drop. As a teenager, I got involved in a Veteran's Rights campaign. I thought he'd be proud of me, but he wasn't. He became distant and avoided being alone with me. He put a great wall between us."

I start to say something, but Madeleine cuts me off with a shake of her head.

"Then there was a time when all my friends were reading the novel *Catch-22*. When I brought the book home, he told me he didn't want me reading it. I got angry and yelled that he couldn't censor me, that this was America, not China. He then went very quiet and asked softly that I not read it in the living room. I did as he asked. His abrupt softness was more effective than if we'd gone another round of shouting."

Again she stops and stares past my shoulder. I feel sympathetic, but we only have a short time. I don't imagine Madeleine will take any phone calls from me in the future.

"Please, Madeleine," I say, but before I can ask anything, she continues.

"Another time, I had a slumber party. My parents had gone out for the evening, but something happened and they came home early. We were a very politically aware little group, all sworn feminists trying to be very hip. We were watching *The Deer Hunter*. My father took one look at the screen and ripped the videocassette out of the VCR. I believe he was about to throw it across the room.

"I yelled at him that the movie belonged to Jennifer's father and he froze. When he recovered, he handed it to Jennifer and quietly apologized to her. He asked that she apologize to her father for him."

"What happened then?" I could imagine the scene so clearly.

She sighs. "He walked to his room and slammed the door closed. A few minutes later, my mother came out and announced we would order pizza and have ice cream. She saved the evening for me, but things were very tense between my father and me for a while."

There is a break again. I have the picture, but I need clues. "Can you think of what might have happened or where he might be?"

"My father is a loner, Will." The lock of hair has escaped her ear again, but this time she lets it swing. "I don't believe he's with anyone. I don't think he's kept in touch with any old army pals. He might have worn an American uniform, but beneath it he is one-hundred percent Chinese. We are his family. We are everything to him. It's not like he even has any brothers or sisters."

I look away, thinking of Li Tzu, the proud uncle she doesn't know existed.

"He certainly doesn't belong to a veteran's counseling or support group." She shakes her head. "I tried to get him involved. Believe me. But, like I said, he's Chinese."

"And he doesn't call you or check in with you?"

"No, not usually. But this is the first time he's gone away for so long. Once he stormed off for a few days, but he called my mother in the evening to tell her that he was okay."

It is ten minutes before three and I feel a wave of frustration. It's all dead ends. The mother, daughter and son have no idea where he is or how to find him.

"What did your father do in the war?"

"Don't know. I'm sure he saw action. There are some deep psychological scars there."

"Didn't he ever get help? Didn't your mother ever suggest it?"

"Not that I know. My mother wouldn't share much with us about our father other than he loves us and he's a great man." She suddenly grabs my arm. "It's not easy to ask for help when you're an Asian man. It's simply not done. And maybe he was frightened to dig up whatever's buried."

She moves her hand away, embarrassed I'm sure, and stares out the window.

"Then there's the bureaucracy involved if vets do want help. Everything's so damn complicated. They think you're after money, looking for an easy ride. They make you think that there's a stigma in going for help; that you're leaching off the state. They can be insensitive bastards, damn insensitive." She stops and swallows. "These are men who put their lives on the line for their country."

She stands abruptly and grabs her car keys from the table. I follow her outside. As we stand on the curb waiting for a car to pass, she turns to me. Her eyes fill with tears, and she whispers: "He's out there hurting, Will, all alone. He needs help, and I can't reach him."

Sitting on the Greyhound bus heading back north to San Francisco, a deep sense of depression engulfs me as I peer through the gathering dusk. Thankfully, there's no one in the seat next to me, and the bus is subdued compared to the trip down. I should sleep most of the way, but I can't.

Though Tzu's children helped fill in the picture, I have learned little to find him. Tzu's son is almost oblivious of whatever his father went through, and his daughter failed to bring down the great walls Tzu erected to protect his children from himself. Madeleine has paid a price for trying, and I feel sympathetic toward her.

I arrive late in the evening and have time to kill before my night bus to the Sunset. As I wait, I see many homeless people gathered around the Transbay Terminal claiming nooks and crannies that might give them a fleeting sense of shelter, if only for a few hours.

Once home, I walk wearily to my room and throw my bag on the bed. I return to the kitchen for a glass of water and see a soft light in Chad's room. At this time of night if the light is on, he's probably entertaining.

I drop a plastic cup into the sink by accident and it bounces. I curse my clumsiness, as I don't want to wake my housemates. I hear a door open and Chad is standing there bare-chested, a long material in various hues of blue wrapped around his waist. The cloth is thin and leaves nothing to the imagination.

"You okay?" He looks concerned. "How was the trip?"

"You got company?"

He nods with a small smile then puts his head back through the door to his room to say something. He returns and sits at the kitchen table.

"How was the trip?" he asks again.

"Depressing. Are you sure you wanna talk?" I nod again to the room.

"It's okay," he says. "We've been having fun."

As he says this, a redhead comes out. She also has a thin cloth tightly wrapped around her voluptuous body. Her hands are behind her head as she ties the cloth ends behind her neck. The light from the room behind her offers a wicked silhouette.

Smiling, she says, "Hi, I'm Jenn." Her voice is very throaty. "Two n's"

"Pleased to meet you, Jenn with two n's. I'm Will, two l's. Sorry if I've disturbed your evening."

"No you haven't. Chad told me about your boss and your attempts to find and help him. I think it's awesome."

I look at Chad. He is smiling serenely. I offer to make them tea, and she joins us at the table. There is a musty smell permeating from them and it turns me on—in sharp contrast to every other vibe in my body.

I recount my trip and they sympathize. "I'm at a dead end."

The kettle whistles, and I jump to silence it. "I've just traveled eight hundred miles in one day for nothing and still have to get up for the morning shift."

"No, I don't think you do," Chad says, and disappears to the living room. He returns with a note. "You had a phone message. Bear wrote it down."

It is from the new barista and says that I'll be working the second shift—that someone wants to meet me at the end. A shiver courses through me.

"Is this it?"

"Yeah, but Bear said you've had other calls this evening. He thinks they were from an irate Asian man. It's your boss, no man? And he apparently didn't want to leave a message."

We each sit in silence and I feel them staring at me. Chad yawns and says he needs to sleep. Jenn comes over and pecks me on the cheek. We have only just met, but the gesture is appreciated.

"He's gonna roast you," she says softly. "Even if he is your boss, you need to stand your ground, but try to stay calm."

"Tell me about it."

She turns and walks from the kitchen. Her hips are swinging and she brushes a finger lightly along Chad's chest as she passes

"She's very nice," I say.

"Yes," he says, and I hear an excitement in his voice that I've never heard. "She really is."

22: Showdown

Aimee, the new barista, is relieved to see me when I enter The Daily Grind. The place is quiet, and she quickly makes the two of us a drink.

"I know he is my boss, Will, but it was really not okay. He was out-of-control on the phone. I mean, jeez, he's never met me, and he didn't ask anything about me or the business. He just demanded that I swap shifts with you. I wasn't even sure that he was who he said he was."

"Don't worry about it." I want to reassure her, but I am tense enough myself. "He's going through a lot. He's a good man, Aimee, a good man who's standing precariously close to the edge."

She sighs. "It's hard. That's all. I see you as my boss. You hired and supervise me. Then I couldn't get through to you when he turned up."

"Don't worry about it," I repeat. "You're doing a good job and I will make sure he appreciates it. Look, why don't you go home? I can take it from here."

She offers no resistance and in minutes she's out of the café and out of my mind. Tzu must know I was in Ventura and that is why he has been phoning and obviously fuming. He must have been in touch with his daughter, Madeleine, after I left her. I rub my forehead as I sip my latte. I'm thankful that I have the café to myself for a while.

Tabitha bustles in late and is surprised to see me.

"Hi, Will. I thought that you were on the earlier ..."

Her voice trails off. She can evidently see from my expression that I'm uptight and assumes I'm in no mood to excuse her for arriving late.

"Look, Will, I've been pulling extra time as well helping to keep things running smoothly. You can cut me some slack too. Okay?"

"Just don't make a habit of it." I snap, wrenching an obscure part of the Beast apart to clean. The new barista is very conscientious and has meticulously cleaned the machine. That also irritates me!

Tabitha busies herself wiping tables, but I can sense furtive glances in my direction. I feel guilty, as she does deserve better—especially from me. I go into the storeroom to check paperwork and hear the front door open and familiar voices greeting Tabitha. Recognizing the two cops, I sigh deeply and stay in the storeroom.

Inevitably, Tabitha comes looking for me. She's biting her lower lip, and I feel even worse at how I'm treating her.

"The cops are here." She forces an apologetic smile. "They want to see you."

"It's okay, Tab." I reach out and stroke her arm. She smiles and pats my hand. "Tell them I'll be out in a minute. Offer coffee."

I take my time shuffling papers, checking orders. We should receive an order of coffee beans today and I phone to confirm the order.

"Why are you calling?" the guy at the other end asks anxiously. "We're always very prompt with deliveries. You had any problems?"

"No." I mumble, feeling bad for him. "The boss is away and I just don't want to screw up in his absence. Thanks." I hang up.

"Busy day?" Mendez looks around the shop, which is distinctly lacking in customers as I slowly approach.

"We have an order coming in today, and I was checking to confirm the delivery." There, I did not lie to an officer of the law.

"Good," said Mendez, nodding. I can't see his eyes behind his wraparounds, but his mustache is twitching. "Organization is the key to good business." He leans forward. "Went traveling yesterday, we heard."

"Your sources are accurate," I say, cringing at the cliché probably lifted from a dozen bad detective movies. "As always."

Mendez seems to likes this. He nods. "Where did you go?"

"Southern California."

"For one day?"

"Under the circumstances, can't afford to take more time off work."

"Mind if we ask what you were doing down there?" Captain O'Connor is sharp with me. I hesitate, and he takes a more conciliatory tone. "You are not required to divulge anything personal."

I weigh my answer. Do I want to start lying? These guys are pros—they'll catch me. "I went to see some people. Research you know. Background I need for my writing."

"Your boss's children live down that way," says Mendez staring at me.

I try not to flinch. "Yes, Mrs. Tzu told me. I've already asked her if he is in contact with them. He isn't. But I'm sure you know that."

"We do." Mendez toys with a toothpick, expertly showing his skepticism. It's amazing what a pro can do with a toothpick. "We do," he repeats.

Captain O'Connor drinks from his cappuccino leaving foam on his mustache. "We came in yesterday to tell you that we have two reported sightings. They are still unconfirmed, but both suggest that Mr. Tzu is alive."

A deft signal from his colleague and the foam is wiped away. I fancy only a writer would have noticed their interaction.

"How long have you guys been working together?"

They stare at each other. Do I detect a moment of macho sentimentalism?

"About twelve years," replies Mendez. "Why do you ask?"

"Research," I say, leaning back in my chair. "Background."

They shuffle in their chairs, and I enjoy satisfaction for momentarily turning the tables.

"You don't seem too relieved at our news," says O'Connor, the first to recover.

"I have no doubt he's alive," I say, surprising all three of us. "He's a survivor."

"What makes you so sure?"

I hesitate and Mendez chips in. "Research, huh?" He cracks a smile, but his partner is frowning.

"Son, what if Tzu contacts you before anyone else?" O'Connor is staring at me. "What will you do?"

"I don't know," I say, trying to appear unruffled. "What makes you think that he'll do that? He has a wife and kids."

"Intuition goes a long way in my profession, kid. I've been doing this for more than thirty years." O'Connor has a deep crease across his forehead.

The big man breaks eye contact and sips coffee. He gives me the distinct feeling of a father who knows his son isn't coming clean. "There's more here than you're telling us. Either you're hiding something or you don't realize what is keeping you so involved. Maybe both. Whatever it is, it's driving you to find him. You're deeply concerned with his disappearance beyond your concerns for the coffee shop and your job. I sense it, and I think Tzu does as well. We know he spoke about you a lot with his wife and children."

I sigh and try to think. These guys are not the enemy. I am not being interrogated.

"What would you suggest I do? He's a war vet. I'm not. He's Asian. I have little experience with Asians. He's old enough to be my father. If you're right, what should I do?"

"You are indeed woefully untrained and unprepared." Suggests Mendez, ever master of the understatement.

"Play to your strengths, Will," says his partner after some thought. "What attracts him to you? Why would he choose you over his family, other war vets or Asians? Maybe because you're a blank slate. You hold no opinions. No prejudices. You're even untainted by American history."

His words speed up as he continues this line of thought. "Maybe it's because you're a writer. Writers are like sponges. They absorb everything around them like a sponge absorbs water. Maybe he'll discover he can talk to you." O'Connor leans in. "Maybe he thinks you can tell his story. He sees something in you. I see something in you. You do research, you look for the truth, and your annoying English stubbornness makes you unable to give up until you have uncovered it."

Despite his sincerity, I can't help but smile.

"Ah," I say. "I see you've read my work."

"No," Captain O'Connor replies without hesitation. "But I will. One day we all will."

23: The Truth

It is nine-thirty in the evening, and The Daily Grind is almost empty. The candles flicker their last reflections on the wiped tables. There is only one couple left sitting in the far corner. We close at ten, so there is little I can do. Wineglasses have been cleaned and toweled dry, opened bottles are corked and oxygen-free. The place is ready to close.

Though she came to work late, I send Tabitha home. Mr. Tzu is probably out there waiting to find me alone. A minute after she's gone, he enters and takes a seat in the opposite corner to the young couple. He is wearing a peaked cap drawn down over his face and a scarf blending with any of ten-thousand other faces on the street. I stare from behind the Beast. Here walks a wounded war hero bumping shoulders with commuters who are oblivious of the warrior that walks among them.

I swallow hard. I must keep control.

The couple calls me over. They would like to take the rest of the bottle home and ask me to recork it. I take the bottle behind the counter, seal it and place it in a brown bag. They are putting on their coats when I return and I remind them to put the wine in the trunk of the car in case they are pulled over. It could be considered an open-bottle offense. They appreciate this, and I appreciate the tip they leave.

We are alone.

He moves to a table nearer the counter, and I bring a bottle of Cabernet Sauvignon. It is a robust wine from the Pablo Robles region located halfway between San Francisco and Santa Barbara. As it is less than one-third full, I figure we can finish it together. I set down two glasses and fill each to just over the bulbous part. Mr. Tzu stares at the glass I've filled for him, and I wonder whether the wine was a mistake. He could bawl me out for drinking the shop's stock, but somehow I doubt this is what's on his mind.

He slots the stem of the glass between the index and middle fingers of his right hand and slowly swirls the deep red liquid around the glass. I note his expertise, very rhythmic, allowing the wine to touch the sides of the glass almost up to the rim without danger of spilling. Ordinarily, one would be oxygenating the wine, bringing it to room temperature or examining its legs—assessing its body by the speed with which the beverage rolls down the inside of the glass. It is easier for my thoughts to focus on viniculture than the man sitting opposite me.

Mr. Tzu knows all this, but I'm sure he's not judging the vintage. He sighs, clearly weighing where to begin. When he speaks, his voice is soft. "How is business?"

"Steady. We're missing you, but the new barista's very competent and conscientious. You'll like her."

"Does she treat the Beast with respect?"

"Yes. I keep trying to fault her but she knows her way around the machine."

No smile. "You have put in many hours." This is said without emotion as a statement.

"Yes. It was not easy deciding to hire someone when we didn't know … didn't know how long … this present situation would continue." Fuck, I'm already sweating.

"Still, I should compensate you."

It is my turn to nod. Yes, he should.

He doesn't thank me and his tone sharpens. "Why are you doing this?"

"You've been good to me, I care about my work and—"

"That is not what I mean." His eyes have not left his glass, and he has not tasted it.

Mine, however, is already empty. I have committed a cardinal sin among wine drinkers. Never gulp your wine. It's disrespectful. There's a winery in Napa built in an old schoolhouse. If they catch you gulping rather than sipping and savoring, they make you write lines on the old blackboard that still hangs there. This is all in jest, I assume, because they are still in business.

But Mr. Tzu is not here to taste wine with me.

"Why do you pursue me?" He almost hisses.

I shake my head. "I've been asking myself that too. Your disappearance has consumed me and, you're right, it's more than the business. Maybe it's a loyalty thing. You trusted me."

He nods but doesn't speak—just continues to stare at his glass. I can't read his facial expressions or his body language.

I try to wait, but I'm not comfortable with this silence.

"I'm sorry about your brother. I really am."

He nods.

"You know that I met him?"

Again he nods.

"I wrote a lot of what he told me. If you would like to see it sometime—"

Mr. Tzu looks down and shakes his head.

"I loved my brother." He whispers. "I loved him very much, but I couldn't help him." His voice cracks. "If I can't help my own brother—"

I open my mouth, but nothing comes out. He continues.

"Before we went into the army, we talked about going into business together. This coffee shop could have been The Brothers' Tzu or something like that. Salvador was with you when you met Li?"

I nod. "He was very cautious about bringing us together. He protected your brother's identity. I believe Li Tzu made the decision to meet with me. Salvador would not have pressed him to do so."

"I trust Salvador. I find comfort in knowing he was there for my brother." There is another silence, before he says, "Did you tell my children about Li?"

So he knows I've met his children. A flash in his eyes warns me not to play games. I take a deep breath. "No," I say at last. "Nor have I told your wife. Li Tzu made me promise before we talked. I am a man of my word."

He nods and lets out a long breath. "Thank you."

"Who are you in touch with? It's Madeleine, right? But why didn't she tell me?"

He doesn't answer.

"Is this a one-way interrogation?" I instantly regret saying it and see his eyes flash again. I need to tread carefully.

But after a few moments, he says, "You are wrong. I am in touch with my son. It is easier that way." He doesn't elaborate, and I think I understand.

"Clear this away," he says. "It is late. You should go home."

He follows me into the back of the store and checks things on his desk. He sees his brother's letter, gasps, and picks it up. Unfolding it, he reads. I see his hands shaking slightly and his fingers almost caress the dirty paper. He opens a drawer and buries the letter deep inside.

I wait for him in front of the counter. He turns the lights out in the back. As he passes, he throws me a furtive glance and I see something disconcerting in his eyes. I tense.

"You must stop this."

I look around the store innocently. He doesn't appreciate my humor.

"You must stop this. It is my life and you must butt out." The t's are spat out. His voice has turned ugly, but somehow, possibly because of fatigue, I don't feel intimidated.

Now glaring at me, he repeats himself.

"You must stop hounding me. This is none of your business. You just work here. You work well and I pay you. That is all this is about."

I feel myself shaking my head. He starts yelling. "THIS IS MY LIFE! YOU HAVE NO RIGHT! I'M TELLING YOU TO BUTT OUT!"

"It's not that simple. I—"

"IT IS THAT SIMPLE! YOU ARE A NOSEY, ENGLISH SON-OF-A-BITCH! I AM WARNING YOU TO BACK OFF!"

I am breathing heavily. From nowhere, something erupts. "I CAN'T." I yell back. "IT'S NOT JUST ABOUT YOU, YOU SELFISH OLD BAST—"

The punch comes from nowhere, and I spin over a table and fall to the floor. Pain and tears blur my vision as I feel him jump on top of me. He is straddling me and raises a fist. I instinctively pull my arms over to shield my face.

But the punch is not delivered. Instead, Tzu astonishingly punches the concrete floor and howls from the pain. He rubs his fist, still clenched, and then glares at the ring on his finger—touching the green stone. Watching the ring, he focuses on bringing himself under control.

He wheezes. "I am ... telling you ... to ... back off. You've ... done enough ... damage." As his breath returns, he whispers vehemently. "You must stop! You don't understand!"

"I can't." I plead. "That's the trouble. I do understand. I am your son who is in denial. I am your daughter who resents the father she never knew, because he thinks he's the fucking Great Wall of China." Then from nowhere I yell in a high, juvenile voice I vaguely recognize. "I LOST MY FATHER. I WON'T LOSE YOU TOO!" I gasp for breath as tears flow down my face and long-buried memories flood back. "I couldn't save him. I couldn't save him."

Tzu climbs off me and pulls me up so we are both sitting on the floor. I'm crying uncontrollably, and he awkwardly draws me to him.

Through strained breaths he whispers into my ear. "I'm sorry, son, but you can't save me either."

24: Among Friends

I lie in bed. The hour is irrelevant—sleep elusive. The truth has surfaced, and it's not only Tzu who was surprised. Fuck! I hadn't seen it coming. Hadn't connected the dots, and I was getting down on Tzu's son for living in denial?

I realize that I'm seeing all this as a revelation—dwelling on the fact that it has surfaced rather than the memories themselves. I know there are many repressed memories that will have to be excavated, but this is not the time. I must repress them again—for now.

I think about Tzu, about how this new aspect complicates matters. I had fancied myself as the objective writer observing impartially from the side. This is no longer true. Perhaps it never was. I feel so stupid—so fucking stupid!

I get out of bed and go to the bathroom. As I wash my hands, I see my reflection in the mirror. The left side of my face is puffed up and bruised. I look closer and make out the imprint of his ring in the middle of the wound.

I go to the kitchen halfheartedly planning to put a frozen bag of peas on the swelling. We always have frozen peas in the freezer. It is a staple part of our household diet. You can't ruin cooked peas.

I hate the idea of the cold and, as I open the freezer door, change my mind. Retreating to the safety of my English roots, I fill the kettle to make a cup of tea.

I open my laptop and stare at the screen. It has been a long time since I could not immediately immerse myself in my writing, but now I just stare at the screen. I know what has to be written. I see the kettle steaming and remove it from the stove before it begins to whistle. It is two-fifteen in the morning, and I won't be too popular if I wake my housemates.

I return to the kitchen chair and sigh. There is a lot to deal with and all I want to do is write. My fingers are suspended over the snow-white keyboard.

Bear is standing at the door rubbing his eyes. His room is nearest to the kitchen and the light has probably disturbed him.

"Hey man, why ya' up?" He has finished rubbing his eyes and is now staring at me. "Jesus! Will, what happened?"

My left hand rises to the swollen part of my face, but I have no time to answer. Bear races to the freezer and yanks out the frozen peas.

"No Bear, I—" Bear is a very big guy, a gym junkie, and his muscular arm glides through my skinny, flailing attempts to stop him. When the frozen veggies make contact with my skin, I manfully scream from the shock of the cold.

I hear movements throughout the house.

"Bear, what the fuck ya' doing to him, man?" Julian is in boxer shorts and thinks Bear is attacking me. When Bear turns to answer, the pack leaves my face. Julian sees the wound and takes control. He got his first aid badge in the Boy Scouts or something like that and always takes charge of dire medical situations such as burns and cuts. This is usually followed by a month of tantalizing self-examination and guilt about whether he should be premed. Apparently, a five-thousand-year connection exists between his Jewish roots and the Chosen Doctors. The guilt dissolves when he sees an inspirational movie that reminds him why he is studying cinema.

Julian's first response is to push Bear's hand and the frozen peas back on my face. My response is to scream again from the cold. Bear is perfectly strong enough to keep the pack on my face despite my resistance. He is very conscious of his strength but, being a gentle soul, is always hesitant to apply it. However, his hand is now directed by Julian's iron determination and resistance is futile.

Chad and Jenn are now in the kitchen. Jenn thinks she has some arnica cream in her bag and goes to find it. It will help ease the swelling. I realize that I've been too self-absorbed to feel any pain thus far. Now that it's being mentioned, I begin to feel the throbbing. There is a dull ache, and I silently curse the attention that I'm receiving.

With the medical situation under control, they sit somewhere around the kitchen table and stare at me. They want answers. They are my housemates, and they are my friends. Harrison, the cat, appears with a stretch and a meow. Human housemates plus kitchen usually equals food. He shows great empathy and rubs against our legs.

I look at their concerned faces. We have been thrown together by coincidence but have become a little family. I wish Jane were here to be a part of it. The icepack is now numbing my face, but I feel a deep cold inside.

I make a movement to fill my teacup and four volunteers jump to assist me.

"Let me—"

"Don't take the pack off."

"I'll make it."

I suddenly feel an overwhelming impulse to cry. Simultaneously, I also think that I would like to be pregnant. This is how every pregnant woman should be treated. Surrounded by loving friends and family spoiling her.

I am, however, not pregnant. I am a man, an Englishman at that, and I can't let myself cry in front of them because, well, I am a guy even if this is San Francisco.

"You can cry if you want," says Chad, staring into my eyes. Jenn is perched on his lap and she puts a hand on my arm supportively. She is wearing that flimsy cloth from the night we'd met and her touch sends currents through my body. I am now additionally racked with guilt, which helps subdue the desire to cry.

"What happened?" Bear has brought me some mint tea and now sits on my other side. He is very concerned. "Are you in danger?"

"No," I say softly. "I almost missed my stop on the MUNI and banged myself on the closing doors." Feeling a need to further embellish, I plow on. "I then seemed to spin outside and fell badly on the metal guards there."

The story sounds flimsy, and their faces show doubt. I have always been a terrible liar, and I can see them all planning the cross-examination that will tie me in knots. I think there is an unspoken collective decision that it's not worth it and move on. But still I feel compelled not to reveal that it was Mr. Tzu.

"Were you attacked?" Bear is very persistent. "Is someone after you?"

"It's the girl!" Julian intercedes, excitedly.

"Jane?" I say, surprised.

"No, the hot, kickboxing, jealous lesbian, Asian ex-girlfriend. She did this, right?"

I laugh though this hurts my face. "Julian, you've been giving this woman a lot of thought."

He blushes, but asks again almost hopefully. "Was it her?"

"No," I say, and then fake a yawn. I want to them to go to bed. "Look, it was an accident and no one threatened me."

"You should drink some chamomile to relax you, not peppermint."

"Let me put some arnica on."

"I'll walk you to work tomorrow,"

"I'll go talk to hot Asian ex-girlfriend for you."

Now I am really yawning. I can feel a throbbing in my face, I'm not sure whether the punch or the peas are responsible, but I want to fall asleep before I get a headache. I look at my friends and their concerned faces. "I'm lucky to have you guys," I say, and mean it. "Thank you."

I stand, walk to my room and lie down on the bed. I close my eyes and, despite the traumatic day, I have a smile on my face. I think of Chad and Bear and Julian and Jenn. I hear Harrison come in purring and he jumps on the bed with me. I think of Jane and—

My eyes fly open. Shit! We are having dinner with Jane's parents tomorrow night!

25: The Swollen Day After

Tired from a restless night, I slowly set up the cafe. The side of my face is throbbing and exhibiting an array of colors. I resemble Neelix the Talaxian, who had a rainbow colored face and, like the TV character on *Star Trek: Voyager*, I need to show a hospitable face.

Thankfully, I am working with Tabitha who is way too cool to make a fuss. Her first response consists of dropping a heavy bag of art materials then hitting me in the head with the cardboard tube she uses to carry her sketches, as I lean down to help her. Fortunately, she hits the other side of my face, and I just wince.

The customers seem fairly oblivious of my disposition. I guess anything goes in San Francisco and only a few ask. I make up some smartass replies: trying a new line of makeup, returning this weekend to Talaxia and, nearest the truth, forgetting to put sugar in my boss's coffee this morning.

However, I am not really seeing the customers, but the faces of Jane's parents sitting across from me at dinner tonight. I will call Jane later and try to cancel. If it were not for my wound, I might have tried to talk to her father about last night. Tabitha is too busy to ask questions and will wait until after the morning rush, so I have time to make up a story.

I groan, hopefully not out loud, because in the crowd I see the big, uniformed body of Captain O'Connor enter and behind him his partner Mendez. They walk toward the counter and stop at the table Tzu had knocked me over. It is, of course, by now upright, but they have noticed, as do I now, that I positioned it too far out. They bend over the side of the table, and I find myself holding my breath.

I move to one side on the pretense of grinding more beans and observe them. They look around the table then lean over the spot. Mendez sits and bends as if picking something off the floor. The Captain makes his way to the front.

He stands in line for coffee and when he sees me, does a double take. When he steps forward to order his coffee, I inquire in my best barista voice what he would like.

"Two drips, medium, and ..." he angles his head to his left parallel with my swollen side, "... a few minutes of your time."

"Coffees coming up." I chirp. "But I'll need you to wait awhile to talk, just 'till we're over the rush."

We both check our watches. Since it's already after nine o'clock, I say with a smile, "Only a few more minutes, I expect."

He takes the two cups of coffee and pays.

"We'll wait for you at the table," he says, as he glances at his change.

Shit! Had he said the table? I pretend not to have noticed. As I watch him walk to the table, I see Mendez is looking closely at the floor again and has a transparent Ziploc bag in his hand. Perhaps he is eating something. I should have offered them a croissant or cake.

I turn to the next customer and smile, "What can I get you?"

The next ten minutes pass too quickly. Tabitha's furtive glances have increased, and I realize I'm sweating. The line of customers dwindles, and I walk to the policemen's table with a heavy heart.

Captain O'Connor is frowning. "What happened, son?"

Despite my preparation, my mind goes blank. I try the Neelix Star Trek joke, suggesting that I am modeling a new range of makeup. Mendez reveals himself to be a sworn Trekkie, though, predictably, prefers the original Captain Kirk series. O'Connor doesn't crack a smile. His expression could be interpreted as either suspicion or worry. Deciding the latter, I feel a wave of affection for the policemen realizing again that I seem to have many friends. Still, something prevents me from revealing that Tzu inflicted this on me. But the Captain isn't handing out tea and sympathy.

"So it didn't go well," he comments, deadpan.

There is a pattern here of O'Connor assuming things that haven't been said and having an amazing propensity for accuracy. He has already caught me lying, or as I prefer to see it, intentionally misleading them. I must tread carefully. I cannot think of anything to say and stay quiet.

O'Connor sighs. "Here's how I see it, son. He came in here pissed off at you for tracking him. You lost your cool and there was an argument. He lashed out, knocked you over the table and maybe a chair—cutting you with his jade ring."

"He has a ring?" Why did I instinctively lie? I shouldn't have walked into it.

"Yeah," says Mendez, leaning in for the kill. "We asked his wife when he first disappeared if he was carrying anything of value. We suspected he'd been mugged or something. He has a green jade ring that's passed through his family for generations." He strokes his mustache and stares off somewhere undefined. "Probably given to a descendant by the Yellow Emperor himself. You know, the one who wrote the first book of Chinese Medicine?"

We didn't know, and the Captain and I both stare at Mendez, bewildered, though this doesn't initially faze him. But when he notices that his partner is possibly glaring, he makes an effort to get back on track and joins in by glaring at me. I recall Tzu punching the floor and looking at his ring, but I still can't stop myself.

"What makes you think I've been hit with a ring?"

"There's a mark inside that beautiful bruise that looks like an imprint," O'Connor says without emotion.

"And you didn't sweep the floor properly." His partner adds waving the Ziploc holding what distinctly looks like a chip of jade. "This makes me suspect that the fight took place at this very table at about twenty-two hundred."

"Go on," I say in wonder, knowing this is against my better judgment. But, ever the writer, I am truly intrigued by their professionalism.

Mendez continues, a Hispanic Sherlock Holmes. "He would never have confronted you in front of customers, so he waited for everyone to leave. You had everything cleared away for closing and had already swept, so when you tried to hide the evidence, your cleaning was clumsy. This is probably because you'd just been whacked. You were afraid and intimidated and just wanted to go home and take care of yourself."

"This is so cool." I admit adding quickly with as much bravado as I can muster. "I haven't denied anything yet because I love watching you work. At what point do you want the real story?"

Captain O'Connor looks at me disappointedly. "Don't bother, kid," he says. "Are you in danger? We're all rooting for Tzu, but this is about a mentally unstable vet who has now turned violent. We've seen our share of sad sights in our line of work."

His partner nods in agreement. "Oh yes, we have—"

"No," I say firmly. I definitely don't want to hear any horror stories. "I'm still as determined to help Mr. Tzu as I ever was." I think of what happened last night—the repressed memories flooding back. "Actually," I add grimly, "even more."

"Jane? You got my message? Look I don't think I can make it to your parents tonight."

"Oh, why not?" She sounds pissed.

"Actually, I'm feeling a bit beat up and I look worse than I feel."

"Shit! What happened?"

"I can't tell you here, but I've made first contact. I'm in the back of the store, and I don't want to be overheard."

"He hit you?"

"Let's just say he left … an impression on me."

"I'll be there in twenty minutes."

"There's no—"

"I've just finished class. I'll take a cab and be there soon."

"There's—"

The line has gone dead. I turn around and Tabitha is standing there.

"I'm okay," I say, unfortunately wincing at a shot of pain. She gives me an enthusiastic hug spoiled only when her face brushes the wound. I jerk backward and breathe sharply.

"Sorry," she says. "You're like a big brother to me, Hemingway. I can get some of my girlfriends from the neighborhood to jump him. Y'want?"

I smile—laughing is still painful.

"I appreciate it, but everything turned out okay, and I think I can help him. I think I need to help him."

"By being his punching bag?"

"He hit me once and instantly regretted it. He won't do it again."

A half hour passes and the café experiences a brief lunchtime rush. By the time Jane arrives, the line is almost gone though the tables are all full.

I meet her by the side of the counter near the bathrooms. She touches around the wound apprehensively then kisses me on the other side. Taking a step back, she punches me in the arm.

"Have you been seeing Susan?"

I am stunned—her ex-Rambo? I stare at her and she bursts out laughing. "What a tool!"

"Well I'm glad you're not taking my grievous wound too seriously."

She stops laughing though it takes an effort.

•

"Oh dear," she says and hugs my arm pulling our bodies together. Feeling her body against mine goes a fair way to appeasing me. Indeed, I am quite the tool.

"Listen," she says, "I'm meeting a friend to go over a paper. She's coming here now and we'll stop when you finish your shift. Then we'll go to my place and you can tell me all about it, and I will pamper your every need. Then we'll shower, dress and go to my parents for dinner."

"Aren't you worried how they'll react when they see me like this?" I point to my face for emphasis. "I mean, your mother—"

An evil grin extends the width of Jane's face and one eyebrow arches. "Are you fucking kidding me?"

26: Family

Despite the growing knot in my stomach, it's easy to enjoy a pampered afternoon at Jane's apartment. I describe the meeting with Mr. Tzu minus my own personal revelation—then we shower together, always a pleasure, and lie on her bed—chilling. She applies an array of soothing creams to my face, and I almost forget our dinner plans.

But all too soon, we're dressed and sitting on a bus. I'm silent for most of the trip and Jane gives me space. Her arm is around my shoulders, and she slowly strokes my neck. I wonder if she suspects there's more than I've revealed so far.

Her father opens the door and stares at my face. He seems to immediately size up the situation as he smoothly invites us inside. Jane gives me a look that clearly tells me not to expect such a similar response from her mother. As I enter, James takes my arm and murmurs. "Progress?"

I nod. He makes a small jerk with his head to my wound, and I nod again. He sighs, shakes his head slowly then leads us into a small atrium. Ever the host, James pours three brandies and passes them out. He then inquires about his daughter's studies and the progress of a paper she's struggling to write. I realize, once again, how one-sided our relationship has become.

"My dears, you've arrived." Jane's mother announces as she enters. Her expression suggests just the right impression of a woman courageously hassled in her kitchen. "I hope James is taking care of ... oh my goodness, your face! What have you done?"

For someone offering smug retorts all day, I somehow freeze up. My mouth opens though no words follow. James intercedes.

"I'm not sure we should hound the young man, my dear. I imagine Will and I will touch on it after dinner." His eyes glance toward the stairs that lead down to his office, his den, his territory. There is something subtle in his tone, something firm and authoritative, and his wife is finely attuned.

"Well, that's all very well then," she says, clasping her hands in front of her possibly in a vain attempt to control them. "As long as you are alright, err ..., Will?"

She remembers my name! This is progress!

"Shall we go in for dinner?" Her arms show us the way, and I ponder the internal power struggle between the brain and its extremities.

James chugs his brandy and puts the glass back on the tray. Jane has already put her glass down, and I infer that one's brandy glass is not a welcome guest at the dinner table. I take another swig and move to put it on the tray. I look up at James and nod soundlessly thanking him. He smiles, puts his hand on my shoulder and gently directs me to the dining room.

The conversation around the table flows and the food is delicious. Mrs. Van Ness serves almond trout, asparagus and salad. James needs to watch his cholesterol, his wife informs us. James makes a grimace at the thought of life without steak, and his wife, though looking at her plate, says sharply, "I saw that, James!"

I wonder if she did, or if she just knows him so well? The wine James selected is a Bordeaux Sauvignon Blanc, and he watches as I examine the label.

"I researched the wine in your honor," he says warmly. "My man at the club promises that a dry white would complement the trout." He smiles playfully challenging me. "What's your opinion, sommelier?"

I clear my throat. "This is very good and certainly accentuates the succulence of the trout," I say in full wine snobbery mode and sharpened English accent. I note my hostess enjoyed the compliment but turn my attention to James. "I'm not a great fan of the Sauvignon as it can get a little dry and sharp. They are so unpredictable, but you have made a bold choice, sir."

James beams at my response, and his daughter rolls her eyes. Mrs. van Ness then explains that she is very active on the charities committee at the country club. Somewhere into dessert, she nonchalantly proposes that I emcee a wine tasting event. Bottles would be donated and auctioned for the UCSF children's hospital, and an entrance fee would cover the wine tasted during the event.

"Your knowledge and English accent would be such a treat. Of course, we would wait until after you're … you know." She points to the side of her face.

"Isn't there a professional sommeliers organization or something?" I am searching for excuses. "Californians know their wine and might have more knowledge than I can offer."

"Sure, but I bet none of them can toast in thirteen languages." Raising her glass, Jane laughs. "Ganbei!"

I blush, and Mrs. van Ness shudders as she visualizes the scene. We agree to think about it, and James suggests that he and I head downstairs.

"No cigars," she calls down after us.

I don't catch James's muttered response, and I hope neither does his wife.

Downstairs, James sends me into his wine cellar to choose a wine. "Take your time," he says congenially. When I return, he is settled in his big chair, a brandy in one hand and a cigar in the other.

"Won't your wife smell the smoke?"

He points to a little machine humming nearby. "Latest technology," he says proudly.

"And it works that well?" I stare skeptically at the heavy fumes gathered around him.

"Of course not," James replies. "No fun in that."

He is surely his daughter's father. We both laugh as I pop open the selected bottle of Merlot and inhale. I love the combination of plums or berries with a subtle chocolaty flavor. Merlot suggests an evening drink with which to unwind.

"So you met him, I see?" James says matter-of-factly. "He got angry with you and took a swing?"

I nod.

"Not many people continue to chase a man they barely know after getting yelled at and whacked. Still want to help him?"

I nod again. I am weighing how much to tell James about that evening. It's not about Tzu anymore. My emotional well-being is at stake in exposing everything to my girlfriend's father. During a long silence, James makes it clear that he can comfortably outlast me. He packs far more experience and is a master of this game.

I soon break. "I'm not sure how to take it from here."

He nods, in no hurry to answer. "Will he see you again?"

"Yes. He said that he needs to think, but that he'll contact me soon."

"What made him decide to meet you?"

I tell him about going to see Tzu's children. "There's more, but I'm sworn to secrecy." James doesn't push.

"But there is more beyond what you cannot tell me. I wonder if our Mr. Tzu is only interested in what you're doing for him, or does he realize what's at stake for you?"

I'm flabbergasted. "W-why do you say that?"

James laughs. He stands and lights the fire. When it has caught, he pulls his chair nearer the fireplace and invites me to do the same.

"What do you know of alcoholics, Will? Have you ever been close to one?"

I shake my head.

"My family comes from a long line of alcoholics. Either you went to war or succumbed to the bottle. Often as not, you died drunk on the battlefield."

"Are you an alcoholic?"

"No, thank God, but I need to be careful. War memories easily depress me, and I enjoy drinking wine with dinner followed by a drink in the den afterward. With my heredity, I'm vulnerable and my wife keeps a steady eye on me. I'm careful about company on fishing trips and vacations. But this isn't about me.

"Alcoholics are an interesting breed, Will, and they're very similar to war vets. It's fascinating that even when they're not drinking, possibly haven't consumed alcohol for years, an alcoholic can always recognize a fellow struggler."

James gazes into the fire.

"They never kick the habit. Decades later, having never touched a bottle, it takes just one unexpected fall to lay waste to years of struggle and discipline.

"And yet, however well they hide it from the world, another alcoholic will recognize them. I don't know how? Ordering a soda when everyone else is drinking a fine whisky. A longing glance at a bottle that lasts just a second too long. A momentary hesitation too short for anyone but a fellow alcoholic to notice."

I shift around in my chair. "Why are you telling me this?"

"It's the same with war vets. The wounds and scars disappear, and though we expend considerable effort on covering our tracks, another vet will sense something. You develop a kind of sixth sense." He stares at me intensely. "And mine is darn good."

There is silence. My mind freezes.

James takes pity. "You don't have to tell me—not now or ever. But if you do, it'll stay between us. Soldier's honor. And Will, I won't think any less of you."

I'm confused, and I think I'm shaking. "How do you know?" My voice is barely a whisper competing with the fire's crackle.

"Many people become alcoholics because they follow in their father's footsteps. This might be genetic or behavioral. Dr. Jane upstairs would know better than me. I think the children of war vets often carry the scars of their fathers' battles."

I stare at him but can't speak. He leans forward. "If you want to tell me about it—now or anytime in the future—you can. That's all I'm saying."

"I would like to hear too." Jane is hovering in the doorway.

She has broken a house rule and knows it. This is her father's world, and even his precious daughter requires permission to broach its boundaries. But James doesn't seem angry, just inconvenienced. He looks at me waiting for my response.

I extend an arm to invite her in. She comes over and perches on the side of my chair taking my hand in hers.

"I've been sent to announce there's a tiramisu upstairs and growing concern about its degenerating condition."

"I guess we should go up then," I say, my voice still shaky. Then I look at James. "Thank you."

Mrs. van Ness is either oblivious of what is happening, or just knows not to broach the subject. She plays the perfect hostess and enjoys the compliments on the dessert.

"Great tiramisu, Mrs. V."

"Yeah," says Jane, raising her wineglass and looking slightly flushed. "Tiramisu and Merlot together—wicked."

The conversation remains light, and Jane's parents surprise us by announcing that they're going to Paris. It's a business trip, but James has suggested they make it a mini-vacation. I wonder if this is a precaution from the drinking culture of the other businessmen.

We are offered the house during the trip though strictly no parties. There is apparently a history here, and I anticipate a lot of fun extracting it from Jane. There is laughter and discussions of the best places to visit in Paris and reminiscences of past experiences. I begin to unwind.

My cell phone rings, and I'm surprised to see that while we were downstairs I missed four calls. I excuse myself and check the others in the hallway. The police are looking for me, have been to the coffee shop and called my house.

I search for Captain O'Connor's number and call him.

"Captain, I hear you've been looking for me?"

"Yes, son. Are you okay?"

"Yeah, thank you. I'm with my girlfriend's parents having dinner."

"Good. The van Ness' are a fine San Francisco family." These cops sure know their city. "Listen Will. After Tzu left you last night, he had a heart attack. He was found on the street about two in the morning. He's at St. Mary's and in stable condition. When we saw him at the hospital, he asked us to tell you."

I collapse on the bottom of the stairs holding my chest and gasping for air. After a minute, I say, "Can I see him?"

"I believe family only for the present and, frankly, given your altercation, you just might be the last person he needs to see now. Give him time."

"Shit. I never meant—"

"And it's not your fault either. Tzu wanted us to make that clear to you as well. He said to make sure you clean the damn Beast."

"Sure."

"Are you okay, son?"

"Yeah."

"We'll drop in tomorrow and see you. You've got the morning shift, right?"

"Yeah."

"It's not your fault, kid."

"Yeah."

27: Confessions

The following morning, Captain O'Connor and Sergeant Mendez enter The Daily Grind with the last wave of our morning rush hour. We talk in private for a few minutes, but I have little to say.

"Did you speak with Mr. van Ness last night?" The Captain asks.

"Yes," I reply.

His partner nods. "A fine man."

We chat, but we are all waiting—just waiting. O'Conner and Mendez can close their investigation, though I suspect it was never an official case. These are neighborhood cops and probably the last of a dying breed. When they leave, I am relieved to return to work.

Mrs. Tzu comes into the coffee shop about eleven o'clock. She seats herself at an empty table, and I bring her a cup of jasmine tea and a slice of cranberry cake.

"You try to make me fat," she says, shaking a finger at me. "You are very naughty boy." But she is smiling.

"How's Mr. Tzu doing?"

"Good, good. Chinese men are tough. Must be. Otherwise, cannot survive Chinese women."

Again she laughs, and I join in. Despite the heart attack, she has her husband back.

"You bring him back to me, Will. I not sure how, but you bring him back. I thank you."

I don't respond—not sure what he's told her and what he's kept back. Mrs. Tzu hears my silence.

"Why uptight? Englishmen always uptight."

I nod but say nothing. She puts her hand on mine.

"I know of secrets. I not know what secrets are, but I know there are secrets between you and my husband. That is okay. Secrets between men. I trust him and maybe I even trust you although you are uptight Englishman. It is good he found you, I think."

"It's good for me too, Mrs. Tzu," I say, my voice cracking with emotion.

"Yes, I think so. Is best. Two souls not complete. Help each other. Yin and Yang not whole alone. In their differences, they help each other become whole."

I stare at her. Mrs. Tzu is a student of Taoism?

She smiles sagely. "You know where I learn this?"

"No."

"On back of Chinese cereal box. Very wise. Very nutritious." Her laughter resonates through the café and lingers after she has left for the hospital.

Jane arrives as I finish my shift and picks up on my buoyant mood.

"Wow, look what my mother's home cooking does for you!" She says, and gives me a warm hug.

I recount Mrs. Tzu's visit, her exuberance at getting her husband back and the invitation I received to visit Mr. Tzu the following evening. Mrs. Tzu told me she will feed him, because hospitals don't understand about feeding Chinese men—then leave us alone.

Jane sits in silence and waits for me to finish. "Do I get you for the weekend?"

"What do you have planned?"

"Paris. We need to enjoy Paris."

"You get inspired by your parent's trip," I say, with a grin that I strongly suspect is stretched from ear to ear.

"You bet." My Goth girlfriend purrs back. "Oh, I filled out a survey for Victoria's Secret a while back, and they sent me a voucher for my troubles." She leans forward and her voice becomes husky. "They have a lot of sexy black lingerie."

"Did you choose anything?"

"No, I thought we could go there together and I could try on a few things. We can decide on something then take it home for a test drive."

Test Drive will never quite sound the same again.

I visit Tzu at St. Mary's hospital the following evening. I have come armed with two boxes of chocolate chip cookies, one with milk-chocolate chunks and the other with dark chocolate and mint.

Mrs. Tzu doesn't approve, and I claim they are for me.

"Two?"

"I might go to Jane's tonight and can't arrive empty-handed."

At the mention of Jane, Mrs. Tzu relents and a smile crosses her face. "She is good girl. You treat her right and she maybe ..." She searches for the right word. "Tolerate you." Her laughter is infectious.

I look over at her husband as he finishes a bowl of soup with what seems a healthy appetite.

My stomach abruptly knots. Last time we met, he yelled and punched me. This, in turn, precipitated his heart attack. I had assumed I'd be welcomed with open arms but now I hesitate.

While he finishes eating—there's no way his wife will leave until he does—he asks me about The Daily Grind. I tell him about the financials from the past week and the order of coffee beans that came in. I mention that we need to place a wine order, and he explains what needs to be done. I take out my notebook and list his instructions.

Mrs. Tzu is in no hurry to leave and begins fussing around the bowls she brought. She wipes her husband's mouth with a napkin, and he jerks his head away. He says something sharply in Chinese and she responds matching his tone. Whatever is said, she begins to pack.

"Will, not too late, okay? Husband still not fit. Plenty time to talk later."

I nod and Mr. Tzu says something to her. Though I don't speak Mandarin, I'm pretty sure his response is less compliant. Mrs. Tzu kisses him on the forehead, and I hear softer tones.

Watching her leave, Mr. Tzu says tenderly. "She is a good wife. She suffers me without complaint."

"She's very funny. The staff looks forward to her visits."

"You are lucky. Her wit is restricted in English but razor sharp in Mandarin."

There is a period of silence as we both consider where to start.

"So," he nods at the cookies, "what flavors?"

Thankfully, Mr. Tzu is interested in the milk chocolate, while I dig into the dark chocolate, my favorite. Mrs. Tzu has left a flask of tea, and we share it. I am told off for dunking my cookie. "This is Mrs. Tzu's tea, you colonialist bastard!"

We both laugh. After a few minutes, I ask, "Where do we start?"

"You gave me a heart attack. Let's start there." But there is softness in his tone that gives me confidence.

"And you messed up my face. I've had to brave the police, the customers and my girlfriend's parents looking like a Talaxian."

"A what?" Mr. Tzu is clearly no Trekkie. Then he laughs. "Tell me about visiting your girlfriend's parents."

"It was very embarrassing." I feign hurt, and he laughs out loud again.

"Serves you right. What story did you make up?"

I tell how James covered for me then stop abruptly as Tzu's face shows shock.

"You told your father-in-law about me?" Tzu ignores my protest to the term father-in-law. "Why?"

"Jane thought—"

"You tell your girlfriend?"

"I'm not like you." I snap. "I can't keep everything inside."

Silence. "I'm not sure about that," Tzu eventually replies. "There are some things you have succeeded in burying very effectively."

I sigh and reach for another cookie. So does Tzu.

"Listen, Mr. Tzu, our relationships with women is different. There are generational differences and," I can hear how earnest I sound, "probably cultural. In my world, we share most of our thoughts and emotions with our partners. It's the glue that binds us together."

He opens his mouth, but I continue. "Jane's father is a war vet himself. Jane arranged for us to have dinner— just the two of us—and, quite frankly, he has been a great help making sense of all this."

"Oh, so now you know what's going on?" He reaches into his bag, brings a big cookie to his mouth and harshly crunches. There is scant regard for the crumbs falling on his bed. Thank goodness I brought two boxes.

"Better than I could have otherwise. He saw action in Vietnam. He is decorated and he also carries scars. He's a good man."

Tzu softens a bit. "Maybe I should meet him sometime."

"I think that's a great idea. I would have to run it past him—"

"We could both bitch about you!" My boss shoots back before devouring the rest of the cookie in one mouthful.

There is another silence, another filling of teacups and selection of cookies. Then, duly armed, he looks at me and speaks quietly. "I am still tired."

"Do you want me to leave?"

"No, but no more fighting. You talk now. Tell me about your father. Your childhood."

I take a deep breath. I haven't rehearsed this.

"My father served in the Second World War fighting the Japanese in Burma. He was captured for, I think, a few months. If he was tortured, he never talked about it. But during captivity, he lived constantly with the threat. I guess that was torture in itself. Their food and water supply was purposely erratic. They could never bathe and lived in fear of disease knowing that the Japanese would kill anyone who became a health threat."

I stop, nibble on my cookie and sip tea. This isn't going to be easy.

"He did speak about the natives, who were caught between the constant advances and retreats of the warring armies. Each time one army retreated, they would take all the food and supplies in the villages then burn crops to prevent their adversaries taking advantage of these supplies. The indigenous people lived in wretched conditions. They had no clean water, decent food or medical supplies. They caught the viruses and germs of the soldiers without the immune systems to deal with them. It sounded pretty horrendous."

Tzu nods. "And he told you about this?"

"A few times usually following some huge argument."

"You argued with him?"

"Sometimes between him and me—sometimes between him and my mother."

"What was her role?"

"She tried to shield me from his eccentricities and tried to allow me as normal a life as possible. It rains in England a lot. I played many sports and came home dirty. I also went camping, fishing and stuff—regular boys' activities. My mother kept the house sterile for him, so me coming home caked in mud from the rugby field was a terrifying prospect for him."

Tzu nods again perhaps seeing the similarities between my mother and his wife.

I continue. "He was paranoid about dirt in the house. Everything had to be kept clean."

"You have brothers and sisters?"

"I have two sisters who are much older than me. That's another thing. They had me very late—a mistake, I suspect, although they vigorously denied it. I'm not close to my sisters and they never played rugby or went fishing. I don't think we ever had friends over to sleep.

Alon Shalev

"It got nasty when my parents fought, and the gloves came off, as we Brits say. When they lost it, they lost it and I'd try and hide, but I couldn't always."

"Why did they stay together?"

"Divorce wasn't something that happened much in England then. Maybe if a spouse was violent or slept with someone else but not because of something like this. They gave each other security. They were very dedicated to their children, and I want to believe they genuinely loved each other. I kept telling myself that it would become easier once I left the house."

I stop. The cookies are calling, and I make a mental promise to hit the gym over the next few days.

"You're not telling me everything."

"What makes you think that?" I try to act casual, but my voice is tense and wavering.

"At the coffee shop, you said you couldn't save him."

I lower my head.

"I don't know if I can talk—"

"It needs to come out."

"What are you, my shrink?" My tone is sharp, and I bite violently on the cookie, splaying crumbs everywhere. Tzu sits in bed, flask in hand, unruffled.

"You are a tight-lipped English bastard, Will. You don't believe in shrinks."

"I'm trying to date one." I attempt to lighten up again.

"Yes, but not because she's a shrink, but because she's sexy and edgy." Tzu grins. I think he enjoys his terminology.

"You've never met her."

"Ahh, but my wife has and she's a very competent judge. Come on. Tell me. Tell it for once in your life. You owe—"

"I don't owe you anything!" I shout, and then stop—ashamed of my outburst.

"That's not what I was going to say." His voice remains calm. "You owe it to yourself. You're bottling it up with all your strength, but I see it dripping out tear by tear."

I wasn't even aware I was crying. There was a long silence before I could summon the courage to speak.

"There'd been some crazy scenes. I'd never heard such arguments. In the past, she threatened to leave him, and she was saying that I was getting older and would soon leave. Then nothing would hold her back.

"He went crazy—first shouting then crying. He sobbed deep into the night. The next day, she had gone out. I don't know why. It was the weekend, and I had rugby practice that morning.

"I found his body in the bathtub. He knew I'd find him as I would bathe after practice. He'd left a pile of towels with scouring soap and pads for me to clean the bath. The bastard."

"Will." Tzu's voice was soft.

"No, you're right. I need to say it. There was a fucking note detailing how to clean up and telling me that he was freeing me and my mother. He wanted me to have the place clean before my mother came home. He didn't want her to see the mess. He didn't want her to feel guilty. His last words on the note were: I can't keep the voices back anymore. I can't."

I look up at Tzu and sigh. "Your brother used these words too before he silenced them forever."

When the nurse comes to tell me to leave, she finds us both crying and picking at the last crumbs of the chocolate chip cookies.

28: Paris in California

"Where are we eating?" I have my passport in my jacket breast pocket as instructed and am carrying two suitcases up the stairs to Jane's parents' house. I am also hungry, no doubt from the long *flight* to Nob Hill, according to my travel partner.

"Mon cheri." Jane looks resplendent in her black Gucci sunglasses and black sundress. She has tied a flowery purple silk scarf over her dyed black hair. She is clearly in vacation mode, holding a long, gold cigarette holder elegantly between second and third fingers. There is a long black cigarette inserted. It is not lit, because Jane doesn't smoke, but this doesn't stop her from elegantly taking a puff and feigning a sexy exhalation through puckered lips.

"Mon cheri," she repeats enthusiastically in what I totally consider a sexy French accent. "Since we are staying at this fair establishment, we shall dine nearby and since we are in Paris, we shall dine at a French restaurant. C'est la vie. It's the least we can do for my poor parents. Oui?"

"Sure." I grin. "Cute idea." I'd agree to anything right now.

"The credit for the idea is mon pere's. He was so tickled by the idea that he booked us a table at the restaurant and probably took care of the bill."

"He did?" James is pure class.

"Will, mon cheri, he really likes you. I'm worried that if I ditch you, he just might leave my mother for you."

We both break out laughing then a thought crosses my mind. I put on my most disdainful frown. "Will I have to drink French wine?"

"You are an English cochon!" She swings at me with her purse.

A half hour later, we are seated in a very elegant French restaurant. James has secured a popular table situated upstairs overlooking the bar and entrance. A waiter with a starched white jacket swiftly brings a bottle of wine to the table.

"Monsieur van Ness ordered the wine for you, sir. Do you approve?" I look at the date on the label. The wine is thirty-years old and probably cost what I spend on a month's worth of groceries.

I nod. "It's very generous of him."

"Mademoiselle?" He inquires, showing her the bottle.

"C'est bien, merci," she replies extravagantly.

We eye each other seductively as the wine is poured. I'm so totally into this French chick. I'm sure the waiter can feel the vibes going between us, because I notice a small shake as he pours just enough wine for me to taste.

I smell the bouquet, then swirl the wine around the glass and smell it again. My nose is completely inside the glass and my eyes are closed. When I open them, Jane is doing an excellent job waiting for my decision and trying not to burst out laughing. I swirl the wine again with confident circular movements, then hold the glass up to inspect the legs of the wine. I smell again, noting the increased intensity of the aroma, the smell of full, ripe plums.

Only then do I sip and let the rich liquid roll about my mouth before swallowing. It is truly magnificent. I can taste the full fruitiness; smell the vineyard. I have never felt this way before—most likely because I've never drunk wine of this quality or expense.

I open my eyes and look at our waiter. I don't need to say anything. He understands and fills both our glasses. I watch Jane as she tastes the wine anticipating her response to such a vintage. She leans forward. "It's very rich. I think I shall add some soda to dilute it."

I almost choke, but she is thankfully joking. Our relationship was, for a moment, in serious jeopardy!

The food arrives. Having lived for six months on Northern California cuisine, it seems very heavy. A thick beef soup accompanied with a crisp, freshly baked baguette is keenly devoured. The entrecote is red and juicy and is accompanied with potatoes and a dish of crisply baked vegetables.

Throughout the meal, I ask Jane questions about her studies and other things she's mentioned always ensuring that the conversation focuses on her. I know she feels neglected, rightfully so, and I listen attentively.

Over dessert, she shares her frustrations.

"My past boyfriends and girlfriends were all social animals. They'd go out to bars, clubs and concerts, stay out late and drink. I'm having a hard time with your preference to sit somewhere and write or dream another plot twist. And this whole episode with your boss is getting to me. It's not like you and I had a solid foundation on which to deal with the intensity of the past few weeks."

I nod, fearing this is a prelude to cutting short our relationship.

"Don't look so worried. I didn't bring you all the way to Paris just to ditch you. What's the matter?"

"I totally understand you. But there's a problem. I'm a writer, Jane. It defines me. I might have many identities: barista, businessman, son, fisherman. But everything is defined by my desire to tell the story. When I'm writing a novel, at some point, it takes over and creates a life of its own."

I take a sip of wine.

"I become a slave to the story. I'm thinking about it all the time desperately negotiating how to leverage my day to find time to write. And if I don't sleep, eat or shower, well, that's okay. The story must be told while it's fresh in my mind. It can't wait."

I realize I'm getting intense, but I can't seem to stop.

"Even after Mr. Tzu, I'll enter periods when the story is leading and I am running to keep up. Those times will affect everything: our relationship, the kids—"

"Whoa, boy!" Jane laughs. "Let's not get ahead of ourselves. You think you can take me to Paris, ply me with expensive wine, and I'm game to reproduce your lineage?"

I'm so embarrassed that I bury my face in my wineglass, hoping the red wine will cover the inevitable blushing. I've been totally caught. "All I'm trying to say," I plead, "is that I'm a writer."

Jane puts her hand in mine and squeezes. She leans forward. "I know," she replies huskily. "I saw that intensity, that magic, in you when I spied you at the wine bar the night I picked you up. It turns me on."

We stare at each other across the table—speechless. Eventually, Jane excuses herself to go to the bathroom. I sigh heavily and wonder at the wine. So this is what vintage French wine does to you! Sweet.

When she returns, Jane sees me staring down at the bar. Our table is perfectly located to people-watch. I note that the majority of people are women. Jane follows my gaze.

"There's a lovely array of women down there. Let's see who is most suited to you." There is a grin on her face, and I don't try to deny window-shopping.

I pick out a woman with a tight turquoise dress that complements her red hair. She's surrounded by a group of seemingly enchanted men.

"Tut tut," says my psychologist girlfriend. She makes a great play at putting on and adjusting imaginary eyeglasses worn halfway down her nose. Then she reaches into an imaginary briefcase and removes a book. She licks her index finger charmingly and leafs through the pages, then looks up and asks, "Do you remember when we were at the hot-springs resort and I told you about Alpha and Beta men?"

I nod, preparing to have my ego crushed again.

"She, mon cheri, is undoubtedly an Alpha woman."

Already defeated, I sigh. "Go on,"

Jane pretends to read from her book. "She is a highly successful businesswoman far ahead of the field for her age. She went straight to grad school, no break, and chose an aggressive MBA program. Alpha female knows that most women and all men will not forget her in a hurry, and she has all their business cards filed and waiting."

"So a Beta male like me should just crawl under a bush until she's moved on?"

She laughs. "You specifically, yes, since you're taken. But generally, an Alpha female is not attracted to an Alpha male. Things will be too competitive, too intense, and too fast. Consider Susan and me."

Jane lifts her wineglass and sips, and then remembers that the same hand was holding her imaginary book, so she theatrically pretends that the book fell on the floor. Once retrieved, she frowns. "Hmmm, it says that she'd be happy with a teacher or artist. She wants a man who won't look for power struggles with her and is willing to concede the spotlight and coordinate around her schedule."

"Really."

Jane smiles. "Are you interested in how she is in the boudoir even if you're not going to make a play?" She quickly flicks a page, her pinkie extended. "Her technique will be very result-orientated and efficient. If you can't find the right spot to attend to, she will direct you. Though she approaches sex in a controlling manner, she can get wild, but you need to help her preferably without her knowing."

"Well, forget that," I say. "Sounds too complicated for me. Say, is this book on your school's booklist?"

"It's on the alternative booklist," she peeks over her imaginary eyeglasses, "put together by the students."

I pick another woman. She has dark, curly hair and has pinned it up flatteringly. From our vantage she seems to be wearing a shiny one piece and looks very sexy. She has an orange-colored drink with a slice of orange on the rim.

"She's not for you," says Jane, a crease furrowing across her forehead. "Look at what she's drinking. It's a dead giveaway."

"What's she drinking?"

"Orange juice," says Jane, shaking her head.

"It might be a screwdriver," I venture.

"Look at her hair and clothes. I mean, what does it tell you?"

I shake my head and wisely keep quiet.

"She looks like she is coming from or is heading to the gym. It's subtle but clear to the expert. She is New Age. A twenty-first century Jane Fonda. She goes to work with a briefcase in one hand and a yoga mat in the other—assuming she works in San Francisco. She knows when happy hour is at the juice bar and orders a high-protein spirulina smoothie."

Jane leans forward and takes another sip of wine.

"Her skin is smooth and gleams. Look at her long, elegant neck. You'll enjoy the thoughtful, meditative massages that you give each other with candles and aromatherapy oils burning. She'll expect you to take care of your body and live a clean life. She'll also expect you to participate in deep and meaningful relationship talks even when your soccer game is about to begin."

This hits me hard. There are limits to how much I will compromise for my soul mate.

"It's no good, Will. These women take great pride in their lifestyle and expect you to fully embrace it. You can't pretend for a few weeks then go off smoking and boozing, you cad!" She laughs at the word, and I think of James using scallywag.

"What about sex?" I ask, ignoring her attempted British accent.

Jane pretends to scan the pages. "She sees sex as an integral part of your intimacy. She'll be happy to try new moves, consult the Karma Sutra—that's when you'll really appreciate her yoga lessons—and participate in retreats with you or watch how-to DVDs. But, my dear Will, she won't be into quickies. Beware, it's gotta be slow and meaningful."

"Next," I say, recognizing my limits and immediately point subtly to a couple sitting at a table near us.

Jane surreptitiously glances over and takes a moment to flick some air pages. This woman is pleasant to look at, wears a flattering yet unrevealing dress with a matching beret cutely attached to her head. I chose her for the beret, because Jane is mentally in Paris.

"Okay," says my Goth psychologist girlfriend. "This woman is the definitive suburban housewife or homemaker. She is modest, loyal and stable. She also has a very clear idea of what she wants, which is a nice rock on her finger and an attractive but successful professional who can provide her with a nice house in the suburbs and an SUV—preferably hybrid—for shepherding their children to soccer practice.

Jane finishes her glass of wine, which a watchful waiter soon replenishes.

"She'll cook for you, launder your clothes and be your loyal wife at business functions or at the club. She'll worry about you and listen to how your day went and generally be good for your ego.

"She attracts guys who had a stable home and a caring mother, as well as those who grew up in a dysfunctional family and spent their teen years swearing to give their children something better."

She looks at me. "Don't look so gloomy. You don't earn nearly enough to have a chance. Anyway, sex won't be high on her agenda after there are a few kids in the house." She pats my hand condescendingly. "She's not for you, my lad."

I concede and look down the bar again. "See anyone else you want to analyze, Doctor?"

Jane scans the room. "You see the two women over there? What do you think?"

"I think they are more interested in each other than men," I reply.

"Sure, but that doesn't stop men showing an interest, huh? The one with her back to the door is the Cultural Goddess. She knows where all the shows are, who is exhibiting in town and which books are current. She'll be good company but expects you to be, if not an expert yourself, then at least capable of listening and offering intelligent responses. It's probably why she isn't with a man.

"You want to be with her because she's cool and takes you to interesting places. She's also adventurous in bed and this is probably worth the culture investment."

"Will they make it as a couple?" I ask.

Jane now pretends to check the index at the back of her book. This is quite impressive because she is trying to balance a very real glass of wine in the same hand. "Her friend could make it work because she's into intimacy. She's similar in some respects to New Age girl insofar as she's committed to discover her inner self as well as those around her. She'll want to analyze everything so it could become too intense. But if you connect, she'll be eager in the bedroom seeing sex as an opportunity for a deeper connection. She'll probably suggest things that you haven't considered. So hold on to your hat and enjoy the ride. She'll be a great kisser and toucher. She'll want to connect with every part of your body. Oooh!"

Jane stops, puts her imaginary book down, raises her glass and swirls the wine around before sipping. Despite the dim lights, I see her cheeks are flushed, and she sees I've noticed.

"It's the wine." She protests, holding up her glass. "It really is trés bon, very trés bon." And she giggles.

29: French Exercises

Jane rises from bed bright and early—far too early for a Saturday. Blame it on the rich Burgundy from last night, but when we returned to her parents' house, we fell asleep as soon as we were horizontal.

She sweeps back the curtains, and I receive a kiss for my groans.

"Bonjour, mon cheri." She chirps, sexy French accent mercilessly flowing. "Come on, Paris awaits and we must have a French breakfast."

I groan again.

"Oui, oui, sorry for falling asleep on you last night. Definitely the jetlag." She throws my clothes at me. "But I have great plans for today, and you'll get your *just deserts*. Now get up. Up!"

When the clothes fail to move me, a tossed pillow yields a livelier response.

Half an hour later, we are sitting outside a French bakery near California and Folsom. I bite into a fresh croissant that melts in my mouth. The strong cappuccino that accompanies it helps clear the nighttime fog from my head.

Jane is stepping out. Resplendent in a black beret, she has actually found an old French couple and is assaulting them with her newly adopted language. They look bewildered, and I am hardly surprised. Not only is her grasp of the language rough at best, but she is insisting that we are in Paris and they should be directing us to Le Louvre.

The old man stares from Jane to me, and I shrug my shoulders. The old woman is a bit more indulgent and some conversation is exchanged. When we finally rise to leave, the woman reaches over and whispers in my ear.

"It is very nice of you to take care of your sister like this. How long has she been ... err ... this way?"

"Since she was born, I'm afraid," my expression is suitably pained. "The doctors have tried everything, but I don't care as long as she is happy. I just wish I could spend more time with her."

She pats my arm and nods. "You know, even with your own wound," she glances at my crotch, "you could still meet a young lady one day and lead a normal life."

Jane is already at the crossroads swinging around a stoplight post.

"I must run," I say, bidding a hasty retreat.

I follow Jane, who is in hysterics. When I catch her, she falls into my arms.

"My wound!" I exclaim.

"I've known for a while, mon cheri." She coos in her thick French accent. "That is why I pretended to fall asleep last night to spare you the embarrassment." After another bout of wild laughter, she puts her mouth to my ear. "But Paris is famous for solving such problems. It is truly a miracle city, non?"

With this, she takes my hand and leads me into a store. It's my first time in a Victoria's Secret boutique, and I'm intrigued by the rows of lingerie. For the next half hour, Jane tries on an array of styles and colors— each sexy, revealing, and full of promise. My *wound* seems to be showing signs of rapid healing, and I find each option more exciting. Jane enjoys trying them on. Strutting before me one moment in a lacey black one piece that plunges to intriguing depths then brushing close to me in a red satin negligee.

"Do you think this is quality material, mon ami?" She pouts. "Please rub the material and tell me if it feels like a quality product."

A sales attendant hovers nearby wary of the growing pile of bras, panties, garters, bustiers, and probably fearing I just might jump my exotic French girlfriend in the changing room.

"Okay," she says, coming out of the changing room in her own clothes. "There is a cute bookshop two-doors down. You can wait for me there."

"I'm not going to see what you choose?"

She comes so close that I feel her warm breath on my neck. "Mais oui, mon cheri, you certainly will."

We are soon heading back to her parent's house with Jane swinging her bag of treasures. At the front door she asks, "Don't you usually workout on Saturdays?"

"Yes," I reply, disappointed at the change in direction. I have, in truth, other physical activities on my mind and kind of thought Jane did too. "I'm not sure there are 24 Hour Fitness centers in Paris," I add, hoping to get her potential workout off the agenda.

"Good boy." She purrs approvingly. "But you forgot the hotel has a gym. Go change."

The *Good Boy* reference sends shivers through my body. I obediently follow orders and am escorted to a sunny room with rubber flooring. I'm impressed. There is a treadmill, a weights machine, a full set of free weights, and all sorts of other gadgets for toning and strengthening the human body. Jane's parents mean to stay in shape.

Most impressive is a flat screen TV mounted to the wall that can be turned in any direction. I soon find an option for music and begin pumping iron to the beat of Alanis Morrisette.

Having finished my usual set, I hit the treadmill. But I'm soon distracted when Jane enters the room.

She is wearing a shiny purple push-up bra and lace panties. She has tied a scarf around her forehead. A single curl of hair has escaped. She twirls seductively in front of me and compliments my choice of music. I await her advances, but she ignores me.

Instead she begins stretching—doing familiar warm-ups I've seen women go through a hundred times at the gym. Except, this woman is doing them in a push-up bra and lace panties and occasionally looking to see if I notice. I stare, probably drool, and realize that if I ever looked at a woman this way in the gym, I would soon have my membership revoked. But then no woman has ever stretched and bent over so provocatively so close to me as Jane is doing.

She walks toward the treadmill where I am running then abruptly changes direction to the weight machine. Enjoying my disappointment, she smiles. Twenty minutes later, Jane comes over to the treadmill with her face flushed and beads of glistening sweat dripping down her cleavage. She reaches over and slows the machine to a gentle jog and then to a walk. She signals for me to remove my shirt while walking. I feel her get on the treadmill behind me and walk in sequence with me, so close I can feel the heat of her body and the warmth of her breath on my shoulders. Occasionally, her breasts lightly rub against me sending electric currents through my body. A moment later, she wraps her arms around my waist and we walk in perfect sync.

Just as I begin to wonder when we'll move on to the next stage, she reaches around and switches off the treadmill. I turn to face her ready to say something, but she puts a finger to my lips. She is in total control and I am both surprised and excited. Taking my hand, she leads me to the bench by the weights machine and has me lie on my back, my feet on the floor and my hands holding the grips above my head.

She straddles me while watching me intensely. Then she slips off the scarf from her head and shakes her hair free. She leans slowly over. I feel her body lightly and progressively touching mine—stomach, breasts and breath brush my face. I close my eyes barely noticing the silk scarf tightening around my wrists.

Only when it is knotted, do I realize my hands are tied to the grips. Automatically, I pull at the bonds and feel them tighten. A wave of fear rises mingling with the excitement. I try to ride it and surrender to Jane's command. I close my eyes as she kisses me, her lips caressing mine, the tip of her tongue darting around my mouth. Her face hovers just above mine, and I lift my head lips poised and ready. But Jane retreats keeping her lips just out of reach prompting me to open my eyes. She licks her top lip with the tip of her tongue.

Jane stands, and, as she pulls away, removes my gym shorts and underwear. I lie there naked, tied, but standing at attention. She turns and, swinging her hips and taking her time, goes to the cooler. With one hand on an arched hip, she pours a cup of water and drinks. Then she refills the cup and returns. Her breasts are full and nipples erect through the shiny material. She shakes her head sending the cute strand of black curly hair from one side to the other.

She offers me a drink, but only a few drops are allowed to reach my mouth. The three middle fingers of her right hand dip into the cup and she brings it to my lips. I slurp the water then lick the remaining moisture from her fingers and palm. She moves the cup to my lips and lets me drink. Abruptly, she spills the rest on my chest. It shocks and I gasp as it makes its way down my body.

Tossing the cup, she peels off her bra—first releasing the straps from her shoulders then revealing her breasts. I stare at their roundness and her stiff nipples. Then she turns her back to me as she bends over and wiggles out of her thong.

She climbs on top of me and begins to make slow rotating motions over my erection. Her eyes are closed and one of her hands massages herself. Whenever I try to enter, she raises her hips.

I futilely try to release my hands but her bonds are strong. I desperately want to break free, touch her, flip her over and take her. I am more and more turned on by my helplessness and her complete power. As a primal groan escapes me, she raises her hips and slides me completely inside.

She rises and falls only twice or three times before I explode. My spasms take her over the edge and she collapses on top of me as both of us breathe heavily.

"J'adore Paris." She whispers in my ear.

"Je t'adore," I reply, exhausting most of the French I remember from high school but needing no more. *Je t'adore* says it all.

30: Closure

Jane and I miraculously return from Paris without suffering from jetlag, and I look forward to future trips with great anticipation. My body is still quivering and the next time I go to the gym will not be easy.

Mrs. Tzu enters The Daily Grind about eleven o'clock and sits at her usual table. I bring her a cup of green tea and she signals for Tabitha to join us. She is full of smiles—a dramatic transformation from past weeks.

"Mr. Tzu soon released from hospital. Maybe tomorrow morning. We not know when he return to work." She turns to Tabitha. "Chinese men very stubborn same as Englishmen."

They nod in unison.

"Mr. Tzu should not come back to work." Her voice is sad. "But maybe he come and sit." I see Tabitha stiffen, no doubt dreading the prospect of having Tzu looking over her shoulder again.

"Check what is going on and spend time with you." She directed this last comment to me. "Maybe best he retire and let you run coffee shop, Will. But go tell Chinaman to retire."

Two days later, Mr. and Mrs. Tzu come into The Daily Grind. He has a walking cane and looks tired. He sits heavily at a table and grudgingly allows Mrs. Tzu to order two cups of green tea. Tabitha fusses over them while I serve a young couple on vacation from Arizona.

After everyone is settled with drinks, Mrs. Tzu approaches the counter with Tabitha.

"Maybe I help Tabitha. Go sit with Mr. Tzu."

I pour a coffee and join my boss. We sit together in silence staring out of the window as harried businessmen and women walk by clutching files, briefcases and yoga mats. This is San Francisco.

I feel very close to this elder Asian man with whom, until a few months ago, I shared nothing in common except a love of coffee and wine. Now we sit comfortably together and absorb the rhythm of our city.

At length, he turns and scans his coffee shop. I watch knowing that he is weighing up a new reality.

"I cannot give it up." His voice is soft but steady. "Not yet."

"Why not bring in someone else with experience? You come in a few times a week, check how things are going, and train the new staff. The business runs, you draw from the profits and one day hand the business to your children to work or sell."

"I am not ready to retire."

"Perhaps your body doesn't agree." I flinch expecting a harsh response, but Tzu just sighs.

"It is not my body's limitations that I fear." His voice remains quiet and measured. "I need the activity, the routine, the distraction. It keeps them at bay."

I nod. He is referring to the voices.

"You are hearing them?"

"After my brother died, I hear them incessantly. That is what brought on the heart attack. No, not our fight," he says, correctly interpreting my look of astonishment.

"They ambushed and possessed me. I fought them until ..." his voice fades and he wipes a bead of sweat from his face, "until I didn't have the strength."

Tzu's words worry me. He sounds like his brother just before Li Tzu took his life. We sit in heavy silence.

"You can't let yourself walk down the same path he did." I whisper—almost pleading.

"I can't stop myself. He is ... was my brother."

"But you cannot bring him back."

He nods stoically. "I know."

"And he didn't want you to die the same way he did. That's why he stayed away. He didn't want to drag you down. He was so proud of you. Don't let him down. Don't let his death be in vain. You owe it to him to fight."

"DON'T PREACH TO ..." He catches himself and looks sharply around the cafe. The young couple from Arizona stares at us.

"I am sorry," he says to them, slightly bowing his head. Then he glances toward his wife and Tabitha. They watch but remain at the bar.

We are silent for a few moments, and I hear his strained breathing.

"Have you told your wife yet about your brother?"

"No, but I must. The funeral is on Friday. They have postponed it a few times because of my health. Will you come?"

"Would you like me to?"

"Yes."

"Then I will come."

"It will be held at the military cemetery. It is in the Presidio—"

"I know where it is. My girlfriend's father took me there."

Tzu stares at me. "Why?"

"For the same reason you are all drawn there: your friends, comrades, officers, soldiers. You keep their memories alive and pay them the respect they deserve." I sip my coffee. "You show them they will not be forgotten."

Mr. Tzu puts his hand on my forearm and gently pats it.

"Thank you," he says softly.

Mrs. Tzu, seeing that we have made peace, returns to the table. Her husband takes a deep breath and turns to me.

"Will, I think the letter is in my desk or maybe in the top side drawer. Please bring it to me." Then he turns to his wife and takes her hands in his. "I have something I must tell you."

I watch them keenly from behind the counter. They are deep in conversation. He reads the letter to her then she takes it and reads it. Again, they hold hands as the conversation continues. Occasionally, Mrs. Tzu shakes her head but for the most part just listens.

Tabitha stands next to me. We are both drawn to the intensity of their discussion. When Mr. Tzu wipes tears from his eyes, so does Tabitha.

"You okay?" I ask.

"Yeah," she says, but her voice is shaky.

"Want to take a walk and get some fresh air?"

"In front of the boss?"

I cannot resist. "Mr. Tzu has a lot more on his mind than an insignificant cog in his business machine."

"Fucking pussycat." She taunts—platonically leaning against me. "I meant you. Mrs. Tzu says he'll promote you to store manager and let you run the show."

"Then you might want to shy away from the *fucking pussycat*."

"Probably." She attempts a smile, but her nose is blocked and she sniffs. "I think I might take ten."

I squeeze her arm. "Meow," I say.

Mr. and Mrs. Tzu leave the café holding hands. When she says goodbye, it is clear Mrs. Tzu is already busy making funeral arrangements in her mind. She has accepted whatever Mr. Tzu told her and is now going about the business of supporting her husband and honoring the dead.

I call Jane's father.

"James, can you spare time Friday afternoon about two? I need the company … a funeral."

It is a gray, cloudy Bay Area day in the Presidio, as it should be. James meets me for an early lunch then drives me to the cemetery. We eat in near silence, and I can only imagine how tough this must be for him. But he didn't hesitate to accompany me. James was a soldier—still is.

The nearest I've ever come to witnessing military funerals have been Hollywood movies. I'm immediately consumed with the intensity as the honor guard solemnly marches to the graveside. These young men are polished and precise. I wondered whether this is a chore for them or whether they truly see it as an honor—a tribute to a fallen comrade they never knew.

The casket is lowered, and I watch Tzu with his hands deep in the pockets of a thick coat. He stands still with every facial muscle, I think, straining to do its duty. Their children aren't here. I doubt Tzu even asked them to make the trip.

Mrs. Tzu stands by her husband's side gazing at the casket of the brother-in-law she never knew existed. I wonder what thoughts are going through her head? Could she have helped? Could she have made a difference by tipping the scales? Could this so easily have been her husband if they had never met, or might it, a depressed suicide, be his epitaph at some point in the future?

But as I watch, all I see are the heavy lines of Chinese history—of suffering etched across her face. As I look, I prefer to picture the laughing Mrs. Tzu siding with Jane and Tabitha to bully me and chiding me for not writing to my mother.

The three-volley gun salute abruptly jolts me from my thoughts. Birds soar from nearby trees. I cringe with each volley and feel James take my arm. I resist looking at him, he might not want me to, but I slightly lift my upper arm to make room for his hand and feel his fingers grip tightly through my jacket.

The flag is folded with impressive precision and offered to Mr. Tzu. He takes it solemnly, stares at it then caresses it to his heart. I think I see tears in his eyes. It is hard to be sure because mine are blurry.

The bugler plays Taps. His notes ring out rising to the top of the pines toward the swollen clouds reaching the partly fog-shrouded Golden Gate Bridge. Then, abruptly, it is over. The few people in attendance are all

Asian save for the honor guard, James and me. We hold back as they pay their respects to Tzu—shaking hands and occasionally exchanging a stiff hug.

When only Tzu and his wife are left, I introduce James.

"It was a beautiful ceremony," I say to Mr. Tzu. "I'm sure your brother would have been very proud."

He nods. Mrs. Tzu smiles and thanks me for coming.

Tzu and James exchange words. It's code to me—battalion numbers and battlefields. Then James glances to the grave.

"You buried him away from the last line. You reserved the adjoining plots?"

"You cannot reserve spots other than for a spouse," Tzu replies. "But when my time comes, it would be nice to be near him."

James nods and looks back at the newly dug grave. "I have a friend. I'd be happy to put in a call. Would you mind?"

Mr. Tzu shakes his head, but Mrs. Tzu answers for her proud husband. "Husband appreciate it very much, Mr. van Ness. Thank you. You have wonderful daughter. You must be very proud."

"Oh, I am," James replies, and his pride shines through the gloomy weather.

Mrs. Tzu nods theatrically at me. "Just not sure of her taste in men." She adds, furrowing her brow.

"She gets that from her mother," his reply is smooth.

As I turn with Tzu away from the grave, the conversation vanishes from my mind.

They stand in two rows—a different honor guard—wearing uniforms of faded, tattered layers. They create a corridor for Tzu to walk through. Salvador is the first of a dozen who have come to pay their last respects to a colleague, a brother of the street, another homeless hero who fought the good fight for as long as he could.

31: Pictures From the Past

Settled in his car, James pulls away in silence seemingly content to listen to some mellow jazz. I lift the CD cover and see that the artist is Stephen Dreyfuss.

"He's a local lad," James says. "I picked that up when he was performing on the street at Fisherman's Wharf."

I smile. I imagine James enjoying being able to support one of the city's musicians this way. After a few minutes, he turns the volume down.

"Do you have some time for me? I have something I want to show you."

I can hardly refuse.

At his house, we head downstairs. Mrs. van Ness is probably at the club planning her latest fundraising activity, and I'm sent to select a bottle of wine.

"Take your time," James says indulgently as always, and I can't help but inspect several bottles before picking one out.

I return with two glasses and an uncorked bottle, a Merlot reserve from a Sonoma vineyard. But I see James cradling a small, stout glass that's already empty. He refills it.

"I really appreciate your coming with me today," I say for the fifth or sixth time.

"I did it to honor a dead comrade." His voice is distant and wavers. "It's never easy going there."

I sit down next to the unlit fireplace and wait. James joins me, a heavy sigh escaping as he falls into his chair, and we sit together sharing an intimate silence.

"Your boss doesn't look good," James says after a while.

"I know. I'm worried."

"Will he be able to return to work?"

"Doesn't look like it, but he'll need to hang around in some limited capacity."

He takes another sip. "You seem competent enough running the business."

"I meant that he'll need to stay involved for himself."

"Yes." James nods. "I understand that. I think my business saved me. When I'm busy, distracted, I can't hear the voices."

I look at him sharply. "You hear the voices?"

"We all do. All who came back. And they are the same voices, whether from Europe, Korea, 'Nam, or the Gulf. But for some, the voices are louder."

"How do you get rid of them?" I ask.

"You don't. You fill your head with other thoughts, other voices, I guess. My business is time consuming, but do you think I couldn't pass it over to a hungry, young hotshot executive? Do you think I haven't considered retiring and spend my days fishing or actually learning how to play golf at that darn club?

He takes another sip. "But what will I think about when I'm waiting for the fish to bite? What will fill my head while I search for the lost ball in the rough?"

He sighs. In the silence, I think he considers another drink. He stares into his glass then sighs again. When he speaks, there is more certainty in his voice.

"My better half," he glances upstairs, "knows to keep a watchful eye on me. She doesn't worry when I'm swamped at work. She fears my downtime and makes sure to fill it. Why do you think she accompanies me to Paris and other far less desirable business locations? She would rather spend her time at the club. Here in the San Francisco social scene she is well-known and recognized."

He laughs. "The second thing she does when I tell her about a forthcoming business trip is to look over the schedule. Then she quickly fills in the blanks."

"What's the first thing she does?"

"Why, check her wardrobe of course. She takes good care of me, but she would be unbearable as a complete martyr."

We both laugh and, again, it is warm and bonding, but I realize that James is trying to tell me something.

"The way for Mr. Tzu to recover is to immerse himself in something?" I ask.

"Yes," James replies, "though it'll never be total or permanent recovery. But if it can provide some kind of closure, then all the better."

"Can one ever become reconciled?"

"You can force the voices into a box and bolt it down good." His voice sharpens. His stare at his glass intensifies. "But there's always a danger they'll slip out in an unguarded moment: the death of an old friend, a dumb war movie shot on location, some frat boy thinking it's amusing to wear his old man's uniform on Halloween or something. All these possibilities can force open your box and let them loose."

With my mouth open, I stare at him.

"You've heard such words before?" he asks.

"Yes," I say in a whisper.

"And you will find them in self-help books and used by sweet, well-meaning therapists as well." He points a warning finger at me. "And you won't repeat that last part to my daughter."

I nod, barely acknowledging the joke. "I have no idea what moves Mr. Tzu. I really don't know him."

"Then play to your strengths, Will. I've given some thought to what you have to offer him. Ask yourself, what does he see in you?" He pauses. "I want to show you something."

He rises, walks to a bookcase and pulls out two copies of a shiny hardcover book. He looks at the cover wistfully and, returning to his chair, passes me one. The cover is white and glossy. There is a black-and-white picture of the Vietnam War Memorial in the center surrounded by mug shots of young men also in black and white.

The title of the book is *The Men of the 7th: Honoring their Memories & Sacrifice*. The author is James van Ness, and there is a foreword by General Andrew J. Goodpaster.

"I never knew you were an author," I say with wonder.

"I'm not. I had a talented young woman ghostwrite for me then a team of expensive editors who connected the text and the pictures."

I open the book. Each page is dedicated to a different soldier. There are pictures of them as children, with girlfriends or wives and as young men in uniform. Each has a short biography and those who died have short obituaries often describing how they died accompanied with a poignant vignette.

"This is really impressive, James," I say. "Your soldiers and their families must—"

"I didn't write it for them." He rasps then quickly regains control. "I wrote it for me, Will, during one of my darkest times. Barbara picked up on the idea from somewhere, and she engineered the whole thing with amazing efficiency. It worked. I spent a long time helping write and edit it. When it was ready, I commissioned a few hundred copies. I tracked down all the families and sent them each a copy with a personal handwritten dedication. I have all the thank you letters carefully filed. Often they would request additional copies, and I printed a second run. Now I have a box of them stored somewhere gathering dust."

Each sifting through a book, we sit and drink in silence. Concerned, I glance at James. He is far away in another world, another time. Then he puts the Scotch glass aside and asks me to fill his wineglass. He is preparing to continue.

He raises the heavy crystal and swirls the rich, ruby liquid. "The whisky dulls the pain quickly. The wine keeps the road smooth for longer. Do you see what I'm suggesting?"

"About the drink?"

"No." He laughs but the sound seems alien. "I mean about the book."

"That I offer to write a book for him? Write about his unit? His brother?"

"Let him decide." James suggests. "And you're not offering to write it for him but with him."

"It's hard for even experienced writers to be collaborative. I don't know if I can do it."

"The mechanics of the writing will probably be your domain. His input will be details and descriptions. He was there, after all, and knows his protagonists well."

I nod, absorbing his words and thinking of what he has proposed. Again, we each retreat into our own worlds. I barely register a far-off door opening or footsteps coming downstairs.

"James? Oh, there you are." His wife's tone is agitated. "Why are you home so early? I saw the car … you're reading the book again." This last is a statement, and I can hear her uncertainty.

I realize that she can't see me. I'm sitting in a big leather chair with my back to the door. I turn my body and lean over so she sees I'm here.

"Hello, Mrs. van Ness. James was showing me his book. He told me that you were the inspiration behind it. It's really quite an achievement."

"Thank you, dear." But her eyes are on her husband and move only to take in the whisky decanter and wine bottle. "Are you alright, James?"

"Yes, my love. It's been a hard day … for both of us."

"I see. Well, I would like you to come upstairs soon into the light. I will have tea waiting." As an afterthought, she glances at me. "You are welcome too, of course. I'll call Jane and maybe we can have an early dinner together."

She disappears and I turn back to James. I'm surprised to see that he has a grin across his face.

"I don't think she remembers your name!" He breaks into laughter. "You fluster her, Will. You're a poor artist, young and unpredictable, and a foreigner to boot. You're one of the last people she wants to pursue her daughter. But Jane loves you, and you and I are close, and she just doesn't see you fading away."

He laughs again. "Don't hold it against her. She cares passionately for her family and her social status."

I smile back. I'm not thinking of Mrs. van Ness. Jane is close to her father, and I'm sure she confides in him. And he just told me that she loves me.

Tea becomes dinner and Jane joins us. The food is good, the wine impressive and the conversation purposely light. I am sure Mrs. van Ness has spoken with Jane and fears the worst regarding her husband's mood. She will probably be very apprehensive knowing James attended a military funeral. Everything just seems too sweet, too staged.

Toward the end of the meal, there is a knock on the front door. James answers and returns with Captain O'Connor and Sergeant Mendez.

"Sorry to bother you, Mrs. van Ness." Captain O'Connor is standing stiffly.

"Good evening, Captain. We have finished dinner. Can I get you some coffee?"

Was there anyone in this city these cops didn't know? The Captain declines and looks to me.

"Will, we called the coffee shop and young Tabitha suggested you might be here. May we have a moment of your time, please?"

In the entrance, the Captain turns to me. "He's disappeared … and he doesn't have his medication with him or his wallet."

32: Unwanted Heroes

"Oh, no!" Jane hears my response and comes quickly out of the dining room.

"Dinner's over." I whisper without looking up.

Jane disappears into the dinner room while I thank the police. It was beyond their duty to come and tell me personally, and I really appreciate it. I don't know what she tells her parents. Jane had driven her car to her parents' house and now we decide to begin looking for my boss at the cemetery. Jane parks the car, and we climb over the locked gates. Jane tries to lighten the mood by pointing out it's a full moon and, the urgency notwithstanding, we might have had quite a date.

"Maybe Tzu is just helping you duck a dinner with my parents?" Jane's tone is flat and our eyes lock.

An owl hoots, and we jump into each other's arms. We laugh uneasily—way too cool to be spooked.

After not finding either Tzu or ghosts, we return to the car and drive down Geary to the financial district. We park near The Daily Grind.

"Why here?" Jane asks. "The police have already checked earlier."

"Yes," I reply, "but it was open then."

The café is dark, and I can feel Jane watching me as I check my watch. "We close late on Fridays if we have customers but they must have closed at least a half hour ago. Maybe he came here after the staff left."

Jane stares at the dark storefront. "It's more impressive with the lights on." Her tone betrays that she is losing her enthusiasm for the search. She knows I'm doing this more to appease my fears than of finding Tzu.

"I knew it was a long shot. Let's go." As I turn away, something catches my eye. "Just a minute. Someone left the light on in the back."

Jane sighs.

Opening the door, I see the alarm either wasn't turned on or has been deactivated. Trying to exude bravery, I suggest that Jane wait outside. She rolls her eyes and pulls out a small cylinder.

"Pepper spray? I didn't know you come armed."

"I guess you've been behaving yourself," she says, and I rather hope I detect some disappointment.

I reach inside the front door and turn on the lights. The place is clean and empty, and I hurry through to the back. A noise abruptly stops me. Something metallic has dropped to the floor. I hear a hissed curse and labored breathing. I move through the café and into the storeroom. Tzu is crouching on the floor by his desk. I see a heavy, metal flashlight rolling toward where I stand. Sweat drips from his shiny forehead, and he is scrambling around. The desk lamp is on the floor near him. On his desk, I recognize his brother's letter.

"What are you doing here?" I ask.

"I own this place, Englishman." He snaps. "I should be asking you the same question." He sees Jane approaching and smirks. "Ha! Brought your girlfriend in for a quick thrill?"

Jane leans against the doorframe one arm high up on the frame and arches her hips. Wearing tight-black slacks, black vest with revealing black bra straps, she sighs dramatically.

"He's not in the mood, Mr. Tzu. I tried it on at the graveyard just now. There was a full moon and it still didn't work." She looks nonchalantly around the café. "Where would be a good spot in this place? Remember, Will's back isn't too strong, but he's very enthusiastic."

There is silence then the old man begins to laugh.

"You are funny, Jane. My wife is right about you."

He extends an arm, and I help him up. I retrieve the flashlight and put it on the desk. He is still breathing heavily as he makes his way unsteadily to the front of the café. He slumps down next to a table. Jane brings him a glass of water and he sips it. His hands are shaking. He looks at me sternly.

"She deserves better than a graveyard, you cheapskate."

"I wasn't thinking of a quickie with Jane when we climbed over the railings," I reply, finding that I am the only one without a sense of humor.

He laughs and leans forward. "She's in much better shape than the rest of them there."

"Oh, Mr. Tzu, you old sweetie." Jane does her best to blush. "That's the nicest thing anyone's said of me in a long time."

Tzu hasn't finished with me. "Never associated uptight Englishmen with necrophilia. Much of a sport in England?"

I am still pissed with him. "You went out without your medicine."

"What's the worst thing that can happen to me?"

"You can die."

He glares back at me—no doubt contemplating a cutting reply but relents. "You're a good boy," he says softly.

"And you're a—"

Jane puts her hand on my arm and wisely takes over. "Will was very worried for you, Mr. Tzu. I think we should call your wife and tell her you're okay. The cops are also out looking for you."

He sighs and takes her cell phone. She takes mine and finds the Captain's number since he rang me earlier. When all calls are made, I look at Tzu more calmly.

"What are you doing tomorrow after I finish the morning shift?"

"I'll check my schedule." Tzu sneers. "What do you have in mind? Dead bodies? Animals?"

"Lunch," I reply. "Let's meet for lunch. I have something to show you."

We drop Tzu off at his house and watch him shuffle in. I look over at Jane. I'm tired and feel like an emotional wreck, but it is Friday night in San Francisco and I want her to have a good time.

"Can we go back to your parents? I want to pick something up. Then we'll go anywhere you want."

"You are planning to show him my Dad's book?"

"Elementary, my dear Watson. I'm impressed."

"Good, we can borrow some blankets as well. The cemetery probably gets cold at night."

We don't try the graveyard—heading instead to a nightclub near her apartment. A few hours of dancing helps me relax.

I have trouble waking up in the morning. Sore muscles from dancing and a hangover means I open the coffee shop a little late, but I enjoy the slow flow of customers and the relaxed atmosphere of the weekend warriors. Even the fucking South of Market writers' group doesn't faze me as they noisily make plans to attend a writers' conference in Santa Barbara during the summer.

About midday, Tzu comes in with his wife. They sit at a table and let Tabitha fuss. When my shift is over, Tzu and I walk Mrs. Tzu to the Farmer's Market that spills out of the Ferry Building on the Embarcadero.

It is sunny, with a few wispy clouds and a shining Bay Bridge. She is armed with recyclable bags and ready for some serious produce purchasing. I often spend time around the Embarcadero on the weekend. I love the array of fruits and vegetables at the Farmer's Market and am fascinated by the mushroom stand and the honey station inside the building. I taste everything offered convinced that I have saved myself the expense of a meal and a healthy one at that.

Tzu and I settle on a small deli near the corner of Market Street. We sit outside enjoying the sun, despite the lack of warmth, and eat sandwiches, chips and pickles with iced tea.

I show him James' book and he reads it carefully.

"He's a good man," Tzu says, nose still in the book, "your father-in-law."

"He's not my—"

Tzu is smiling without looking up. One-zero.

He reads the book until the food comes then hands it back to me. We attack our sandwiches in silence. Mine disappears quickly and Tzu suggests that I order another. I decline.

"It's my treat." He grins. "I know how little you are paid. And I screwed up your Friday night. I guess I owe you something."

Some smartass responses come to mind, but I settle for another sandwich. I polish off my second as he finishes his first.

"You eat too fast. All Caucasians do."

"I have an idea." Ignoring his comment, I wipe my mouth. "You need to do something to close this chapter of your life; reconcile yourself with your brother, share with your family and force the voices back into a secure box."

Tzu is watching me intently. "Go on."

"You should write something as James did. I can help you with it. Ghostwrite for you maybe."

He thinks. "I mean no disrespect to your father-in-law." He relishes using that phrase though this time I don't take the bait. "But I'm not sure what a fine book like this could do for me."

I think for a moment. "If you wanted to tell the world something, what would it be?"

He takes his time gathering his thoughts. "I would want them to know of my brother and his struggles. I would want them to know of our relationship and how I lived a lie and denied even my precious brother's existence because I was afraid he would drag me down with him. I want America to know that heroes come in all shapes and sizes—not just Hollywood's Chuck Norris or Schwarzenegger."

His face is serious. Focused. A single bead of sweat runs down the left side of his forehead.

"We are Asian, but we are also American, and we have paid dearly for our membership. Just like the blacks, the poor, and Latinos that sign up today. We're crazy and homeless, but we're still goddamn heroes and they need to respect us."

His eyes seem unfocused and far away, as he picks his words.

"They need to know they can't sweep us under the carpet, or more likely, under the bridges and into shelters. They should be ashamed that a man risks his life for his country but can't get medical or psychological help. He has to prove to insensitive bureaucrats that he deserves benefits earned in the jungle and the prison camps."

His face is stoic and he shakes his head—perhaps to himself or to me.

"They should know to treat us as heroes, to treat us with respect. We are the ... unwanted heroes."

He stops to catch his breath and reaches for his iced tea. Unnoticed, I have been madly scribbling for a few minutes. He smiles. "Well, Hemingway?"

I show him a page filled with phrases, arrows and frantic scribbling then snatch the pad back and write at the top of the page in capital letters: "UNWANTED HEROES." My pulse is racing. "Let's get to work." I whisper.

Tzu and I talk for hours. I phone the coffee shop where a frantic Mrs. Tzu is pacing the store. At some point, my pen runs out and the waitress gives me hers.

Tzu picks up my plastic sixty-cent pen. "You are a cheapskate," he says warmly, but we soon return to the story.

I scribble. He talks. Occasionally, I ask questions. Another phone call and Mrs. Tzu announces she's coming to the deli. The temperature drops as the sun's rays fall behind the looming buildings of the financial district.

Mrs. Tzu arrives. Her hasty walk betraying concern. She gives her husband his pills and a few choice sentences. The pills he washes down with iced tea diluted from long-melted ice cubes. Then he turns back to me to finish conveying his current thought, and I write for a minute or so longer. When I put the pen down, I shake my hand, which tingles as blood tries to reach my cramped fingers.

There is silence. Then he says in a quiet voice. "Okay, Will, you have work to do." I hear a quiver of excitement in his voice.

"Yes," I reply. "We both do. Buy yourself a damn notebook and start jotting things down."

He looks at me as if I am an idiot. "You think I'm crazy? I write on a computer like normal people."

We stand to leave. I pick up my Timbuk2 bag and ironically feel the weight of my laptop. I watch my boss walk with his wife holding his right arm. He is talking with animation, and I believe I detect a slight bounce in his step.

Tonight I will write. It will be a long night, but I can't wait to get home and start.

33: The Wine Auction

James van Ness is wrong about his wife. She remembers my name. Unfortunately, she also recalls that I hadn't rejected her suggestion of hosting the wine-tasting fund-raiser at the country club.

"Will, thank goodness I caught you." Her voice comes clearly through my cell phone. "A tragedy. A terrible tragedy."

I'm putting soup bowls on the table at home and quickly sit. Chad and I have been concocting a gourmet supper of macaroni and cheese, but all hunger pangs disappear abruptly. "What's happened, Mrs. van Ness?" A vision of Jane in a hospital is followed by one of James hanging from a noose.

"Regarding the fund-raiser at the country club for the UCSF Children's Hospital? Well, I thought it prudent to find another emcee, more, shall we say, experienced with such occasions."

I sigh deeply trying to shake the tragic images burned into my mind.

"Will, are you there? Will?"

"Yes, I'm here." I sip from a bottle of cold water.

"So, dear, I booked Harvey Bromard from Sonoma and now he is canceling on me two days before the event. Can you believe it? He's finished in San Francisco. I'll see to that. I have sixty couples coming to the event. I have the wine ordered for tasting. The bottles that you'll auction are already at the club …"

The word *you* settles slowly into my consciousness.

"Mrs. van Ness," I say, and she stops. I can tell she's flustered. No one usually interrupts her when she is in full flow. "You said *you*?"

"Yes, dear. I need you to step into the breach and take charge of the situation. Jane will be so proud of you and, of course, she'll be there. James too." She laughs. "How could he not?"

"What day are we talking about?"

"Saturday, dear. The day after tomorrow."

"I'm busy. It's a friend's birthday, and I'm organizing—"

"A friend's birthday?"

This is absolutely true. It's Chad's birthday and we, his housemates, have offered to hold a party at the house. We spent the best part of the last week working out which of his ex-girlfriends we should invite. Just because they all remained friendly with Chad after breaking up doesn't mean they appreciate each other.

Together with Julian, Bear, and Jenn, who has proved quite resilient in the process, we interrogated Chad every evening and finally settled on inviting only every second consecutive girlfriend, so no ex would have to confront the ex she blamed for stealing her guy.

Julian is quite excited at the prospect, because Chad has always had excellent taste in women. Jenn exudes composure and, as I mentioned, we're all very impressed with her.

"Well, dear," says Mrs. van Ness, gathering herself, "it's only a party."

Chad is watching me hearing only my half of the conversation. He is looking worried, probably for me, and this steels my determination. "Chad is my best friend. I can't let him down two days before his twenty-fifth birthday. That's a quarter of a century."

"Believe me, Will, I'm painfully aware of that. Here's what we'll do. You bring your friend Chad to the fund-raiser. I'll buy him a birthday cake, and we'll all sing Happy Birthday. Then you can take him to his party. Our function will be over by ten o'clock. You youngsters haven't usually worked out what you're wearing by that time. You'll still be early for your party."

Fair point, which is confirmed by my silence.

"Well, that settles it. Jane will drive you here. She's known at the club. James will take you out for lunch on Saturday and treat you to some clothes. Thank you, Will. The poor, sick children will appreciate it."

A few minutes later, Chad thinks this is hilarious and has no problem with the change of plans. He serves the food and we share an open bottle of Pinot Grigio. Chad stares at his glass and tries an English accent.

"A daring combination, Will. The Pinot is the natural choice to partner a complex Italian pasta dish like mac n' cheese." We burst out laughing. "So," Chad asks, a mound of pasta stuck on his spoon about to disappear, "what do you have to do?"

"Make comments like that, I think," I answer glumly. "Apparently, there are several lots of wine that I will auction off. Barbara will drop off the list along with comments from the wine sellers at the coffee shop tomorrow."

"Barbara? You've never called her *Barbara*."

"After agreeing to do this, I'll call her whatever I fucking please."

He laughs again. "I don't recall you ever getting a chance to agree or disagree." He thinks this is hilarious and almost falls off his chair. I attempt a swing to ensure he does, but I miss.

"No protein there," says Bear, his huge physique filling the small kitchen as he checks the food on our plates. "Powdered cheese won't cut it." He puts a huge sandwich with a dead animal rolled up inside on the table and reaches into the fridge for mustard.

Chad recounts the last five minutes, freely embellishing, and, when Bear has caught up, asks me to continue.

"So, I introduce each wine, and we have a taste. Then I auction the cases. I think I can handle this, but—"

There is a knock on the door. Bear answers and Jane appears. She has an apprehensive look on her face.

"Did you speak to my mother?"

I nod.

"Still my guy?"

I nod again. "Just about." Then I wrap an arm around her waist as she perches on my leg.

"So," Chad says seamlessly, "you auction the bottles and take the good folks through the wine tasting. What else? What's worrying you?"

"I need to entertain them, provide cute stories or facts that will soften them, warm them to me and encourage them to spend more money. Where am I going to find that kind of stuff? It's knowledge that you collect over a career."

"No problem," says Chad, and he steps out of the kitchen returning with my laptop. "Blessed be the Goddess Google," he says reverently.

"Ladies and Gentlemen." The microphone squeals, and I jerk my head back a few inches then clear my throat. "Ladies and gentlemen, please take your seats and let us begin." I look at the table on my left where Jane gives me an encouraging smile. James, already holding a glass of wine, looks relaxed, Barbara anything but.

"The Oscars are approaching," I say, swallowing nervously. "Francis Ford Coppola, who directed many movies including the Godfather series, once said: The two professions, filmmaking and winemaking, are almost the same. They both require source material and take a lot of time to perfect. The big difference is that wine-makers still worry about quality."

I receive a generous round of laughter and subconsciously brush the lapels of my new velvet jacket that James bought for me on our shopping spree earlier that day. He also offered some material gathered, he complained, from a lifetime of charity wine-tasting events.

"We have some fine quality wines to taste and auction," I say. "All proceeds, as you are aware, go to the UCSF Children's Hospital."

Two more people have joined the van Nesses at their table. James rises to shake hands with Mr. Tzu, who stands stiffly in a dark, starched suit. James then invites Mrs. Tzu to sit next to him.

"Our first bottle comes from one of the rising stars of California, Spencer Rolson, who uses old, almost-forgotten grape varieties to produce unique wines. Let's taste our first wine."

This is a signal for a small army of white-jacketed men and women to descend on the tables and fill the first wineglass. There is a great deal of swirling and smelling with each person conscientiously aspiring to strike a fitting somber pose.

"What are the legs of wine, you wonder?" I am holding my glass high in the air letting the rich red wine swirl and the light catch the crystal. "The legs of wine are the rivulets that drip back down the inside of the glass after we swirl. Good legs such as these imply that there is glycerin, a natural component in well-balanced wine.

"Taste it, swirl it around your mouth and close your eyes. Remember the images that it brings up and make an offer for a case of this excellent wine."

The bids come in and the first wine sells for what I'm sure is four times the price at BevMo. The bidders know this, but they have to show good sportsmanship and philanthropic willingness. More important, Barbara van Ness is taking careful notes of whom bids—and probably who doesn't.

"Congratulations," I say to the winner as I let the gavel fall. I glance at my flashcards for prompting. "Who can tell me what the most expensive bottle of wine was and how much it sold for?"

There are a few mumbles but no answers proffered.

"The most expensive bottle of wine ever bought was a 1787 Laffite, which sold for $160,000 at a Christie's auction in 1985. The bottle was reputed to have been owned by Thomas Jefferson, who passed it up for a bottle of two-buck chuck."

I received a resounding round of laughter because of my referral to the two-dollar bottle of wine from Trader Joe's that recently won a double-blind tasting contest held in Napa.

"The next wine comes from nearby Napa Valley, now renowned around the world. But who can tell me what was Napa's primary fruit crop during the 1940s?"

Several exotic fruits are congenially yelled out.

"Prunes," I reveal, "undoubtedly a secret weapon for the war effort."

And off we go with the bidding.

"The next wine beckons from my homeland. As the only author who became famous without Oprah's help once said: The wine cup is the little silver well, where truth, if truth there be, doth dwell."

"Shakespeare," someone calls out.

"Oh, so you've heard of him over here," I reply and receive generous laughter. I realize I'm subconsciously stressing my English accent. "Let's taste the wine."

The army of waiters appears by the tables filling a second glass of wine as I read the information provided by the winery. Another case of wine is enthusiastically bid on, and Barbara is smiling as she writes the results.

After the fourth case is sold, Barbara comes up to the microphone. She thanks everyone for coming and makes a plea for people to continue supporting the cause as the auction continues. I get a chance to join Jane,

"Very smooth." She whispers in my ear while squeezing my thigh.

Mrs. Tzu is beaming. "Will, you look handsome."

"And for work he turns up like a shloch," her husband says.

I once had a Jewish girlfriend and picked up some Yiddish during our time together. However, I'm always shocked how all Americans know the rudiments of the language. Hearing a Chinese American shticking the Yiddish to me in an exclusive and rather white San Francisco country club only adds to the bizarre scene.

Barbara is at the podium and invites Chad to join her. He is wearing a creased, white, buttoned shirt with no tie or jacket and has unsuccessfully tried to rein in his long hair. But his shy smile is more than enough to appease the dinner jackets and evening dresses, and a cake appears on cue. We all sing *Happy Birthday* and Chad stands there so totally out of context but beaming. Barbara van Ness, I discover, is true to her word.

I return to the podium and switch on the microphone. "A slice of cake to anyone who can tell us the five-deciding factors in the production of fine wine."

A tall, handsome gentleman rises from his chair. He pushes back his silver hair and announces in a rich baritone: "The terroir, the soil type and its quality, the weather, the quality of the grapes and the actual winemaking process."

"And I understand this is your first-time wine tasting?" I quip, but my tone reflects the awe I feel. I take a plate of well-earned cake to his table and he gives me a bone-crushing handshake.

The event proceeds smoothly until the ninth or tenth round. As I turn to pick up a new bottle, I nearly fall from dizziness. I haven't been spitting out the wines that I taste.

I look at my audience and realize that they haven't either. There are a significant number of reddened cheeks scattered around the room, and I realize the bidding has spiraled progressively higher.

We conclude the auction and Barbara comes to the podium. She reminds everyone of the single bottles donated by the country club on a table that can be bought without auctioning—all money going to the poor, sick children, of course. She suggests that drivers have some coffee before they get behind the steering wheel. Her cheeks are also flushed. She then proceeds to thank me landing a big smacking kiss on the cheek.

I return to the family table suitably stunned, and Jane puts her arm around me and says into my ear. "Quite a kiss, you slut! You just might be my first to make it past the tolerated stage." She then plants a kiss of her own. "Still, you earned it."

"Yes," I say somewhat perplexed. "Quite a show of appreciation."

"No," Jane whispers in my ear. "We have another party to go to. Then I'll show you *appreciation*."

34: The Dream

Gunfire!

The constant fire of machine guns comes from all directions. My knuckles are white as I grip my M16 with one hand and hold my ill-fitting helmet above my eyes with the other. I stumble and land on my knees. My joints lock from fear.

To advance or retreat?

Our gunfire. Theirs.

Someone yells. "Fall back! Fall back! The Huey is gonna toast 'em. Fall back!"

Loud thuds of a mortar firing. Heavy M2 Brownings meant to provide cover. The enemy is all around us. The jungle's crawling with 'em. Gotta fall back.

Soldiers run in all directions. I have advanced and retreated too many times to count these past months. The searing scream of a jet or helicopter strikes as much terror into me as Charlie's gunfire.

I stumble to my knees.

As I rise, I glance down to see what tripped me. Horrified, I look into the face of Timmons, a cocky Irish bastard we all hate. I can barely recognize him—a black-painted face; unblinking bright-red eyes.

I stagger on. One hand extends in front flailing to clear a path. The other holds my too-large helmet high so I can peer out from underneath. My M16 swings and bangs into tree trunks as the strap constantly tangles with brush.

I am running without knowing where I am going. I scream—

"Will! Will, what's happening? Will! Wake up. You're dreaming." Jane pulls me into her arms, then involuntarily lets go. "You're soaking wet, Will."

Recovering, she extends her arms, and I cling tight to her. The smell of gunpowder and humidity is replaced by Jane's soft skin and musky scent. I'm still gasping, and she holds me.

After a few minutes, she releases me, but I'm too scared to lie down. Wanting to catch my breath, I swing my legs over and sit with my back to her—my shoulders slouched forward.

Then I make my way unsteadily to the bathroom and splash cold water on my face. Staring in the mirror, I gasp, expecting to see boot polish, but my face is pink. "I'm here in San Francisco." I whisper. "Here in San Francisco."

Jane is behind me with a glass of water and when I take it, she throws a towel over my shoulders. I collapse on the toilet and gulp the water. I watch drops of sweat drip on the floor.

"What time is it?"

"Three-thirty," she replies, and I hear the concern in her voice. "Will, what happened?"

"Just a bad dream," I say as calmly as I can. "Shouldn't have finished off the Mexican food after we got home."

No laugh.

"Get in the shower," she says. "I'll change the sheets."

The warm, comforting water trickles down my body relaxing contorted muscles. I regain control and take my time hoping Jane will fall asleep. I don't want to answer questions, and I won't go back to sleep.

I towel dry slowly appreciating the softener Jane adds to her laundry. With the towel tied around me, I open the door and see that she is indeed asleep.

I creep through the bedroom and into the kitchen. I put the kettle on and open my laptop. I don't start writing until the water has boiled. I do not want the kettle to whistle and am relieved that Jane lives alone.

I make a cup of peppermint tea and take it to the table. I close my eyes for a moment. I must relive the dream. I need to write it down. The details were so vivid that I can't risk losing them by waiting until after work later today. I am a writer. I must go back.

After an hour of furiously pounding the keys, I feel it's done. Still mopping sweat, I read it. I ignore the red and green squiggly lines under all the misspelled words and incomplete sentences. I'm only interested in capturing the detail—the intensity. Spelling corrections and grammar can wait. I save the document and wipe away tears that I only now discover are there.

I sit upright stretching my suffering back muscles and pick up a half-cup of cold peppermint tea. Looking over the computer, I jump. Jane is sitting on the only armchair in the kitchen wearing a loose white blouse. She has her legs tucked under her and is leaning on the arms of the chair.

She is hugging a steaming cup and staring at me.

We say nothing for a few moments as we study each other. Finally, Jane asks, "Have you finished?"

I nod.

"This isn't the first time is it?"

I shake my head.

"Is this why we've been sleeping together less frequently?"

I nod again.

"I guess I should take comfort from that."

"I'm very much in love with you, Jane," I say, hearing my conviction. I've never said something so vulnerable like that so easily. I am, after all, an Englishman. But this isn't the time and Jane has other things on her mind.

"You dream about scenes that Mr. Tzu describes to you?"

"Yes. I'm also reading other books, seeing films and stuff. I'm immersing myself in war and, I guess, this is the reaction. I'm also listening to a lot of stories. When I dream, it might be a mergence of these stories. It sort of blends together."

"It was so intense." Jane shakes her head. "I thought you were having a fit or something. I was frightened to touch you."

"I'm sorry."

"How many times has this happened?"

I think for a minute. "Four or five times. Five."

"Does Tzu know?"

"No, and I don't want to tell him."

"Why?"

"He has enough to handle. His dreams are far more vivid. A shower and cup of tea and I can move on. It's not that easy for him."

"Who else knows?"

"All my housemates, I'm afraid."

There is silence and I struggle to grin.

"Chad has twice come into my bed and slept hugging me. I'm not sure what his girlfriend thinks, and she was sleeping over at least once."

"Why haven't you told me?"

"I … didn't want to worry you."

"Silly bastard." Her attempt at a British accent sounds forced. "Silly English bastard." She's trying to laugh, but she's pissed. Sarcasm gets the better of her. "Selfish, in fact. I could do my fucking dissertation on you, don't you think? Post-Interview-Over-Identification-Syndrome. People win prizes for things like this."

I force a smile. "I'm sorry. I feel like the story has possessed me. No question of that. I dream about it, think about it, see the characters, and learn names I'll never—"

I turn around and look for my bag. What I want isn't there. I look at Jane.

"Do you have a copy of your father's book?" My tone is intense, and Jane looks a bit freaked.

"On the bookcase in the living room."

I retrieve it and go to the index at the back skimming the names: Tanster, Tenshaw, Timmons. I scramble to page eighty-two and stare at the photo.

"Oh, my god—"

Wearily, Jane stands and looks over my shoulder.

"Did you dream about this one?"

"Yes." I whisper, as I read *killed in action*. It is not clear if he died of enemy fire or our napalm. Timmons was a big man and the soldier who found him, Private McGarry, couldn't carry him back.

I return to the index and search for McGarry. He was found wandering in the jungle the day after the scorch. He was delirious—crying that he wasn't strong enough and had to save himself. McGarry was admitted for psychiatric observation and never saw action again. He was honorably discharged and sent home.

I put the book down and start shaking. The tears soon follow.

"He ... couldn't carry him. He ... was a small guy and his own equipment and webbing was hard enough. His ... fucking helmet was too big. It kept slipping down the front of my face. I couldn't carry him. I tried. I—"

Jane grabs my arm. I can feel her nails penetrate my skin.

"Will, it wasn't you. It never was! You weren't there, Will! Snap out of it! You're here with me, Jane, in San Francisco. Let it go!"

She is shaking me, and I fall into her arms crying.

"Come on, baby." Her voice is soft now. "Let's go back to bed."

She tries to pull me toward the bedroom, but I don't budge. I pull her toward me and kiss her hard. I feel a wild, manic passion erupting. She is wearing only the oversized blouse, and my hands are all over then under it.

I grab her buttocks too hard. She gasps then slaps my hand.

"I'm sorry," I say, breathless.

"It's okay," she replies, her breathing showing she is also aroused. "Ride the emotions but remember I'm here too."

I try to unbutton the shirt, but my hands are shaking and after two, I give up. Her breasts are delicately defined, erect nipples clearly silhouetted through the thin, white fabric.

I lean down and clumsily suck at a nipple. She lets out a groan and maybe winces. I move to my knees. Jane wears no panties, and I lick her roughly for a moment. I desperately want to please her. Everything suddenly seems so critical—so life-or-death. Breathing hard, she leans back with her elbows on the counter.

I stand, rip my towel off, lift her to the edge of the counter and enter her stroking hard. Jane's cries are harsh as her heels dig into my ass. Her hands cling to me for support. Her nails scratch my back. My eyes are closed. I feel the pain but on a detached level.

"Don't wait, Will." Sensing my impending climax, she cries. "Don't wait." And I explode inside her.

We maintain this pose for what seems hours. When our breathing calms, I open my eyes. She is staring at me, and I look away ashamed. We have never had sex like this. I have never had sex like that ever. It wasn't making love. It was all about me and only me.

It was Timmons or maybe McGarry. I feel as if I had violated her, hurt her. Jane is staring at me. I can feel her gaze, and I am embarrassed to return it.

"Will, look at me." She moves her untidy black hair out of her face.

"I'm sorry," I say. "I've never done it like that before. It was …"

"It was raw, Will, very raw. But it's okay. You didn't force yourself on me."

"But it was only me." I whisper, while the faces of dead soldiers pass through my mind. "We weren't making love. It was very … very—only me," I say, trying to convince myself.

"Yes." She whispers, pulling me to her chest. "It was very raw, but it was never only you. It was always us." And we hold each other like that for a long time..

35: The Cabin

"You can't use my brother's real name." Tzu pounds his palm on the table. "We must respect the dead."

"But this is a tribute to him."

"We'll write that at the beginning, but this is a work of fiction. You're only a fiction writer, Englishman, and I must work with what I have."

I look and discover Tzu is smiling. I've brought him a potential first chapter. I hadn't wanted to show it to him, but he insisted. I try to explain what writing coach Anne Lamott calls *The Shitty First Draft*, but he won't be denied.

Looking quite distinguished with reading glasses perched on the end of his nose, he reads my five pages. When he finishes, he glances at me.

"Not bad." He concedes, his voice betraying a slight quiver. "It's really not too bad."

I smile modestly, but inside I'm bursting with pride. He doesn't know it yet, but there are another sixty pages finished. The book is flowing, and I am riding its wave.

"You must work faster!" Tzu says. "I've been thinking how we can give you more time. I'm going to give you a paid vacation over the Easter break. I have arranged for you and your girlfriend to stay in a friends' cabin."

"What makes you think I'll be productive with Jane around?" I'm excited at the prospect—a paid vacation to write and be with Jane.

"Her finals are coming up," he replies flatly. "She'll keep you in line."

"That's true." I admit. "Seriously, Mr. Tzu, I appreciate your generosity."

"This is not for you, stupid Englishman." Tzu yells, then pauses to gain control. "I need you to finish this project. I need to move on, to close the book and get on with my life."

I pause. "Are you having nightmares?"

"Yes, every night. You can't imagine."

I nod. "Who will work my shift? Easter can get pretty busy."

He inclines his head toward Tabitha. "Teach her to open and close. She's due for a promotion. I'll come in for the busy period of her shift. We'll get through it."

I remember that I had actually taught Tabitha to run a shift but never told Tzu. I smile to myself. I'm going to enjoy telling Tabitha that she's getting a promotion and will spend a week telling Mr. Tzu what to do. She won't know whether to laugh or cry.

Tzu continues. "There's a young man who worked here before going to grad school. He's coming back for the spring break. He's a good boy. Tabitha can boss him around. You need to write faster, Will. I want us to spend a lot of time together in the next week. I want to give you all the information I can, then this torment might leave me alone."

He stops and stares out the window—holding his breath, frozen. I have seen him do this numerous times recently, but it still freaks me out. When he drags himself back, he stares intensely at me. "If you work hard over Easter, how long until you finish?"

"I don't know. I've never written like this and never had a week to just write. Maybe I'll finish the first draft by June. Then a few months to edit and show it around." I scratch my head. "After that, I need to write a synopsis, a cover letter and a pitch. Then I'll begin approaching agents. It's going to take time."

"Why all this? It's just a goddamn novel."

Tzu stares at me. I watch his eyes go out of focus. I'm sure he's back in the jungles of Vietnam—his mind precariously bridging two worlds. And I know that while I could have a lot of fun with Jane in the cabin, I will spend my Easter vacation writing as fast as I can.

Highway 17 winds through the mountains from San Jose to Santa Cruz with thick forests guiding its path. Jane drives and my left hand intermittently massages her neck. She needs to negotiate both the sharp bends and the erratic drivers.

American drivers are in a class of their own even compared to the crazy Italian drivers I encountered in Europe. Italians take bad driving very seriously plunging it down to a level that can only be defined as an art form. When they cut in front of you, it is planned meticulously, and the satisfaction derived from your screeching brakes sends their Mediterranean blood coursing through their veins.

In contrast, American drivers don't consider the possibility that you even exist. The road is theirs. When they cut into your lane, there is no preconceived or malicious intent. They are simply oblivious of your presence alone in their own little world. It's not about the cell phone, the GPS or the self-help audio books on their iPods plugged into the cigarette lighter. It's all about them: pure and simple. Other drivers simply don't exist in their sphere of consciousness.

Jane pulls over at a gas station designed to look like an old log building. A sign advertises coffee and jerky. We don't need gas, but she wants a drink. Returning to the car, I'm already regretting the coffee I've bought. Perhaps it's part of the Wild West persona because the coffee tastes as though it was brewed during the Gold Rush. Jane has an orange juice: 100% natural fruit, no preservatives or additives. I should trust her judgment more.

A few minutes later, we leave the winding highway for a dirt road with sharp curves. As Jane negotiates the slow but steep descent, she must also deal with near darkness as the mountainside blocks the sun and the trees almost interlock overhead. She constantly flicks her sunglasses to her forehead and back over her eyes.

"Creepy," I say.

Jane smiles. A moment later she swings the car to the side of the road and parks. Opening her door, she grins. "Come."

Holding hands, we walk into the forest. Jane guides me—her body vibrant and happy. I note how she swings her arms and body more than usual as if she were a little girl. After a few minutes, she turns to me and instructs me to sit—gently pressing my shoulders down.

"Close your eyes," she says.

Crouching behind me, she covers my eyes with her hands. I'm aware, as ever, of her body pressing against mine, but this isn't what she has in mind.

"Focus," she says, sensing my arousal. "That'll come later. What do you hear?"

The babble of a stream fills my ears, and I hear water bouncing from one rock to another. I become aware of a strong smell of moisture and note it is chillier here than where we parked the car.

"Keep your eyes closed." She purrs and stretches me forward immersing my hands in the water. I gasp as my fingers tingle from the cold. "That's not all." She whispers. "Taste it."

She cups water in her hands and I lap it up. I can feel the refreshing water as it makes its way through my body—an invigorating experience. It tastes so distinct that I imagine I can actually taste the minerals.

"Mmm," I say, "a vintage year."

We laugh as Jane washes her face and arms with the spring water. I'm not so brave as to splash the cold water on my body, but I happily drink more.

"How did you know about this?" I ask when we are back in the car.

Enjoying the mysterious net she is casting, she ignores me. "We'll go over a sweet little bridge around this corner. It's almost a century old and is still sturdy enough for us to drive over. I hope."

Just past the bridge, we turn up a smaller path and Jane focuses on avoiding potholes. I realize then that she hasn't referred to a map. When she announces that we have arrived, the cabin is still moments from view.

Jane gets out of the car, surveys the scene and sighs deeply.

"Jane." I smile. "Have you been here before?"

She has a broad grin and nods.

"This land has been in our family for three generations. We use to come here a few times a year. The men would hunt, shoot, fish and do the other things men do." She sighs again. "I have very fond memories of this place. My mother rarely came, but my father was a different man here cut off from business and technology. For a few days, I would bond with my real nurturing, loving father."

"I thought that Tzu had—"

"You said that a friend of Tzu's had offered him the place for you. I think you'll find that my father and Tzu are seeing each other behind your back. Don't get jealous. It frees you for me."

As she opens the trunk, knowing it will piss me off, Jane adds almost wistfully. "I lost my virginity here."

"But I thought I was your first." Refusing to be baited, I feign hurt.

She turns, puts her arms around my neck and kisses me passionately.

"Of course you were, sweetie," she says as patronizing as possible but then seriously. "In many respects you still are." She squeezes my butt and nods to the suitcases. "Now start hauling."

The cabin is out in the wilds and possibly has not been used for some time, yet there are no signs of dust. The fridge is stocked with vegetables and cheeses, while a dozen bottles of wine fill a wood wine rack and there is a large pile of logs waiting near the fireplace.

James is taking care of his daughter and me as well.

Best of all is a heavy wooden desk facing a window that peers over a tree-filled valley. Right now, late in the afternoon, rich rays of sunlight fan out over the area. This will be my desk and no writer could ask for more. I really can't wait. Above the desk, to the right, is a clock made from a slice of redwood trunk. It is beautiful and the time is accurate. Time to write.

Jane plants a pile of books and files on a nearby table. She won't have the window, but this doesn't seem to bother her.

"This desk is amazing," I say.

"Come see the other highlights." Jane takes my hand.

There are two bedrooms. One is sparse with mattresses strewn on the floor, but the other boasts a four-poster bed.

"Sweet," I say, my work ethic swiftly dissipating.

"Yes, but we are here to work, and I promised my father that we would have separate rooms. He doesn't admit to knowing that we have become," her thin jet-black eyebrows jerk conspiratorially, "familiar."

"Familiar!" I laugh. "Okay." I gently shove her into the empty room and walk into the master bedroom. "Enjoy the mattresses."

But it doesn't end there. A door leads from the bedroom to a wooden platform. From the hot tub, there's the same impressive view that I have from my desk. I turn to Jane with as serious an expression as I can muster.

"This book could take several months to write."

Despite the obviously romantic environment, it is surprisingly easy to be productive. Jane's approaching finals provide a needed element of discipline. The fresh forest air has us at our desks by seven-thirty in the morning with coffee and toast keeping us going until around eleven o'clock.

Then we take walks along numerous paths appreciating the spring foliage and new growth. Each carries a special memory for Jane who speaks a lot about her relationship with her father. Returning to the cabin, we cut up a salad that we eat with cheese and bread.

Then we return to our desks until dusk. With fatigue mounting, we break for supper. We have brought simple foods, primarily soups and breads, but temptations wait for us in the fridge and we don't expend too much energy resisting. After all, we rationalize, the fridge will have to be emptied when we leave. Shame to let anything go to waste.

We open a bottle of wine over dinner and finish it in the hot tub later in the evening after a few more hours at our respective desks. I spend that time editing and by the end of our third-full day I have written an astonishing twenty-thousand words and completed a first edit on everything previously written.

In the preceding week Tzu drove me mercilessly to record as many notes as possible. He came to the café every day, and I had spent four evenings at his house in the Outer Richmond. I have everything I need to finish a draft, but he'll probably add detail and description.

After three full days, however, I'm feeling exhausted. It's the first night that I lack a desire to make love. Jane suggests that the next morning we go into Santa Cruz for half a day.

"We can relax by walking along the beach or the Boardwalk. We'll hang at bookstores and coffee shops. Do whatever we want."

I'm not sure. It feels like playing truant.

"We'll take our books and laptops." Jane suggests, sensing my dilemma. "At some point we can pitch ourselves and write or study. We need a bit of a break."

I take a deep breath. Jane is right, of course. I need to pace myself, but the faces of Tzu and James seem to be hiding behind every tree.

"Just half a day," I say, and stare at the redwood clock. Its ticking suddenly fills the room.

36: Santa Cruz

Santa Cruz is typical California: sun, surf, wild college town with many cool places to hang out. In Rome, I'd made close friends with an American woman, a Women's Studies major. A proud graduate of UC Santa Cruz, she'd enthusiastically painted a picture of the perfect California college town. I'd considered moving here and, had I not found work with Mr. Tzu so quickly might have done so.

Jane drives along Pacific Avenue looking for Zachary's, a place she has declared perfect for breakfast. She is resplendent in a new black outfit—tight shorts, silky black blouse tied in a halter neck behind her neck— revealing her navel and flat stomach. Accessories include elegant sunglasses, black bandana, and leather-laced sandals with leather boot straps that twist up her lower legs.

This breakfast venue might be legendary, but thankfully we only wait a few minutes to be seated and even score a window table. The menu offers every kind of egg alternative including many without eggs. The list of juice and smoothie combinations is almost endless.

Having decided on our order, we settle into some serious people watching. The field is rich. To our left, two middle-aged women are so completely involved in their conversation that neither has removed her bicycle helmet. Across from their table, four people, all with shaved heads and flowing robes, sit in silence slowly drinking. In contrast, by the door, wearing shorts and sandals, sit aging hippies with long, gray and braided hair. At the adjacent table sit young, carefree, tanned students, UCSC blazed across vests and T-shirts. When one walks past, I note the logo stretched across the back of her shorts.

A handsome, blue-eyed and peroxide-treated young man, pierced and smiling, takes our order. Troy is charming and eloquent as he guides us through our choices. "From the City are you?" he asks smoothly, and I hear the capital "C" clearly. No doubt the correct emphasis helps garner the bigger tips from San Francisco visitors.

While we wait for our food, Jane brings over a pile of newspapers—freebies that follow you around US cities. Focusing on one, she opens straight to the comics.

"This is Comic News," she says, hidden behind the pages. "It helped shape Gen X and now the millennial generation on the West Coast, or at least in the college towns." The ensuing silence suggests she too is being shaped.

Troy brings us our freshly squeezed OJ soon followed with the required caffeine reinforcements.

"The coffee is organic and free trade," Troy says. "We buy from a local roaster."

The coffee is strong and hits the spot. Jane is deep in the comic pages, an occasional wicked laugh the only sign of life. I sit back and try to relax. She is right. I need the break, and I can feel some tension ebb away as I watch the college crowd outside.

On the other side of the road is a Salvation Army thrift shop and farther along the Greyhound bus station. There are few people walking about, and I watch as three homeless men congregate on a bench outside. All three have shopping carts stuffed with plastic bags and blankets. More bags hang on the outside. Each cart has at least one American flag flapping vigorously.

At first glance, they look familiar with heavy beards and long-matted hair that tumbles out of faded baseball caps. One wears a thick red lumber jacket and rolls a cigarette—something I haven't seen since coming from England. He lights it and hands it to another, who takes it with a violent shaking of his hand. This man's second hand steadies his first and guides it to his mouth. His two compatriots watch his struggle.

Then the first rolls two more cigarettes and passes one to the third man. A policeman approaches them and a discussion ensues. I can follow the gestures of their arms but not the conversation.

The first homeless man, the one wearing the red lumber jacket, seems to be the spokesman, but the conversation is not about him. He continually gestures to the shaking guy. I watch and try to absorb their clothes and expressions.

Before I know it, my laptop is out, and I am hammering keys, typing choppy sentences across the screen while continuing to observe the exchange across the road. I am aware that Jane has noticed, but she says nothing.

When the food comes, she encourages me to close the laptop, unaware of the scene outside. I glance covertly, a habit I have picked up from many writing experiences when I am observing people often at the next table.

I absently nibble the toast, organic—sprouted and seeded—but don't touch the rest of the huge plate. With growing annoyance, Jane tucks into her food. She had been excited to share Zachary's with me.

I finish enough of my description that I can fill in the gaps later, smile at her, sip some coffee, but stop abruptly as it is cold and pick up another slice of toast. Troy is on the ball. He comes with coffeepot at the ready and deftly produces a new cup from somewhere under his apron when he sees that mine is half full. Barista-to-barista, I am suitably impressed.

I look at my plate but my appetite has disappeared.

"Troy, I'd like to box this, and can I have three plastic forks, please?"

"Sure." He smiles and picks up the plate. "I'll box it for you. Was there a problem?"

"No, thank you."

Jane is staring at her plate, and I sense that my woman in black now has a dark cloud above her head. I reach out and take her hand.

"Give me five minutes then we'll dive right back into our vacation day." I promise.

Troy brings the boxed food, and I leave the restaurant and cross the street. As I approach the three men, I feel a wave of awkwardness. "Here guys, I lost my appetite and haven't touched it."

Red Jacket takes the box and thanks me with a deep drawl. He immediately hands it to the others, then, seeing the shaking guy struggle to open the box, leans down to help.

"What did the cop want?" I ask.

"Why d'ya wanna know?" He signals to the third man to help the shaking guy and turns back to me.

"I dunno. I was watching from over there." I nod towards Zachary's.

"Not no social worker or anything'?" Red Coat asks.

"No," I reply.

"I-I-I-I-I d-d-d-don' needs h-h-h-help," the shaker says to his friend, and his frustration is palpable.

"We can hang out on the street if we stay invisible," says Red Jacket. "Shanks here makes folk feel uncomft'ble, so they say. Uniforms always come looking f'him. He wore a uniform before they's still having their noses wiped by their mothers. They forget that."

"I'm sorry," I say, not having anything else to add.

"Ain't you been harassing him," replies Red Jacket.

"Are you all vets?"

"Nah, none of us ever worked with animals, only eat'n them." It's a joke probably used frequently to people butting in like me as only I laugh. I look at him embarrassed, and I sense he takes pity.

"Yeah, we're war veterans. Answered our country's call. Sure you ain't from the o'side?"

"Yes," I say. "I—"

"Best be moving on, son. We appreciate the breakfast, but there ain't much more you can do."

I stand there, shifting from one foot to the other, struggling with what I want to say.

"It's not right," is all I can manage.

"Sure ain't, but that's the way it is. An' Santa Cruz ain't a bad town. Get on with your day, kid. Thanks again."

He turns his back to me, not rudely, but the message is clear. I start walking away then stop and turn around.

"I'm writing a book," I say, picking up on my desperate tone.

All three stare at me.

"Sure y'are kid. We thank you f'that too."

His eyes lock to mine. They are dark brown, nothing unique, but they pierce me. I feel as if he wants to tell me more but not here or now. Most likely, he just wants me to go.

I nod and turn to cross the street. A car's horn pulls me abruptly out of my reverie. On the wall by Zackary's, a mural catches my eye. It shows a row of storefronts, all small family-owned businesses: a general store, an auto-supply shop and a real-estate office. In front are cars dating from, I think, the fifties. The people are all clean and fresh and it occurs to me, these men I just left would have been kids then and grown into the contented folk in the mural had they not been doing their duty.

Jane is waiting patiently for me. "Our vacation day isn't going to start here," she says, and a sigh escapes. "Let's go."

I feel bad. Jane had wanted us to unwind in Santa Cruz and for me to loosen up. She is angry but there are no recriminations and maybe this is worse.

"What now?" She asks, seated in the car but staring ahead.

"How about that spa you told me about? The Zen place, you know? Would you like a massage?"

"Sure." She drives off.

At the spa, we spend a half hour sipping green tea from tiny, exquisite porcelain cups before being ushered to a room with a garden. It has a hot tub, a sauna and an outside deck to lie on. We shower and get into the tub but say nothing.

Ten minutes pass and there is a knock on the door. A young woman, thin with blond hair tied back, enters our suite. She is dressed in white slacks and a loose plain white T-shirt, and she efficiently sets up a massage table on the deck.

"Hi, I'm Myra. Who's first?"

Jane exits the tub and goes to the table. I watch the massage feeling the conflict of emotional exhaustion vying with the slow turn on of watching her relax. I head for the sauna. The muscles in my shoulders slowly relax—muscles I hadn't realized were knotted. Then it starts. Tears rise from deep inside, and I shake. I focus on keeping it quiet and let it ride. I don't want to disturb Jane's massage. Wiping away tears mixed with sweat, I reaffirm to spend the day relaxing concentrating on Jane.

Later she enters the sauna gloriously naked. I hope the steam hides my swollen eyes. "Do you want a massage?" I shake my head, and she pops her head out to thank the masseuse. Back in the sauna, Jane closes her eyes and sighs.

"I'm sorry about breakfast," I say.

"I know," she replies, but I hear an edge in her voice that I've never noticed. "Will, how long until you finish?"

"I don't know. At this pace, maybe in a month but don't tell Mr. Tzu's friend."

She nods, no smile. I leave her in the sauna and sit on the deck.

By the time we leave the spa, I am hungry. I haven't eaten breakfast and, as I wait for Jane in the reception area, I stare across the road at a watering hole with a beer garden. A shiver goes through me. The red, lumber jacket is rolling his cart away from the corner. I follow him with my eyes but resist the urge to accompany him as Jane returns. I say nothing.

She suggests we head downtown and are soon walking through funky, vintage clothes stores and thrift stores. Most of our time is spent in a particular one where everything is black. Jane plans to shop and sends me next door to an independent bookstore. By now, my stomach is rumbling and I consider sneaking out for a granola bar or bagel.

I'd already made the mistake of asking Jane if she was hungry, and she'd replied sharply how satisfying her breakfast had been. I say no more but contemplate stealing some chips from a little tyke wandering around the bookstore happily munching and leaving a trail of crumbs.

Jane joins me with a few bags in hand and seems noticeably happier. Declaring the bookstore browsed, we step outside and turn left. But as my eyes casually glance toward the junction to the right, I see a group of homeless guys hovering together. One, his back to me, is wearing a red lumber jacket and baseball cap.

"Jane, let's get out of here."

"Why? Aren't you enjoying the …?" She stares at me with worry stretched across her face. "Okay." Her tone is mild, and she takes my hand. I grip hers harder than usual. As we walk toward the car, she asks where I want to go.

"To the beach. Let's walk along the surf then eat fish n' chips."

"Comfort food?"

"Yeah, at a place where they have malt vinegar."

Soon we are walking hand-in-hand on the beach, the waves lapping at our ankles and our sandals slung over our shoulders. Seagulls quarrel above us. I can't help but glance around looking for red lumber jackets, but the beach is almost exclusively ours.

We eat our fish n' chips nearby with malt vinegar, and there is Guinness on tap. I begin to unwind and ask Jane if she has plans for the summer after graduating. I assume even post grads celebrate a last summer of freedom.

She shrugs. "Maybe Europe. You've given me the taste for Italy. The wine, women and Italian drivers."

"That would be nice," I say. "But no losing your virginity there." It is a poor joke.

"I'm thinking of going alone or with a friend from school." A third choice, me, has already been rejected.

"I guess I'm not much of a vacation companion, huh?"

She shakes her head. "You've got to see this project through, Will, for Tzu and yourself. My graduation will be after you've finished writing, so you shouldn't have the nightmares anymore."

"I'll always have Chad to crawl into bed with if I do."

"True."

Pause. "You're not thinking of splitting?"

"No, I don't think so." *Don't think so!* "But I'm thinking about what the next stage of commitment is and my trip away will give us both some perspective."

"I won't be like this after finishing the book," I say.

"How will you be?"

"Conceited, arrogant, lapping up the literature prizes they'll throw at me. Obnoxiously mentioning my round of golf with Letterman at every opportunity."

Jane laughs, and it is a welcome sound. "You don't play golf."

"For an interview with Letterman, I'll bloody well learn."

She laughs again then instantly turns serious. "That's the guy I met, Will. That's the guy I fell in love with, and that's the guy I want back."

"He wants to come back to you as well." I promise. My voice quivering.

We leave the restaurant holding hands. I have a renewed determination to finish the book and walking to the car, I resist the now paranoid urge to look over my shoulder to see if the homeless guy in the red lumber jacket is nearby.

I know he's there.

37: The Book Doctor

I could have stayed longer in our cozy mountain cabin, not just for the ambience but also indulging the drive to complete the book. Previously, I'd been writing for Tzu, for James, and others like Red Lumber Jacket and his friends. But now there is a new element. I realize that this project, which brought Jane and me together, could tear our relationship apart. I love Jane, and I fear that this book might claim another victim—us.

Three weeks later, I announce to Tzu that I had finished the first draft and was editing the book.

"Why?" He frowns. "Run the spell-check and let's publish."

I smile, though fleetingly, as I realize his urgency. Tzu is a burning fuse; there is nothing self-indulgent here. I start to explain the editing process, then the pitching and marketing process that follows. He's not interested.

In the time that has passed since my trip into the Santa Cruz Mountains, he has aged considerably. His eyes are puffy, and I learn from Tabitha that he sleeps in the afternoon at the café just playing catch-up from the bottomless pit of night where the fear of falling asleep and dreaming keeps him wired until morning.

Tabitha has endured a nightmare of her own—Tzu looking over her shoulder. After only three days, she'd considered quitting rather than work under his uncompromising gaze and Tzu shows no sign of letting up on my return. But a student without cash reserves rarely relinquishes a job during the academic year, and Tabitha is relieved when I'm back.

She pushes me to say something when he yells at the staff, but I'm not sure if this is a boundary I can cross. Tzu has scant patience for me as well. I shield Tabitha as best I can by assigning her to the evening shift when Tzu isn't around, but her studies don't allow this for more than a day or two a week.

Tzu is looking away as I try to show him a well-worn copy of Stephen King's book *On Writing*, the novice writers' bible. The first half is memoir, but the second half is a no-nonsense toolbox to improve one's writing skills. Although I'm in midsentence, Tzu stands abruptly—his chair falling to the wooden floor with a clatter.

"Just get it done." He mutters and disappears into the back of the store.

I'm not seeing much of Jane these days. Her finals are only a few weeks away, and she has scant interest in anything else. Dark sacks under her eyes blend well with the thick-black makeup, but her vivaciousness has disappeared.

We meet for dinner near her place on the weekend but even if I'm invited to stay the night, one of us falls asleep over keyboards or papers before we make it to bed. I grit my teeth and libido taking scant solace from Jane snuggling when we finally hit the sack.

With the weekend approaching, Jane calls and asks if I will join her for dinner with her parents on Friday night.

"I'll understand if you don't want to," she says apologetically. "I know I've been neglecting you recently."

"It's fine," I reply, excited to be her boyfriend again for a night. "I understand your priorities. Finals are finals. Don't sweat it."

Dinner at her parents is no longer such a trial. I have learned enough about Barbara's charities to ask the right questions or at least grunt at all the right moments, and I have an ally in James. I look forward to heading downstairs to his study for drinks.

James is still on his low-cholesterol diet, and we are treated to an impressive poached tilapia dish. It is very refreshing. I'm sent to the wine cellar to do the honors and select a Swanson Pinot Grigio from Napa in honor of the lightness associated with the impending summer.

The meal passes uneventfully, but Jane is unusually tense. I put it down to exam nerves, but I am wrong. I glean references to an earlier conversation to which I was not privy. An old boyfriend is back in town. He is from a good family, longtime members at the club, and his parents have started inviting James and Barbara to cocktail parties and dinner. They would like Stuart and Jane to meet—to renew their friendship.

I don't understand why Barbara's clumsy attempts at match-making ruffle her daughter's feathers. I'm sure this isn't the first attempt. Come to think of it, I'm not sure why it doesn't get to me. Perhaps it is because of Barbara being so outlandish, or maybe because Jane has no time for anything but her finals. There's no time to talk at her parents' house and even when I corner Jane in the kitchen, James finds us and is eager to invite me downstairs.

"Give us a moment, Dad."

James retreats diplomatically. I turn to Jane. "Is it this guy, Stuart?"

"No."

"Your mother?"

"No."

"So what's the problem, Jane?"

"I just need to get through my exams and for you to finish the damn book." Jane nods in a downward direction. She will not deny her father his pleasure. "Please go join my Dad."

James leads me downstairs, and I select a complex Merlot. The fire is not lit and the windows are thrown open. The sounds of the city drift in making the room less reclusive.

"How's your writing coming along?" James asks.

I tell him about the book focusing on the editing process.

After a minute or so, he cuts me off. "How long will it take, Will?" There is a clear sense of urgency in his voice.

"I ... don't know. I've never actually got this far. Preparing a manuscript for publication is very different from just finishing a story. As a first-time author, I want every word, sentence and paragraph to be perfect."

"You don't have much time," he says bluntly, and I wait for him to elaborate. He doesn't.

"Are you okay?" I am worried. Deep in thought, he looks beyond me.

"Oh, I'm fine, really. Business keeps me occupied, but your boss isn't so lucky. He's fast approaching a junction. When he gets there he must make the right choice."

I swallow hard. "What do you mean?"

"I see Tzu once or twice a week." James stands as if preparing to deliver a planned speech. His tone becomes formal and businesslike. "He will soon need to leave the city. His wife wants to retire down South to be near the kids. He needs a fresh start to open a new chapter in his life. He must go and the book must help him sever the ties."

He leans forward. His voice is quiet but strong. "This might not be the time to write the perfect novel, Will. Have you thought of going to a doctor?"

"A doctor? I'm fine. Why do you—"

He laughs. "I mean a book doctor. They exist. I used one. I can put you in touch with her. If you two don't gel, she'll suggest someone else. While she works on the manuscript, you can craft the synopsis and cover letter. Then she can tweak that for you as well."

I make a face. "I know what they do, James. It's just—"

"This is no time for ego, Will." His voice has become more forceful. "That book needs to be out by the end of this summer. Tzu must be out of here by then. Jane will be back from Europe too. You are not the only player in the game."

I can clearly see the successful business leader sitting opposite me.

"It's not just ego, James. These people probably charge thousands of dollars. You tie them up for a month, and they need to pay their rent."

"I'll help you there. If the book sells, it'll be a loan against your royalties. If not, then it was a bad investment for me—not one of my more significant losses."

"I don't know if Mr. Tzu will agree."

The reply is instant. "He already has."

I stare at James not sure whether to be happy or angry with him. But no apology is coming. He leans forward.

"This is war, Will. For all of us. Everyone is jostling for positions, everyone has something to gain and everyone is vulnerable. Tzu has fast-tracked you. You will be a published author in a few months, and you agreed to do this for him. So you need to watch out for him and his needs. Moreover, you now understand that you must move on from this book."

"I know. 'One book doesn't make an author'."

"No, that's not what I mean, Will." He stands again—this time ready to rejoin the women. "By the time Jane returns from Italy, you'll need to be back in your genre, back to the comical, witty satire that you were writing when you met my daughter. You need to recreate the guy you were when you two got together. Get what I'm saying?"

Got it!

I should consider myself fortunate. Any aspiring author would jump at the opportunity to have their manuscript checked by an experienced book doctor. Think of the learning curve, the time hopefully saved in depressing rejections, the priceless opportunity to hear the voice at the other end of the line saying she or he is interested.

I meet with James' book doctor but she only works with nonfiction writers, so she gives me a few names to contact. The third person I call sounded interesting and suggests we meet near his home.

Samuel Meinsch is in his sixties, I think. He looks very comfortable ensconced at a small coffee shop in Inner Richmond where one of the UCSF Medical School campuses looms on a hill. As he flips through my first pages, people periodically stop to greet him. He is polite but clearly focused on my work. I sent him the first draft of a synopsis and the first ten pages—a similar combination soon to land on the straining desks of dozens of agents in New York and other places.

Samuel teaches creative writing workshops, healing workshops, lectures at San Francisco State University in the MFA program, and runs a writers salon from his house.

More important for my subject, Samuel served in the military in Vietnam. He never saw extensive combat and assured me that he is not one of what he calls 'the haunted'. However, he has enough insight to see when something is not accurate or possible.

He finally puts the work down and says, "What is it you want from me?"

"I want to finish the editing and polishing as quickly as possible. I need to craft a marketing package for agents or publishers and get it out quickly."

"You're very earnest, young man. You know that these things take time especially for a first-time author."

"I don't have that luxury. I want someone who'll prioritize the project, go through it meticulously and advance it as fast as they can."

"That's quite a demand. You're a very pushy young gun."

"I am," I reply, "but this is not about me. There are others who depend on this book seeing the light of day."

His smile instantly vanishes behind his silver mustache. "Are they vets? Men who hear the voices?"

"Yes. This has been part of a … a kind of therapy for them, but it's fragile."

"I see." Meinsch strokes his goatee. His hair is hoary and thin, greased back into a ponytail. "I finish teaching all my classes at the end of this week. I have to admit that this is great timing, but it will not be cheap."

He wants three-thousand dollars and will finish it in a month including the synopsis and cover letter. "We'll meet twice a week and go over my corrections and suggestions as we go." I hear an excitement in his voice and know I have the right man. "By the end of the month, we'll have a finished product assuming there are no major structural changes."

I call James to get his approval of the price, and a handshake seals the deal. Meinsch asks questions about my motives. I tell him about Mr. Tzu, his brother and James. I don't provide many details. He can fill them in. There is a pause, and then he is all business again.

"Start researching agents and publishers. List their requirements and anything that might get you in the door. Go to bookstores and libraries. Start looking for books in this genre. List the books and authors and browse through the acknowledgment pages. Look for the author thanking his or her agent or publisher and make a list of these agencies or companies. You will need this information to know whom to pitch your book to."

He has become absorbed in my work, and I am excited too. Neither of us cares about the foam from the latte on his mustache.

"Don't wait for me to finish my editing. You have a lot to do if this is going to unfold at the pace you want."

"That's great information. I appreciate it."

"I think you have something with this, kid. I was there and though I never saw what your boss and his brother saw, I knew many who did. This book isn't just for your boss or your sponsor. It just might silence the voices for many others."

He stands and puts my papers in a briefcase. Then he extends a hand.

"And I know of Colonel van Ness," he says with respect. "We all do."

38: Moving On

I want one specific person to read *Unwanted Heroes*, so I print out an extra copy of the manuscript and hit the streets. I have no idea why I am doing this, but I feel a strong sense of certainty. I can't find Salvador at our past haunts. When I ask other homeless men, they all agree to pass on a message but eye me with suspicion. Some probably remember the events that followed my *chat* with Li Tzu.

Captain O'Connor and Sergeant Mendez come into The Daily Grind one sunny morning in June. They are both in short sleeves exposing muscles and hairy forearms. I notice this kind of thing as I painfully lacked both as a teenager. I once actually stopped dating a girl because her forearms were hairier than mine.

The policemen have mastered the knack of missing the coffee shop's rush hour, and I join them bearing gifts of yesterday's baked goods.

"How's your boss, kid?" Mendez's ever-present sunglasses are more in place now that summer has arrived.

"Not great," I reply. Tzu visits the café about every other day and we all dread his visits. He lacks any patience with the new staff and with the end of the school year there has been considerable turnover with five of the

295

seven moving on. When I try to intercede, he just barks at me to finish the damn book. "It's intense." I admit.

"When will the book be finished?" The huge figure of Captain O'Connor leans in, concern stretched across his face.

"I don't know." I sigh. "We're two weeks into the month with a book doctor, and he's finding plenty of faults. I'm seeing him three times a week, and he's relentless. He has me rewriting whole scenes and pushing me to generate more leads on agents."

"The book is the key," O'Connor says. "I don't know what will happen to your boss if this doesn't work."

"We've seen a lot like him." His partner echoes, a stoic expression across his face.

I look from one to the other. I sigh again and shake my head. This responsibility is getting to me. Something snaps and my tone becomes more of a hiss. "Do you guys know how hard it is to get published as a first-time writer? Then the publisher does not help with the promotion. I don't see how this is going to play out. At best, there will be a first run of a few thousand that will languish in Barnes and Noble for a month, then be returned to the warehouse and pulped."

"You'll do better than that," Mendez says confidently. "You have friends. And this might not be New York, son, but it's the next best for the literary world."

I stare at Mendez. How on earth would he know?

"Do you have a marketing plan?" O'Connor asks, all business.

I shake my head. "I'm revising what the book doctor returns and researching agents. I need to find an agent who'll find a publisher. I haven't got time for anything else."

"Where's your young lady?" He doesn't miss a beat.

"Italy."

"You gonna go after her?"

"I'm planning a fucking book tour there."

They laugh. Gaston continues. "Didn't split too well, huh?"

"Let's just say she has an open ticket."

They nod. Men of the world. They get the double meaning.

"Competition?"

"Yeah, some rich jet-setting jerk whose parents are members of the *Club*." I say it with a distinct capital C. "And he has Jane's mother and probably the City aristocracy on his side." Another capital C.

Again the sympathetic nods.

"Listen son." Gaston puts his big hand on my arm. "Concentrate on the book. It is the key to everything. Get her father to put one of his MBAs to market it. Get Tzu preparing to be the front man ready to give talks and interviews. He'll need to practice for it, and that will do him good."

He sips his coffee before continuing.

"Get the book behind you, Will. Become a success. Especially in Jane's father's eyes. Her mother may be very … domineering, but your Jane will listen to her father. Mr. van Ness is an icon in his house as well as the City. "

I stare at them. Not for the first time, I am amazed at their worldly wisdom.

"You married?" I ask the Captain, realizing that I've seen nothing beyond the uniform.

He nods. "Twenty-eight years." I can clearly hear the pride in his voice. "I have three daughters. They are all too young for you, but if they weren't, I'd be proud to have you as a son-in-law."

"Thank you," I say swallowing hard.

"Are you writing to her?" Mendez's tense face muscles show that he has been doing some serious thinking.

"Yeah, e-mails, y'know. But it seems a bit staid."

"You're a writer," he says with so much force his mustache twitches. "Play to your strengths."

I look at him skeptically.

Mendez doesn't flinch but leans forward again peering over the black frames of his wraparounds. "She hit on you because you're a writer. Use it. Don't just write about the weather and the Giants. You once said you've fallen in love with the City and that Jane loved you for this. Write a story or a … diary … with a perspective like they have on NPR. Send her a chapter at a time. Send them erratically. Have her waiting for the next e-mail."

We are both staring at him and, because we can't see his eyes behind his Raybans, I note that his moustache twitches are speeding up possibly from embarrassment.

"That's a smart idea," says his partner, ever loyal, and then they look at me.

Something clicks and the writer's mind slips into gear—A Writer by the Bay.

"You're a genius," I say, when I realize they are both watching me waiting for the spaceship to land. "A fucking genius."

I find Salvador two days later or rather he finds me. Whether it was O'Connor and Mendez or the homeless people passing on the message, I see him hovering outside The Daily Grind around midday. I run out to him though the lunchtime pace is hectic.

"Do you want to come …?"

The professor is already shaking his head. "What time do you finish, young man?"

"Two-thirty."

"Good. I have a free period then. Meet me between the Ferry building and the bridge? I will try to find us a bench, but you know how enthusiastic tourists are at this time of year. My students have stayed in the classroom."

I assume he means that his cats are staying in the relative quiet under the bridge. "Thank you. I'll be there."

I arrive at the meeting place with two iced coffee shakes in hand. I update him on the book, Mr. Tzu, and Jane. He shows genuine concern for Tzu and my relationship with Jane. I try to shrug them off, but Salvador's expression shows that I can't lie to this wise vagrant.

"Professor, please read the manuscript. I would appreciate your feedback."

He ponders his answer, but I think I see a glimmer of pride.

"You know, I have been working hard with my students these past few months. The summer is a time for the academia to relax and recharge their intellectual batteries."

His defense isn't too forceful.

"I realize that, but the book can't wait. Tzu can't wait and, frankly, I need to put this behind me. I don't think I can win Jane back unless I move on from this project."

"Ah, the battles of the heart." Preparing to lecture, he strokes his wild beard. "They have destroyed stronger men than you, young Will. Beware. You cannot write for her. For Tzu. For anyone. A writer must always write for himself. Later, when the story has been tamed and forced on paper, it can be adapted for a wider circle, go commercial, and become widely read and all. But ultimately, you must write for yourself. You wrote this book," he holds up the manuscript that I thrust into his hands, "but you wrote it in the shadows of giants—of heroes. You wrote this for Tzu, his brother, and Colonel van Ness—men who need you to do this, and it is a noble cause but a cause that must by necessity become historical."

Salvador's eyes sparkle with clarity. "This is why the young lady burned out and why you will too." He pulls on his beard and reaches a decision. "I will read this. Not for you but for them. You, however, must release all that is still bottled up inside. Unleash the creative force, son. I suspect that this," he taps the manuscript, "is merely a warm-up."

He leans back and smiles. "Over my long, academic career, I have developed a good nose for my students and you excite me."

We stare into each other's eyes—his so powerful, so wise, and I realize I am holding my breath.

"I will." I whisper and clear my throat. "Thank you, Professor."

Ernest Hemingway never drank wine or wrote at the Vesuvio wine bar off Columbus near Broadway but others did. Jack Kerouac frequented this establishment and he has an adjacent alleyway named after him. No doubt other lights of the Beat period also met here. Still, in honor of Hemingway, I am drinking a glass of robust red wine from the Chianti region of Tuscany—a dear memory of my travels in Italy. Hemingway's reputed favorite wines came from this region made from an untraditional blend of Cabernet and Sangiovese. They are called Super Tuscans for their deep color—another irrelevant thread that made up the complex tapestry of this giant of the literary world.

A mixed crowd surrounds me. Many young people sit absorbing the vibes emanating from the literary and political ghosts of San Francisco. At least two would-be writers are pounding the keyboards of their laptops. A group of college students drink nearby: noisy and intense in the moment. They are undoubtedly debating the issues of the day different only on the surface from the debates that locked Kerouac and Ginsberg in verbal combat. Europe became Korea became Vietnam became Iraq. Castro still rules and the rich are richer, plunderers of Gaia's treasures soon to be depleted forever. A new reality is ushered in or so we are convinced each time anew.

At another table sits a young couple. He drinks a red and she a white. The table candle sits between them—a light of hope and expectation. They hold hands. Their elbows are firmly planted on the table as they wonder about their future.

This is Vesuvio, wine bar and cafe, a permanent background in the City's rich history. It has stood for decades witnessing many such scenes. Is the next Dylan here? The next Ginsberg? The next President of the United States? Dare I dream of being crowned the next Kerouac?

This is Vesuvio, channeled on the very pulse of creativity that feeds our great city, here on the Bay.

Hemingway: A Writer's Summer on the Bay.

I read through it again making changes here and there but not much. It needs to stay raw. Kerouac would have demanded nothing less. I cut and paste it into the e-mail. No other message.

Click.

39: The Ticking Clock

My last meeting with Sam Meinsch, the book doctor, is at a Chinese restaurant on Clement Street in the other Chinatown, where those who are financially successful have moved and transformed the street into an array of Asian restaurants, supermarkets and utility stores. The Green Apple, a hip used bookstore, and a few clubs have added their flavors to make this a diverse and lively neighborhood.

Meinsch treats me to dinner and orders a considerable array of dishes. As we wait for the food, I show him a list of thirty agents I've researched. About two-thirds live in New York City, with most of the others on the West Coast.

He knows about a dozen, either because of their famous protégés or having met them on the conference and teaching circuit. He makes a few comments that I scribble next to the relevant name. He hands me back the synopsis, pitch and cover letter, all carefully checked.

"How many are you going to send out in the first batch?"

"I don't know," I reply. "The books I read suggest a half dozen but …"

He is already shaking his head. "Will, send them all. You don't have the time."

I don't reply. Meinsch and I have discussed the need to move this quickly for Tzu's sake. I have covered Tzu's imploding scenario with too many people.

Our order arrives and Sam takes me through each dish. My plate is piled high, and I focus on the food. Thankfully, he does as well and there is no discussion for several minutes.

Meinsch scans the bowls of food that remain and judging by his sigh I think he realizes that he has eaten enough. He looks across the table.

"Do you have your next project lined up?" He is loosening his belt a notch.

"Not clearly. I feel I haven't finished with San Francisco."

He nods approvingly. "You could spend a lifetime writing about the complexities of our City." There is undisguised pride in his voice. "But you must start another book. Being a writer is too new for you to sit back and relax. If this book does succeed, you need to be ready. One-book authors abound and the publishers are rightly suspicious of them. Have you been writing at all since you finished *Heroes*?"

Heroes has apparently become the abbreviated title, and I wonder if this will become the final one. I tell Meinsch about the e-mails that I've been sending to Jane. I have now sent five of them—one every three or four days. He is smiling.

"Writing for a woman? Dangerous stuff. Courageous, but dangerous nonetheless. Is it any good?"

"I think so. This time it is from the heart. It's my story. I'm enjoying it."

"Good. Follow your heart with your writing and your women."

He raises a beer and we toast. "To the heart," he says. "Always the heart."

Then, after taking a deep gulp, he hands me a large-brown envelope. It is more a symbolic gesture given that we live in the digital age, but one that has been done ten thousand times by a thousand authors and coaches. I have everything in my laptop backed up on a thumb drive. But tradition demands the ceremony.

"It is finished." He declares with gravity.

Two days later, on Monday morning, I take thirty brown envelopes to the Post Office. All contain a cover letter and synopsis. Some have the first three chapters; others, the first ten pages or whatever that agent's submission guidelines demand.

Now I wait and write two more passages that I send to Jane. In one, I pay tribute to Chad and Buddahood. In the other I recall a trip on the ferry to Sausalito and the Italian fishermen. The latter trip was actually taken with the law student who had an aversion to Janis Ian being played at the coffee shop during finals, but this part I happen to leave out. It had been a pleasant afternoon, payback from her point of view, and I sought nothing more.

Jane occasionally thanks me for the stories and tells me about the places she is visiting. She is on a cultural spree, which will end on an island beach off the Italian Riviera before coming home. There are no hints or references to other men or women, and I'm determined not to dwell on them as I read and reread the e-mail several times.

The envelopes begin to trickle back after two weeks. The first few are standard replies: *we are not accepting* and *not our genre*. Gradually they change to contain more personal notes: *perhaps another*, *matter of taste*, and *good luck*. Someone has actually read part of my package and, for a moment at least, considered my work. Progress!

I try to take these rejections in stride. It's part of the trade, and I think I'm prepared. Following Stephen King's example—he is one of my writing role models even if I am too much of a wimp to read his novels—I have put up a huge spike on the wall and skewer the rejection letters with different levels of vindictiveness.

But it is not just about me. These rejections portray more than personal failure. I'm failing Tzu and James and might have lost Jane. My SFPD fan club believes in me, as does my professor, the wise old man of the streets.

In the second month, as the number of replies dwindles, I receive one request for the entire manuscript. I am ecstatic and absurdly optimistic but resist calling Meinsch, James or even Tzu.

I send the package that same day and now eye my e-mail box hourly. According to the many books I've read on writing, rejections come through the post and acceptances through e-mail or the phone.

As more rejections come in, I reluctantly prepare another thirty submissions to agents. Another agent requests the entire manuscript and my hopes soar again. Time spent at work passes quickly as I dream of imminent success. Even the pretentious SoMa writer's group that meets at the café on Saturdays becomes barely tolerable. I even regard them sympathetically as they arduously debate character versus plot.

September catches us unaware. Summer on the Bay should still continue for another six weeks or so, but this morning is cloudy and cold. As I walk from the bus stop to The Daily Grind, I wrap my flimsy jacket around my body.

Tzu appears at the shop around eight am. There is something different about him, something ominous, and I feel the staff tense up. Nothing is said as we deal with the rush of commuters picking up cups of coffee on the way to their offices.

Around nine-thirty things begin to calm down, and I head to the storeroom to locate a new sack of coffee beans. Raised voices drift in from the café.

As tones spiral out of control, I relinquish my search and hurry to the front of the café. The scene is confusing. Tabitha is chewing out Tzu while a young girl we have just hired is red-faced and close to tears.

"It's her second day. Jesus. You should be teaching her. Not tearing her apart."

Tabitha stops when she sees Tzu's expression. His face is bright red and suddenly he explodes turning his anger on Tabitha.

"Who are you to talk?" He yells. "You've been here a year and still can't tell the difference between lattes and cappuccinos. You have no idea how the Beast works or how to clean it, and how many times have I shown you? That certainly hasn't helped. I don't even know why I keep you on. I do know why. You wouldn't have lasted a month if it wasn't for Will covering your sorry ass because he's fond of you."

Though her eyes are still fiery, she now stands silent as he rains insults on her. I am also stunned. Mercifully, there are no customers and I hesitate—not sure how to react. I want to defend Tabitha. What he is saying is simply not true and quite unfair considering that she carried more than her share of the responsibilities when he disappeared.

As I see two businessmen approach the café, I take a metal jug and bring it down sharply on the stainless-steel surface of the counter. It breaks their focus even as the doorbell rings signifying people entering. There is a tense silence and even the businessmen stop their conversation briefly and look around.

I receive their order and, thankfully, they take their drinks to a distant table to continue their discussion. Wiping my hands on my apron, I say softly, "This is not the time." I turn to Mr. Tzu. "You're breathing heavily. Go sit and I'll bring you a cup of tea."

Though Tzu is my boss, I hear myself say this with authority. He glares at me, then shuffles to a table, and I scrutinize Tabitha—still red-faced and ready to rumble. Tough kid.

"Take a walk. Come back in half an hour."

"Will he be here?"

"It's his café, but I'll try to move him on." Looking at the new girl, also still red-cheeked, I say, "I need you behind the counter. Go wash your face and have a drink of water, but I need you here. If there is anything you can't handle, call me."

She nods and disappears to the bathroom.

I make Tzu his tea and struggle to plan what I'm going to say. Tzu has chosen a table as far from the businessmen as possible. He does not acknowledge his tea, but his breathing is back to normal.

"You were out of line," I say softly.

"This is my business." He hisses back though clenched teeth. "I can hire and fire as I please."

"Yes, you can. And Tabitha can stay or leave if she wants. So can the new girl." Tzu opens his mouth to speak, but I say, "And so can I."

He closes his mouth without speaking and I continue.

"Before you received your brother's letter, before this … consumed you, you were firm with us but always fair. When you criticized us, it was with the aim of teaching. Tabitha has stuck it out and I've told you a few times, maybe not enough times, that she has always been willing to pick up the slack since you went AWOL."

He harrumphs and looks around. "Where is she?"

"I gave her a half hour to walk it off."

Another harrumph.

"Mr. Tzu, listen. You need to come in here and work. You need this for yourself. I have staff to handle the rush, but allow me to take charge. Come in and clean the Beast, inspect the beans, chat with the customers, but let me run the show."

We sit together in silence. I see the tight lines engraved across his face. He is struggling—still fighting a war that ended more than thirty years ago. He has been fighting it at home, in his family life, and now it confronts him even here. This is his café. It has been his sanctuary, a steady boat in the sea of insanity.

"When is the damn book coming out?"

I want to reply that it will be soon, but I can't. I tell him about the rejections and the new submissions. "This is the way it's played."

"Then find another way." He growls. "I can't hold out much longer." He stands and walks out of the coffee shop.

As I watch him leave, my hands reach across the table and touch his still warm cup. I recall a discussion with Meinsch. What would I do if time runs out? He talked to me about the print-on-demand industry. They produce good products, but the major outlets won't stock the books as there is no return policy. These companies give little help with promotion or marketing, but even the major publishers only roll out the red carpet for a select few that already have a fan base.

Meinsch advocated for print-on-demand given the time restraints, but my pride had ruled them out. Now it is time to make a difficult decision.

From the back of the store I call James' office. He is in a meeting, but his secretary promises he will return my call soon.

"Do you know who I am?" I ask, frustration getting the better of me.

"Yes," she assures me. "I will tell him when his meeting concludes. It will be in the next half hour."

"It is very important."

"I know who you are, Will. I know what you're doing."

I take a deep breath and say through clenched teeth, "Thanks."

When James calls back in twenty minutes, the pleasantries are short and awkward. I learn inadvertently that Jane has returned to San Francisco because James is excited to have lunch with her. An embarrassed silence ensues. I move on.

"James, I need your help. The book is getting rejected. It's not moving. Tzu was in today. He's sliding. We are losing him.

The voice on the other end is quiet and measured. "I can make calls."

"I know you can."

"I don't think we have a choice. I know you never wanted it done this way, but we don't have a choice. This is not about you, unfortunately."

"I know."

"I'll make the calls."

"Thanks."

I put the phone down heavily. This is so not what I had hoped. I want a pile of rejections, then the offer of exclusivity. Then a grace period while an agent reads through my work and tentatively shops the novel around. I want the adrenaline rush. I want the call from the agent that he or she wants to sign me up, then later the call that the rights to the book have been bought by a major publishing house.

I crave that rite-of-passage, after which I can show the world my scars and declare that I am an author. I want my own war stories to tell at writers' conferences, book signings and, of course, to reluctantly share with the fucking pretentious SoMa Writer's Group.

But there is no time left for that. This book was written for my boss, and I can't forsake him now. He is an American hero, a warrior, a giant. But he's slipping.

I had sworn an oath to his brother under the Bay Bridge the night before Lao Tzu had succumbed. I couldn't save Lao Tzu, but I swore I would do everything I could to prevent my boss, his brother, taking the same route.

James will make the calls.

40: The Goth, the Writer & the Wine Bar

Flashes of sunlight shimmer on the water and reflect off the Bay Bridge and tall buildings in the Financial District. Today is a rare, bright, crisp morning. At this time of year days often begin wet and foggy clearing into a warm Indian summer. The San Francisco commuter, ever prepared, is therefore destined to return home in the late afternoon laden with layers of clothes that—while essential in the morning—are shed through the day.

But I am basking in sunlight of a different kind. Yesterday, the San Francisco Chronicle published a third consecutive article by me in the cultural section of the Sunday papers under the heading *Emerging Talents*.

It had been Tabitha's idea. She was at my house watching a movie. I was making tea and left my laptop on the kitchen table unprotected. Tabs sat at the table and, without permission I should stress, read one of the e-mails for Jane.

"What's this?" she'd asked, sitting in my chair.

"Something private," I had replied. "Thanks for asking if you can read it."

"You're an author, asshole. You live to have people like me read your work."

"People like you?" I feigned disdain.

"Yeah, adoring fans." She theatrically blew me a cheek.

"Anyway, I'm not an author yet. A few more weeks, I'm afraid."

"A few? Weeks?" An exaggerated grin had stretched across her face. "Let's see. How many days exactly?"

"Twenty-nine," I said—too quickly. She could have asked me how many hours and received as fast a response.

"So what is this?"

"One in a series of short pieces from the diary of a writer in San Francisco. You know, insights into the city, arts and culture, coffee shops and psychotic coworkers."

She ignored the dig. "And you send these to Jane?"

"Yeah. She needs me to move on from *Heroes*. To be the edgy, funny and sexy writer she'd met before Tzu snapped."

"Cool, I'd also like to meet him."

She received a playful punch on the arm for her efforts. "Actually," she added contritely, "I think this is pretty sweet. Let me read more."

I opened a few excerpts, and then responded to the shrill call of the kettle. When I returned with the steaming cups, she didn't respond, and I saw that as a positive sign. I sat opposite her and ignored the newspaper on the table. I wanted to give Tabitha the freedom to read while I analyzed every muscle movement on her face.

Chad had come home alone. He was still with Jenn, surely a record, and this meant that if they weren't together that night, he would not entertain. I had no complaints as it has enabled us to grow closer.

He threw his bag in his room and came into the kitchen to forage.

"Hey man. Hey Tabs. What y' doing?"

"We were going to watch a movie I rented," I said as nonchalantly as I could muster. "But she got distracted."

"Come here Chad," Tabitha said intensely. "Read this."

She slid over, and he moved another chair next to hers. They read in silence. Twenty minutes later, I prepared Chad a cup of tea and started warming leftovers.

We didn't see the movie that night.

Things are quiet at The Daily Grind. Mr. Tzu still comes in and helps with the morning rush, then he cleans the Beast, inspects the stock and heads home. He is quiet—ominously so. He speaks only to me and to customers. If something needs to be told to another member of the staff, he defers to me. Around ten o'clock, Mrs. Tzu comes in with empty shopping bags, and they enjoy a cup of green tea with some baked goods. When they leave, everyone breathes a silent sigh of relief.

Ironically, I find his silence just as intimidating as the eruptions. Tabitha and I exchange worried looks but say nothing. It is the calm before the storm. We know it. Mrs. Tzu knows it, and Tzu … I don't know what he thinks.

About 9:30 one morning, Mr. Tzu answers the phone.

"The Chronicle? Of course. You want to write a piece on our little café …? Oh, well that is good too …. I am his boss, and I say you are welcome to come and see him …. Yes, perhaps not around lunchtime when we get busy …. He is our barista, you know …. Very important

...! Yes, the next half hour is fine. I can stay and cover for him. By all means, please come now."

Tzu puts the phone down and turns. He has a big smile on his face—a proud father. To the entire café, he says, "*The San Francisco Chronicle* is coming to talk with our writer, Will." He turns to Tabitha. "Come." Still smiling, he invites her. "Let me show you a trick to cleaning the filter base of the Beast."

Then he turns to me. "Go wash your face and put on a clean apron, English scruff bag."

"Tell me about these articles." Jerry Baton is not what I'd expected. He might be in his thirties but not by much. He wears an orange sweater and brown sport jacket. His hair is blond and dyed—I think. It is casually spiked showing considerable artistic effort. Jerry's eyes are blue and sharp.

He had presented me with his business card, and I'd presented him with a macchiato. We now exchange brief bios and I tell him of my impending book launch. He asks several questions about the book before moving to the passages I sent him.

I tell him the story behind the passages playing down my desire to bait Jane. Instead, I stress my love affair with San Francisco. I have been writing two articles a week, and I still have plenty of ideas.

"How open are you to criticism?" he asks. "Do you see these as finished products?"

"I'm young and my ego hasn't yet been inflated by success—though I'd be happy to work on that."

He laughs politely and tells me that the Chronicle is interested. They have a sophisticated method of researching how an article floats. The online version of the newspaper accurately shows how many people visit an article, and they have time-honored ways to know how many read the printed paper.

Jerry pulls out one of the articles from a folder that I had sent him. It is full of scribbled comments—evidently from more than one person. "I'm going to the bathroom. Read through the comments if you can decipher them. I want to hear your response."

When he returns, I ask his help not only to decipher but also to explain some of the comments. I take out my notebook and write things down.

"It's always like this at first." He reassures me when we have finished. "You'll see that we'll suggest fewer changes as you write more so try to learn from this."

I nod.

"We want to run three articles—one in each of the next three Sunday papers. We want the New Orleans street musician to start with and the pickup at the wine bar. After that, we'll choose a third. If there is a good response, we'll make it regular. Sound good?"

I can only nod.

"Make these corrections to the New Orleans one tonight and e-mail it to me. Tuesday is our preferred deadline for our permanent columnists."

Permanent columnist! San Fran Chronicle! I gulp and mumble something as indecipherable as the editing comments I have just struggled with.

We stand and shake hands.

"Will, I like your work and this will help position you when your book comes out. Good luck, man. As we say in the business: *Good Writing.*"

"Well," I say, unsure of myself. "Fancy meeting you here."

Jane smiles. Our first meeting since her return from Italy feels awkward, and she has chosen the location—the same wine bar where we first met. Or more accurately, the wine bar where she picked me up. It was also featured in yesterday's *San Francisco Chronicle* column titled: *The Goth, The Writer & The Wine Bar Pickup.*

I have no idea what made her think this was about her—about us! My fictional protagonist wore black and picked me up at the same wine bar. But other than that … Tabitha thinks I'm in for a flogging.

Julian, my ever-loyal housemate, has valiantly offered to come along in case Jane brings Susan, her kickboxing ex-girlfriend. To be fair, Susan had threatened me if I mistreat Jane, but when I remarked that Susan would make short work of him as well, he just smiled serenely.

"Tight." He purred.

But I have come alone and unarmed: no laptop, no notebook and no pencil. Jane is already there when I arrive. She has a table and two glasses of wine waiting—a wise move considering the place is crowded. Tucked in a dark corner, we are anonymous.

"You look great," I say, and mean it. She wears black—everything down to the lace gloves. I haven't seen Jane for a few months and a wave of loneliness engulfs me. She looks just the same. Only tanned.

"And you're the talk of the town, Hemingway." Her tone is uncharacteristically fierce. She doesn't continue.

I try diplomacy. "How's Corporate Ken?"

She glares. "Is that what this is about? Anyway, his name is Keith."

I knew that.

"Actually," I say doggedly, "you convened this meeting. I'm just trying to fill in the spaces. I heard Ken joined you in Italy."

"How did you …?"

"A writer never reveals his sources."

"Jerk."

There is silence again as Jane seems to struggle with what to say next.

"Look, Will, Keith's been a friend since we were kids. We probably bathed together naked when we were four. Not that it seemed to influence him. Keith would rather get you into bed than me. We're just good friends.

"His parents make mine look like *The Waltons*. They don't know he's gay so this escapade is very convenient for him. We went out for dinner a few times and met at the club. Then he flew to Italy to join me, and we had a great time sightseeing in Rome. When he returned, he told his parents that it wasn't going to become a relationship, and we would remain good friends. They couldn't fault him for trying. Satisfied?"

"Satisfied."

"How's the law student?" She continues without missing a beat.

"How do you ..." I try another track. "There's nothing there," I reply. "I'm waiting for your decision, Jane, before I let the hordes break down my door. I haven't even looked at another woman." Then remembering what a terrible liar I am, I add, "Well, I look but nothing more."

Her facial expression softens. "That's nice to hear." She smiles. Then she probably remembers she's pissed at me. "That was a shitty article to write," she says, trying to get angry again, but the candles on the table catch a glint of moisture in her eyes. I notice a folded copy of the *Chronicle* poking out of her bag.

"Really? You should have seen it before the editors got their markers on it. But I thought the vocabulary was crisp, the syntax succinct and ..."

"The article was great, you bastard. You know what I mean."

"I said I am waiting for your decision, but I never promised to be passive about it." I feel a sudden air of confidence. I'm not going take a tongue lashing.

"Is that what all these articles are about?" She tries cynicism. "The e-mails? You're trying to impress a girl?"

"Sure but not just any girl. You're over in Italy deciding whether you want to get serious with me, while leaving a trail of sexy Italian machos in your wake. I can't see you; can't touch you. I can't seduce you with my good looks, my masculine presence or my bad Italian accent. I go to the only weapon I possess. My laptop."

"Pathetic. And all of San Francisco must bear witness to your love trials?"

"Whatever it takes, Jane," I reply, then—realizing my voice is husky—I quickly sip the wine. I had initially considered the Pinot Noir she'd selected as too heavy and melodramatic for an encounter such as this, but now I find her choice comforting.

"Anyway, it's not all of San Francisco. It's my housemates, the staff at the coffee shop, your parents and the interview I did for the Country Club monthly." I make a sign of headlines with my hands, and say, *"Author Reveals All Behind the Chronicle Columns."*

She doesn't laugh, and I realize this meeting can't drag on. I contemplate finishing it before any damage is done and regretted. "Am I still in the equation somewhere, Jane?"

"Do you wanna be?"

"Are you reading my columns?"

No smile. Stupid comment.

"How much?" She asks, arching a thin-black eyebrow.

"What do you mean?"

She leans forward intensely. Jet-black hair falls over her face, and she flicks it back. God, I miss that flick. There is a defiant tone in her voice. "Would you give up writing for me if it came to that?"

I frown and lean back. Where the fuck had this come from?

"I thought you were attracted to me because I'm a writer." Where was the edgy Goth that had strong-armed me into a relationship? Then I'm hit by a wave of doubt. "No, I don't think so. It's something inside of me, Jane—perhaps like alcoholism or drug addiction or depression. It's part of my identity, my fiber, perhaps even my DNA. You might not be attracted to me without this creative drive. I wouldn't be the same person. No, I won't give it up."

She nods—her expression hard, caught perhaps between conflicting emotions.

"I know." She whispers. "I just don't know if I'm willing to lose you so totally every time you get sucked into a plot. Tzu is the first, but he won't be the last. San Francisco is full of wrongs waiting to be exposed. And when you've finished here, the rest of America and the world are waiting."

There is no cynicism here. She is right. But while my self-assured Goth therapist confronts a maelstrom of emotions churning inside her, I feel a strange calm—a solid sense of purpose.

"Were you craving that side of me when you made your move at the bar over there?" I nod to the very seat that is ironically vacant.

We both stare at it for a moment. We have reached the crossroads. I take a sip and return my wineglass to the table.

"I have a talent," I say, "or at least I think I do. I am not driven to write a series of meaningless romances and mysteries or describe elves and unicorns I will never meet. If I learned anything from what has happened with Tzu, it's that I want to use my gift for good.

"I want to write about what matters. Right here and now. The beatniks that bounced between New York and North Beach never consciously created a social agenda. We can do that in San Francisco. If we can't get it right, here of all places, where else will it happen?"

I lean forward and hear the passion in my voice. "Jane, this is the magic of San Francisco, and the hope of the world. I want the energy of gays and Goths, of creativity and anger. I want to parade and party and protest. I know I can be intense. I get too involved, but that's the energy I feed off.

"The rebel Goth I fell in love with has to accept me as I am."

I loosen my grip on her hands without withdrawing. I'm giving her the choice. The candle softly illuminates her face defining between dark and pale—Mission Goth and Nob Hill facing off.

Jane whispers something I don't hear, but her head is bowed and a tear drops into the deep-red Pinot. Then she looks at me, holds my stare and her fingers tighten around mine. A quivering smile is struggling to blossom.

"Okay, Hemingway, but not now. After Heroes, we will live life together on the edge."

41: The Book

I should feel elated. The sun is shining, the sky a deep blue, and hanging in The Daily Grind is a framed copy of my first published article in the Chronicle—put there proudly by my boss. I plan to rearrange the tables on Saturday, so the SoMa Writer's group has no choice but to sit under it. Jerry said if I can keep this up I might be in line for some emerging writer's award.

Later today, forty review copies of *Unwanted Heroes* will arrive at the café, two weeks before launch date. Yes, I have every reason to feel elated.

But I'm not. It's been three days since anyone saw Mr. Tzu. The police have been in, the usual questions have been asked, and Mrs. Tzu spends an hour or two each morning sitting at her regular table.

It seems different this time—she seems different. There is no brave "he'll be back" rhetoric as there was in the past. Everyone feels it, but no one dares mention it. Mrs. Tzu just sits there occasionally joined by staff members who take their breaks sitting in silent support at her table.

There is nothing to do but wait. Mrs. Tzu holds a letter from her husband—a wild scrawl oozing with guilt and apology. The letter is so much scarier given what happened after his brother wrote him something similar.

Last night I dreamed I was sitting with Tzu as he wrote the letter. Actually, I saw myself as Tzu, and I held the pen as it raced across the paper.

I'm losing the fight. I'm drained and feeling empty. I betrayed my brother and now my family and friends. I should be stronger, a warrior. I have betrayed you, my ever-loyal wife, and you, my children. Chinese men should be tough and resilient. I should have been able to cast the memories away and banish the voices ....

I must find my brother, track him down, walk his path, and apologize. You don't turn your back on family. You don't leave your brother. We should have stuck it out, opened the business together. I must find him and set things right.

And you, my wife, I am most of all sorry to you. You have always been a loyal Chinese wife. You have stood by me through thick and thin. You deserve so much more. We should have retired and headed south to the coast. Pismo Beach would have been near enough to play with our grandchildren, but far enough away not to interfere in our children's lives.

You must leave the City, go south, and begin anew. You deserve to enjoy the rest of your life. You don't deserve me, so weak, not a man, not the Chinese husband you wanted. I am sorry, so sorry.

I must walk my brother's path. I must make amends. I must silence the voices, once and for all ....

I awaken breathing hard and struggle to free myself from the dream. I am sweaty, breathless and alone. After a shower and a cup of tea, I walked through the city heading toward the Financial District. It's still dark and the streets seem empty. The air is chilly. The city holds its breath and waits to reclaim one of its own.

The letter comes out every half hour or so and Mrs. Tzu scans it each time for a clue—a glimmer of hope. I have read it twice and Tabitha probably knows it by heart. The letter's presence casts a heavy net inside the café as does its owner's absence.

FedEx delivers the parcel with fifteen minutes remaining until noon. It is forty-five minutes late, two-thousand-seven-hundred seconds, but who's counting. The shop is almost empty. Cruel though it is, I resent Mrs. Tzu's presence. She will stifle my elation.

The staff gathers around the table, and I open the box with shaking hands. The picture on the front cover has two layers. In the background is a faded military cemetery, and the rows of white tombstones climb a hill to a statue and a wind-battered flag. There is an elliptical layer in color. It is a photo of a young soldier holding a folded flag in his hands and looking into the distance— perhaps the future. The cover looks impressive.

Unwanted Heroes is typed in bold black print and below the title are the names of the authors: Chang Tzu and Will Taylor. I feel a lump in my throat and stare at the book. Then, swallowing hard, I take a copy to Mrs. Tzu and put it on the table in front of her. She stares at it for a moment, then looks up and smiles a smile that seems ten-thousand years old. She doesn't touch the book. But a few minutes later, ever considerate to those around her, Mrs. Tzu silently leaves the café. The book has gone too.

I had called James after Tzu disappeared and told him what happened. James had been seeing Tzu, and I hoped he might have an idea where to find him. That evening I receive a call from Jane asking if I am okay.

"Let's talk about something else." I can't even get excited at Jane calling. "How's your job?"

"To be honest, pretty shitty." Jane started working at a high school not far from San Francisco State. "I have no idea what to expect with each new case or even from one session to the next. I had a session with a student and her mother yesterday. I made a connection with the student, quite a good one in fact, but I had no idea how to get to her mother. I felt useless, and the student was disappointed. She didn't say anything, but I felt it."

"I'm sorry. I guess the first year is going to be a challenge. There are things they just don't teach in a classroom."

There follows an awkward silence as we search for something to say avoiding what needs to be said.

"When is the book due out?"

"A few weeks. I just received the review copies."

"My father is very excited."

"Yeah, I'm looking forward to giving him a copy."

"I'd like to be there when you do."

"I'll have the kettle on."

The lunchtime crowd is heavy. Pleasant weather makes people reluctant to return to their cubicles, and The Daily Grind is full of vibrant conversation. It's Friday. Clarence the street musician is moving about the café, and his sax is ripping through the crowd. The New Orleans Aid jars on the tables receive their dollar bills and sometimes more.

"It's not just the money." He calls out between songs. "Y'all need to know and shout that New Orleans is still healing, that people still can't return t' their homes and begin rebuilding, that businesses still ain't functioning. The water may have subsided, but it'll take a lot of love and prayers for the healing t' flow. But the money is important too, so I thank y'all on behalf of ma city, brothers and sisters." He launches into another song.

A few minutes later Clarence comes over for a glass of water. I proudly show him the book, and he gives me a big hug. Then he turns around and lets off a dramatic riff from the sax creating instant, shocked silence. Thank goodness nobody spilled a hot latte over his or her lap.

"Ladies and Gentlemen, y'all know him as y' barista, purveyor of mighty mochachinos, but may I present to y'all the hottest new literary talent in the Bay Area, the famous Chronicle columnist," he points with his sax towards the framed article on the wall, "Will Taylor and his just-published novel *Unwanted Heroes*."

I receive thunderous applause. At least it sounds like that to me having never been applauded before in my life except at the country club's fundraiser. I blush and give Clarence another hug. He hands the book back.

"If my current agent doesn't work out ..." I do not finish the sentence.

Sirens blare outside, blue and yellow lights streak through the building and the door opens. Captain O'Connor's massive body blocks the entrance and a natural corridor quickly opens. His face is red. He booms.

"Will, come now! We've found him!"

We shoot out the door. I jump in the back of the police car with my apron still on and book in hand. The tires screech; sirens wail. Mendez is master of the road weaving between cars and negotiating junctions.

I try to ask what's happening, but the police radio is blaring—intermittent instructions crackling through the static. In the mirror I see O'Connor, his face strained as he listens. When there is an opening on the radio band, he booms into the microphone.

"I have the kid. We'll be there in a minute. Clear the entry to the freeway."

We skid onto the on-ramp. The bottom half of the Bay Bridge has been closed and all I can see are police cars, ambulances and fire trucks.

The car jerks to a stop. We get out and O'Connor grabs my arm, but I yank it away.

"I started this." I yell and glare at him.

He points with his head, and we move to a ring of police cars. As I pass through the cars and officers, I wonder whether they will allow me to get near him, and if they do, what will I say? I see a small, hunched figure on the edge of the bridge. An officer holds out an old-fashioned megaphone, a cone-type device with a handle and trigger to turn it on. It is orange. The kind you see at demonstrations, and I recognize my writer's desire for detail, even in this crazy situation. As I bring it to my mouth, I remember that this is why Tzu sought me out. I am a writer.

"It's Will, Mr. Tzu." My voice is now strangely calm and authoritative as though deep inside I always knew it would come to this. "I'm coming over."

There is a halfhearted attempt to restrain me, but O'Connor barks at his fellow officers. A bright-orange life jacket is slipped on me, and I hear something being clipped to the back of the jacket. As I walk toward the lone figure on the ledge, I feel a rope dragging behind me. There is a strong wind up here on the bridge despite the warm weather in California. I climb out on the outer rim about four feet from him and stare at the Golden Gate Bridge. It is gleaming, a message of optimism, of promise, of a false dawn. In front of it, the island of Alcatraz, ominous, gray, a symbol of incarceration. Tzu needs to leave his own Alcatraz and swim for shore and freedom despite the freezing water and sharks.

He stares west as I do. Does he see the bridge or the prison?

He turns his face to the water, and then glares at me. His eyes are wide, blood red, and sweat drips in rivulets down his shiny forehead.

"Go away." He hisses.

"No," I reply. I swallow trying not to vomit from fear while my fingers squeeze themselves around the cable. "You can't do this, Chang Tzu." I don't think I have ever called him by his first name but seeing it in print next to mine has changed something.

Using his full name is not lost on Tzu either, and he struggles to catch his breath.

"I can't go on. I can't silence them."

"And you never will. You know that. None of you can. You told me that. I wrote it in the fucking book."

I raise my arm, and he glances at it. I realize the book is still in my hand, and he hasn't seen it.

"We've done it, Chang Tzu. The book is out. In a few weeks we can spread the word. Hell, Clarence all but held an impromptu book signing back at the café just now. It's Friday. James has found us a fancy publicist in New York and probably has half his own marketing department making contacts. We have work to do—a message to spread."

"The book cannot banish the demons." He snarls exposing his teeth. Spittle drips from the left side of his mouth.

"No, but it can help with the struggle. It can help confront the voices instead of running. It can help people like you force them back in the box and clamp it shut. Make a stand."

"It's too late for my brother." The whites in his eyes seem to grow larger.

"Yes, but it's not too late for your children or your wife. For God's sake, Tzu, she deserves better. You said that in your fucking note. Your brother loved seeing you with her and your children. He was proud of you. He made me swear to keep reminding you. And I'm making good on that promise now. I'm hanging from a fucking bridge keeping that promise. You can't save him, Tzu, but you can give him something to look down on from heaven and continue to be proud of what he sees. The dedication in the book is to him. Don't let him down now. Don't fail him at the point where his and your heroism is about to be recognized."

Tzu hesitates, looking from the book to me, to the water and back again.

"The book contains the voices." He sounds delirious and shakes his head. "But it can't silence them."

"No, it can't." I am desperate. My voice is becoming hoarse. The icy wind has numbed my fingers, and I am shit scared. "Take the book and make your decision. The book contains the voices. Throw the book in the water. Drown it." I am yelling at him and the wind is battling with my words. Tears blur my eyes, and I don't know whether it is from the wind or the situation. "Let the guilt go this once! Let it go!"

Hesitantly, he reaches for the book with a shaking hand. He holds it and stares at its cover. He wraps his other arm around the post and uses his free hand to open the book.

"Read the dedication, Chang Tzu. You fucking wrote it!" He is staring at the page. I know it by heart and shout it to him.

"To those who fought and to those who are fighting still. To those who conceded and to those who struggle on. All heroes. Unwanted but always heroes. To my brother Li Tzu, who fought until he could fight no more."

And farther down the page, a passage from the Bible that Tzu chose. My throat is burning, but I shout louder. *"And I set before you life and death, blessing and curse, choose life, saith the Lord."*

"Choose life!" I plead, my voice squeaking. I am panting from the effort. "Please!"

Tzu turns slowly and stares at the water. He has arrived at the junction. He raises his hand that holds the book above his head and lets out a guttural scream—perhaps words, perhaps Mandarin. I fancy that I hear his brother's name. Then Tzu throws the book in the water. We watch it fall for what feels like a lifetime. Then it floats for what seems an hour, an ominous white dot from our vantage, before it sinks out of sight and Tzu faces me.

With tears streaking his face, he says softly, "I have chosen. Stop crying. Let's go and clean the Beast."

I smile. "I've already cleaned it."

"I know, but let's go check again. I'll find something you've missed."

Epilogue: One Year Later

The Daily Grind is full of people. Tables have been stacked in the back, and we rented thirty additional chairs with people still standing and hugging the walls. The speaker is just finishing. His voice is not strong, but people listen closely.

He talks of his time in Vietnam stopping several times to sip water when he mentions his brother. It never gets any easier and it shouldn't. Hung proudly near the makeshift lectern is a poster-sized cover of his book, our book, *Unwanted Heroes*. The cover is well known in San Francisco and all over the US.

Heroes started selling slowly through the late summer and winter experiencing exciting bumps when one veteran's association or another featured it. Then, four months before Memorial Day, we were booked for a TV interview on a special Memorial Day show.

Our *publicist*, a marketing whiz kid that worked for James, quickly tied up additional appearances on other shows, radio and television. Then there was the momentum all authors dream of. In the week leading up to Memorial Day, the book hit *The New York Times Best Sellers* list, and Barnes & Noble followed with feature posters in their stores nationwide. *Unwanted Heroes* was in demand with a vengeance.

Mr. and Mrs. Tzu moved south to Pismo Beach buying a modest and beautiful red-tiled cottage, and he handed the reins of the store to me. Once a month, he travels to San Francisco to keep an eye on the Beast and visit his brother's grave.

Today, he is here for a double occasion. *Unwanted Heroes* was celebrating its first anniversary and, with my mother, enjoying her first trip to the West Coast, he would stand with a groom at a country-club wedding on Sunday.

The previous night, Mr. and Mrs. Tzu took me, Jane, and my mother out to dinner where he spoke with pride of how I had helped him through the book. He told my mother of the nominations for literary prizes and the contract that a publisher was now offering me. Then he presented my mother with an album containing all thirty-six columns of *A Writer by the Bay* published in the *San Francisco Chronicle* that next spring would become a book in its own right. When my mother seemed embarrassed accepting the gift—she is English, bless her—Mrs. Tzu confided that they had an identical album at home.

Finally, Mr. Tzu had a gift for me. It was a contract declaring The Daily Grind now owned by the partnership of Tzu and Taylor.

"I thought we could rename the coffee shop The Vet and the Bull-Headed Englishman," he had said, but Mrs. Tzu thankfully vetoed the suggestion. We settled on remaining 'The Daily Grind'.

Back to the present: as the book reading ends, Mr. Tzu receives applause that leads to an emotional standing ovation, and I am urged by photographers to stand next to him holding our book with the poster behind us.

Through the blinding flashes of the cameras, I scan the room and see Captain O'Connor and Sergeant Mendez still wearing his sunglasses—each clutching copies of *Unwanted Heroes* as they wait for Tzu's autograph. Next to them is Salvador, the proud street professor watching his student graduate. He shares a thought with Clarence who introduced us and will entertain when the wine begins to flow.

Chad is leaning against the wall. A wide, harmonious grin lights his face as he gently rubs Jenn's shoulder. She is equally radiant. Bear lifts a massive hand to wipe tears from his eyes and receives a sympathetic hug from Julian, who is determined to see the book become a movie should he ever graduate.

In the front row, Barbara is whispering emphatically in her husband's ear. She probably doesn't understand why he didn't arrange for the event to be held at the country club. I'm sure she is chiding him that the café is too cramped and she could easily have bullied another hundred people to be there. James just smiles and nods, but he is looking at Tzu and, well, I wonder where his thoughts are.

To our left, Tabitha is hugging Mrs. Tzu, the old woman ever proud, and always watching her husband.

I am gently turned around and receive a passionate kiss from my fiancé, who is back, as ever in black. Jane has been in difficult negotiations with her mother about the color of her wedding dress. I have thankfully been kept in the dark regarding the outcome.

As the applause dies, Tzu puts his arms around us. Seeking some privacy, he guides us behind the coffee counter. Mrs. Tzu is waiting and hands him a small box. He turns to me.

"When we die, my other son and daughter will inherit our wealth, such as it is, but this is an heirloom that has passed down through my family for thirteen generations. I want you to have it."

"I can't. I am not your ..."

"Yes you are." He whispers. "More than you can imagine. And just maybe I am the father you finally helped save."

My hands shaking, I open the box. His jade ring has been smoothed and polished with no sign remaining of the chipped stone from when he punched the café's hard floor while pounding my face.

"Just promise me," he says, "you won't chip it. Not even when some stubborn English kid really makes you mad."

###

Message from the Author

Dear Friend,

If you are reading these words, you have probably arrived with Will, Mr. Tzu and myself to the end of the tale. These characters have become my firm friends and I will continue Will's journey into Unwanted Heroes sequel, which continues in San Francisco and focuses on his relationship with Professor Salvador Espinoza, the homeless professor.

I know your time is valuable and am honored you decided to spend some of it reading *Unwanted Heroes*. Please consider leaving a brief review if you purchased this book online. I would love to hear from you at **alshalev@yahoo.com** or sign up for my weekly blog post at **http://www.leftcoastvoices.com**. I also tweet at **@alonshalevsf**.

Thank you once again for reading *Unwanted Heroes*,
Alon Shalev
http://www.alonshalev.com/

By the Same Author:

The Accidental Activist
A Gardener's Tale

www.ingramcontent.com/pod-product-compliance
Lightning Source LLC
Chambersburg PA
CBHW062018170626
46813CB00001B/207